D0947271

FIVE-CARAT
SOUL

FIVE-CARAT SOUL

JAMES McBRIDE

RIVERHEAD BOOKS

NEW YORK

2017

RIVERHEAD BOOKS
An imprint of Penguin Random House LLC
375 Hudson Street
New York, New York 10014

Library of Congress Cataloging-in-Publication Data

Names: McBride, James, author.
Title: Five-carat soul / James McBride.
Description: New York : Riverhead Books, 2017.
Identifiers: LCCN 2017007480 (print) | LCCN 2017013199 (ebook) | ISBN
9780735216716 (ebook) | ISBN 9780735216693 (hardcover)
Subjects: | BISAC: FICTION / Short Stories (single author). | FICTION /
Literary. | FICTION / African American / General.
Classification: LCC PS3613.C28 (ebook) | LCC PS3613.C28 A6 2017 (print) | DDC
813/.6—dc23
LC record available at https://lccn.loc.gov/2017007480
p.   cm.

International edition ISBN: 9780525533252

Printed in the United States of America
1 3 5 7 9 10 8 6 4 2

BOOK DESIGN BY MEIGHAN CAVANAUGH

To Sonny Rollins,

who showed me the Big Picture

CONTENTS

THE UNDER GRAHAM RAILROAD BOX CAR SET

sell vintage toys. All kinds of toys. I sell sheep that belch popcorn, dolls that whisper secrets, papier-mâché Santa Clauses, Halloween masks, Little Bo Peeps, and puppets. I sell toy parrots that say "Here comes a nigger," 1823 fire engines that say "toot!" and windup clocks from 1834 that say "Time's up, Gramps!" I sell tricycles from the Depression, toy coffee grinders from World War II France, and two types of the original 1964 Rock 'Em Sock 'Em Robots, including one that looks like Peter O'Toole and another that looks like Sammy Davis, Jr. I sell tin soldiers, steel trains, wooden cars, cardboard airplanes, ceramic piggy banks, and pinball machines. If it's a vintage toy, I sell it.

I am a sole proprietor. I buy toys on commission from collectors. They love me. When I call on a prospective client, often an ancient widow selling off her husband's collection or an ailing toy collector who made a killing on Wall Street and now is about to go kaplooey, I look the part. I'm not like my competitors from Sotheby's and Christie's who arrive wearing crisp pinstripe suits over starchly pressed shirts, the women with their hair carefully coifed, the men clean shaven, with their nails just so. Instead I play an antiques professor, a man of letters. I arrive ten minutes late. I knock on the door wearing a bow tie, a button-down shirt, and penny loafers, adjusting my glasses and scratching my beard. I fumble my way from the living room to the kitchen, dropping my pen, saying "Excuse me" to walls that I bumble into. I am a lost professor, a toy savant, expounding on the attributes of the dollhouses built by the great toymaker D. U. Edwards of 1851 Germany while losing my spoon in the bowl of chicken soup that I accept with the humblest of thanks from my generous host. I preach the gospel of the precision pinball creations of the Frenchman J. D. Gourhand, circa 1834 Paris. I crow with tears in my eyes about the wondrous, glorious, dazzling tin rooster creations of T. J. McConnell of Belfast, killed in the Irish Uprising.

Toy collectors love enthusiastic, absentminded professors. Absentminded professors are goofy, forgetful, and cute: They give sellers the misguided notion that they're getting the best price. That's why they love me.

I've done pretty well over the last thirty years. Not bad for a Jew from Queens who started out as an actor trained in Shakespeare and then toiled unappreciated in the small towns of upstate New York where I plied my trade in summer theater, best described as continually shouting "Blow thou winter wind!" to retired New York garment workers who wouldn't know iambic pentameter from a pair of pliers. I slaved that way for more years than I have fingers. Thankfully, my audiences these days are far more sophisticated.

Still, no toy collector from Amsterdam to Anaheim can resist my charms. No weeping widow holding her late husband's valuable train collection of Herman Beavers Specialty Trains can resist me. No millionaire CEO teetering on the brink of ruin or the edge of life, clinging to his valuable collection of series 922 Henry Ford Toy Racers, gathered over a lifetime of savvy negotiation from Spain to Selma, can say no to me. Entire toy divisions at Sotheby's and Christie's shudder at the sound of my name: Leo Banskoff.

Toy collecting is a small world, and in that world I am Pete Rose, Henry Aaron, and the Babe, all rolled into one. My batting record over the last twenty years is close to 1.000. I have never lost a client. No one can resist my blend of knowledge, perception, and most of all, profit. No one can resist my charms.

No one, that is, except one.

I first heard of the Reverend Spurgeon Hart by way of an old friend, Milton Schneider, a New York tax attorney and investor who handles estates and divorces with a degree of skillful discretion that has earned him considerable sums over the years. Milton is a clever, joyful fellow and from time to time, while trawling through the shattered portfolios and economic wreckage of his wealthy clients laid bare by divorce, he has occasionally uncovered a pot of gold in the toy arena that he sloughs off to me. Young millionaire ex-wives don't care about toys, especially those rising from the wreckage of a marital disaster, most having served as the third or fourth notch on the marriage totem pole of the aforesaid wealthy client's love life. Milton sniffs these out with ease, and if he gets a whiff of toy gold, sends them to me. I do the dirty work, query the prey, find the mark, make the initial visit, talk down the sale price, sell off the toys, take my commission, and fork over a small remuneration to Milton for his trouble. Everyone is happy. It's a win-win.

Such seemed to be the promise of the Spurgeon Hart case, which arrived at my place last fall via an overnight package from Milton wrapped in a brown paper envelope bearing a note that said, "This is a long shot. But no harm no foul." I was suspicious, for Milton had previously struck out three times straight, and I'd recently informed him that he'd have to lighten his wallet in my direction should this lead prove to be another bust, for the last had cost me no small amount of time and dignity, as I'd been shown out of the home of an elderly Upper East Side widow posthaste by her new boyfriend and personal trainer, an African-American fellow about the size of Milwaukee. He was offended by my opinion of a rare toy in her collection, a doll replica of a famous boxer named Joe Frazier. The doll wore boxing trunks and the headdress of an Indian chief, with a towel draped over his shoulders that read "Thrilla from

Manila with the Gorilla." When you pulled the towel his tongue came out. It was a delightful piece—not vintage, but a rarity. There were only fourteen made in the world before the manufacturer was stopped by a lawsuit. But after six weeks of research and extensive discussions with the manufacturer, I determined that the doll was a fake made in Taiwan. That roiled this widow's paramour—he was a big fan of Smokin' Joe—and after several hot comments about my Jewish background, race, motive, and bearing, I was forced to leave the home with explicit instructions not to return, as well as candid descriptions as to what would happen to various parts of my anatomy should I venture to that cause in the future.

But I'd made a fair amount of money with Milton over the years, so when this brown paper package arrived I opened it immediately. Wrapped inside was a dusty vinyl portfolio containing the stock holdings of one Rev. Spurgeon Thelonius Hart, of Springfield Gardens, Queens, whose holdings had been discovered in a circular file by one of Milton's young law clerks. I sat down and thumbed through it. Apparently, the good Reverend's mother had worked as a domestic for the Von Klees family, one of the wealthy families of 1920s New York City and its cousin, the Hamptons. The stock holdings, along with a few family heirlooms, were gifts for her years of service, before the family died off.

Apparently, the Von Kleeses' wealth died off with them, because there seemed to be nothing of worth inside the portfolio: a wandering bond or two, a couple of mutual funds, some old securities that predated 1927 and were stamped "Prerequisite," which meant they were probably worthless. I was about to toss the portfolio back in its envelope and return the whole business to Milton when I noticed, attached to the rear inside cover of the portfolio, a faded black and white photograph.

I almost fell out of my chair when I saw what it was.

It was a toy train. But not just any train. An 1859 Smith-Deckert 2350 Blue-Tone, Single Engine, Steam Powered, Piper-Coal Locomotive. And a set of four box cars. Also known as the Under Graham Railroad Box Car Set. In immaculate condition.

Let me explain to you about the worth—and value—of antique toys. I have an art collector friend named Muriel, and we occasionally debate which of our respective trades is more lucrative and important to world history—an argument Muriel almost always wins. But one evening during one of these talks, after consuming a considerable amount of bourbon (which I'd generously supplied), I said: "Muriel, name me one piece of art in the world that is almost beyond wealth in terms of its worth, a piece that captures history's impact on the present. Name me one."

Muriel sat back thoughtfully, smoking a Gauloise with one hand and holding her glass in the other. "I can think of several," she said. "The Sistine Chapel. Michelangelo's *David*. Various Impressionists. Monet. Van Gogh. Those are priceless. They all import some kind of history to the present."

"But do they have some kind of intrinsic value? One that you can assign money to?" I asked.

"I suppose so," she said.

"Aha!" I said, pouncing on her weakness. "Therein lies the difference. Antique toys don't work that way. Toys are priced based on emotion. The ones in the best condition have the saddest stories. The sadder the story, the more valuable the toy. That is a human element and it's one that no painting has. The specific history of sorrow or joy in a child's life, when determining the price, means the sky's the limit. Because there is no limit to sadness at a child's suffering, or the happiness a parent feels at a child's wonder. Thus the emotion contained within the product, when determining the worth of a child's life, is tied to a child's innocence, which gives that product infinite value."

"I'm not finished," she said. "There are other factors. Say you found a sketch by Jesus himself. Or discovered the Ark of the Covenant. Or a cloth napkin used by Mohammad the Prophet upon which he'd sketched with his own hand. Those would be beyond value. Those things are not merely art. They are human history. They would then be worth, say, all of Argentina. Throw in Spain and Portugal. You're not talking millions then. You're talking hundreds of millions. Perhaps even a billion. Can you think of any equivalent in your field?"

I could think of only one, one that bears both the stamp of crucial world history and the infinite value of a child's innocence. And I was staring at a picture of it.

The Under Graham Railroad Box Car.

That set is unlike any box car set ever made. Most toy trains, even rare ones, are made in sets. For example, the Chestnut Rozinki Locomotives set made in Brussels. It's one of four sets, one of which was owned by Winston Churchill. Or the Budskin Promethian by the great Flemish toymaker Noel Tobias Eisenhauser, one of four sets owned by George IV. Or the extraordinary Cuddinsky Router Chugger, a set of eight trains created by noted French toymaker Jean Pierre DuBlanc Rudan, of which there are only two left in the world, one of which is reputed to be owned by the King of Saudi Arabia.

The Under Graham Railroad Box Car Set, however, is unlike any of those. It is one of one. There is no number two. And it is a special one. To put it simply, it is perhaps the most valuable toy in the world.

Its value is tied to history, naturally, and complicated by time, war, and the unreasonableness and the emotions of a child's joy and sorrow.

It was a gift from General Robert E. Lee of the Confederate Army to his five-year-old son, Graham, who died before he could play with it. But it is not just the toy itself, nor the tragic death of Graham, that gives the toy its special value. There are other factors. For one, Lee actually commissioned the toy in 1859, just before America's Civil War, for the unheard-of sum of $3,100 from the weapons maker Horace Smith, he of Smith & Wesson fame and who himself was an amateur toy collector and was considered the Fabergé of Toymakers.

The future commander of the Army of Northern Virginia knew that war was coming. He was also aware that Horace

Smith, whose designs were later borrowed by the German gun-maker Franz Wilthgaard to create the weapons that powered the German war machine during World War I, was considered a weapons-making genius.

Smith turned out a masterpiece. The train consisted of five cars, an engine with coarse rubber wheels, three coaches, and a larger-than-usual coal car equipped with a tiny coal burner and a tiny compressor the size of a man's thumb that fed water via a metal tube to a tiny steam box. The train was powered by steam, and was said to be able to run on a specially made looped track at a top speed of twenty-five miles an hour for four hours on a full tank of water and a single lump of coal—faster than any horse and carriage could sustain at any length in those years. It was an extraordinary miracle of engineering.

But fate or providence got in the way. The train arrived at the Lee family home two days before war was declared, much to the delight of Lee's young son Graham. Two days later, war descended upon the nation, and Lee was called immediately from his Arlington, Virginia, home to organize Confederate forces along the Georgia and South Carolina seaboard. Two weeks later, while in South Carolina, he received a telegram from home bearing devastating news: His beloved son Graham had suddenly taken sick and died of consumption. Further-more, the beloved boy's new train and the female slave who tended to him—both valuable items, as slaves held consider-able monetary value in those days—had both disappeared, the woman having escaped to freedom in the North. A double loss for the general. Triple, if you consider that the woman who had tended the child apparently had been a trusted family member and much loved by the poor departed boy—and had now absconded with his toy.

The great general was outraged. He vowed to find the thief, and spent a great deal of money both during the war and after toward her capture, but with no success. He came close in 1863 when a hired detective discovered that the thief had made her way north via the Underground Railroad and had landed for a time in the Hell's Kitchen area of New York City. But the trail ended there. The war ended two years later and the general died in 1870 not knowing what had become of his beloved son's lost toy.

The specific facts of the thief's life were never fully ascertained thereafter. But there is no doubt that the train actually existed. A painting of the train was known to be in the general's home in the ensuing years after his death, and design sketches for it still exist. Those sketches were discovered among the papers of several prominent weapons makers in Germany and France—its basic design was used by artillery designers in Germany's war department during World War I and was referred to in the letters of the general himself.

Which leads to the second reason for the intrinsic value and importance of this tiny mechanical device. For within its tiny loops and doll-like cranks and widgets lay a weapon of war. What other mechanical device, powered by a tiny piece of coal and a small amount of water, allowing a tiny engine to propel it twenty-five miles per hour for four hours, faster than any horse and carriage could sustain, existed during those years?

As the war progressed, the general realized that if the train's technology was made available to the engineers of the South, the fate of the rebellion could turn. A full-sized steam engine using that same technology could toss cannonballs for miles, pull armed Southern troops by the thousands, cart supplies, horses, and ammunition for miles without refueling—not to mention be further developed to create newer, more efficient cannons and guns that would wreak havoc on Northern troops. Indeed the possibilities of the technology were so great that during the war, the general convinced Confederate president Jefferson Davis to send spies to Connecticut to kidnap Horace Smith, the train's creator, with the goal of forcing him to reproduce the train as a weapon of war. The foray was unsuccessful and further complicated by the fact that once the war began, Smith, now realizing the true purpose behind the general's commission, suffered a burst of guilt and wrote a letter to the general denouncing the South and declaring that he was an abolitionist. Furthermore, he demanded that the train be returned to him at once since the general's son was dead and no longer had any use for it, and insisted that the cost to develop the train had actually far exceeded the $3,100 commission since the train was, after all, one of a kind.

The general was understandably angry. A flurry of outraged letters between Virginia and Connecticut followed. Another front of the war might have erupted between those two states had not a curious reporter at the *Hartford Courant* gotten wind of the dispute and poked around, asking questions, nicknaming it in one story he wrote "The Mysterious Under Graham Railroad Box Car Set," a cruel play off the name of the general's son and the manner in which the train made its way north, reportedly one train riding the other. Thus the train got its name and withdrew to a silent place in history, for the threat of additional publicity caused both sides to scramble to their corners immediately. If Smith & Wesson was discovered even discussing the business of selling weapons to the South—or cooperated with that idea in any manner—Horace Smith would have faced a firing squad. Conversely, had Davis's government admitted it rested the Confederacy's military strategy in part on the fate of a toy train stolen by a Negro who had absconded to New York City via the Underground Railroad, it would be the laughingstock of Europe, from whom it needed to borrow money to finance the war effort.

With these points hanging in the air, both sides clammed up, and the matter died down. History did the rest. The war ended. The general passed away, and in 1893 Horace Smith died as well.

The train then vanished from history, never to be seen again. Stories of its existence popped up from time to time. A French toymaker in 1923 claimed he'd procured it, but it turned out to be a fraud. In 1945, a Negro seamstress from Baltimore swore her grandmother had it and produced a picture, but that, too, turned out to be a fake. There had not been one credible sighting of the Under Graham Railroad Box Car Set in over 130 years.

That is, until that balmy afternoon in 1992 when I sat in my office and found myself staring at an old photograph in the weather-beaten portfolio of the Reverend Spurgeon T. Hart.

I WAS SO STUNNED I sat in my chair for several minutes, staring at the photograph. I got up, collected myself, stumbled into my kitchen, and shoved a shot of bourbon and a spoonful of peanut butter down my throat, a combination that usually dulls my nerves. It tasted like sand. Still, when I sat down at my desk again to review the photograph, I could feel my racing heart slowing, and my fast, shallow breathing deepening. I again stared at the picture.

Finally I swung into action. I turned on my computer, scanned the photo onto my hard drive, and compared the photo with the sketches available on a private-access toy website. When they matched, I canceled all of my appointments for the following week. I called in both my assistants, then telephoned a fellow toy collector who sent over two more helpers. With this army in place, I laid out my war plans.

I sent one assistant to the Library of Congress in Washington, D.C., to check its files. I sent another to Washington and Lee University in Lexington, Virginia, where Lee served as president, to procure a copy of a drawing of the train made by General Lee himself. I dispatched my top assistant to Norwalk,

Connecticut, to check the Smith & Wesson archives of Horace Smith's descriptions and early working sketches of the train. Then I sat down and studied the photo again.

I studied it for a full day. It was of a dark-skinned, African-American boy, perhaps six or seven, seated next to a barren, beaten Christmas tree. He was wearing tattered pants and a tattered button-up shirt. He sat with his legs crossed Indian style, staring up at the camera. In front of him, in a neat row, lying on their sides so the photographer could catch them more clearly, were the three passenger cars, the famed coal car, and the locomotive engine of the Under Graham Railroad Box Car Set.

I sat staring at that photograph a long while. Then I placed it on my bookshelf just above the desk where I could stare at it. It was nearly midnight when I finally went to bed. I fell asleep dreaming of trains, and frauds, and fools who chased millions. I slept not like a log but rather like a frog, with my eyes open.

The next morning I rose and took the image to a well-known photography expert I know to have it analyzed. He took less than two hours to confirm that the photo was real and warranted further study, which required a series of tests. I hastily agreed.

A day later he called me to say that, given the age of the photo paper and the sparse furnishings around the child—part of a chair was the only furniture that could be seen, and the narrow wall behind him—the picture was most likely taken in an uninsulated structure, perhaps a cabin of some kind. Using a magnifying glass, he identified several detectable slivers of light seeping into the home from the wall behind the child, which appeared to be slats of wood.

"My guess," he said, "given the type of wood construction, composition of the floor, and light angle, is that this was taken in the South sometime in the late 1930s." He based this on several equations using a ruler, a spreadsheet, an astrology table showing the position of the sun and the moon at various times during the year, and a cheap dime store calculator, which he also used to tally up his fee, which was impressive.

All told, during those first two weeks, I spent several thousand dollars on the Under Graham Railroad Box Car Set—a healthy sum, but a pittance if the train proved to be real, which I was certain it was.

With that evidence in tow, I set out to contact Reverend Spurgeon Hart, the owner of the photograph, whose address was procured from the portfolio. I telephoned first to break the ice and deliver the good news. I got Mrs. Hart on the line. I was delighted to learn that her husband was alive and well. I identified myself as a friend of the firm that held her husband's portfolio and asked if I might drop by.

"For what?" she said. She seemed suspicious.

"I am a toy collector and am interested in the toy train that is pictured in your husband's portfolio."

"Oh, that thing," she said.

I nearly fainted, my heart was pounding so hard.

"Does your husband still have it?" I managed to gurgle out.

"Oh, Spurgeon's got that old thing laying 'round some-place," she said.

At the words "laying 'round someplace," I felt dizzy.

"Do you happen to know where it would be right now?"

"Course I do."

"May I come see it?"

"You got to ask Spurgeon. I'm sure he don't care."

"May I speak to him?" I asked.

"He ain't here, mister."

"And when may he be in?" I asked, willing myself to sound calm. I was scared. Afraid of disappointment, I think. I had begun to dream high. Was it wrong of me to believe that I'd stumbled onto every vintage toy collector's dream? I had no children. No wife. No dog. At fifty-seven, I had become my father. I even walked like him, with a kind of drifting, wandering look, my pants always loose around my stomach, my face configured into a puzzled, bemused, locked-in grin. I'd become my worst fears: a drafty, ancient-looking geezer, motoring around lovely Bucks County, Pa., in a newly leased Mercedes-Benz that lives in front of my converted 1726 barn, which like its owner looks bountiful and prosperous from the outside but on the inside is hollow, worn, unsound, and filled with useless old things. I wanted a cause. A purpose. And a decent pension, too, for God's sake. And for the first time in my life, I was circling the door to all those things and more, and this woman on the line held the key.

I heard a crash in the background and two dogs barking. "Hold on," she said. I heard a lot of yelling and some cursing, then more barking. After a few moments she got back on the line.

"Now what do you want again?" she asked. She seemed flustered.

"About the train," I said.

"Oh yeah," she said. "Well, I ain't got time to talk about it just now. My dog is whipping up on the neighbor's dog. You know a Rottweiler ain't worth two cents? You ever own a Rottweiler?"

I confessed I hadn't. "About the toy. Could you mention to your husband that I want to see it?"

"Mister, you want to talk to Spurgeon 'bout that old piece of junk, you better put your foot in the road and come here yourself. Myself, I ain't got time to chat about some toy."

"Can I come today?"

"Come anytime you want."

"When will he be home? Your husband, I mean."

"Can't tell you. Old Spurg is hard to catch. He's always on the job. Working for the boss, like they say."

I could feel beads of sweat forming on my neck. "Who's his boss?"

"The Son of Man."

She hung up.

. . .

IT'S A FOUR-HOUR DRIVE from my gentleman's farm in Bucks County to Springfield Gardens, Queens, where the Reverend Hart lives. I made it in three. I would've made it in less, but I had to get my stage props in order. I tossed aside my usual absentminded professor getup in favor of a tailored suit, tie, shiny shoes, my Mercedes, of course, and $90,000 stuffed into a briefcase in carefully packed wads of $9,000 held together with rubber bands. It was all the cash I could muster quickly. Also, I'm told by an accountant friend that any bank deposit under $10,000 will not draw IRS attention. I assumed there would be some negotiation and depositing of accounts on the Harts' part. By starting with 9K, then increasing my bid by the same increment, I could draw $9,000 clips out of my suitcase without mistakenly drawing more or less, and at the sale's end advise the Harts about the wisdom of making their deposits at a clip of $9,000 per deposit, thus keeping them off the IRS radar and convincing them at the same time that I had their best interests at heart. I also brought a release form. I meant business.

I drove to the Reverend's address and parked out in front of the Hart home. It was a tiny red house that sat at the edge of a pack of small, claptrap houses, which but for the grace of God and the airport designer's pen would have sat dead along the middle of Runway 12 at Kennedy Airport had there been a need for more tarmac space. The sight of massive 757s just three blocks away, the giant logos of the airlines that owned them gleaming in the sun as they made their final turns just beyond the airport fence, gunning up to takeoff speed, added an unnerving roar to everything. Talk about bad location. The place was fresh out of a real estate agent's listings garbage pile.

I approached the house and noticed a sign atop the front door that read "The Lord is listening to your junk!"

As I climbed the rotted, beaten steps to the front door, I glanced behind me and noticed my Benz suddenly had suitors. Several young men who when I pulled up had been lounging on a battered stoop across the street, listening to the infernal racket of rap music from a giant boom box, now had risen to their feet and were slinking toward the car, nodding approval and gazing at it admiringly. I ignored them, aware that I was carrying what amounted to my life savings in cash in my brief-case, and focused on the door. I knocked loudly.

After a moment an enormous creature answered. Six feet, six inches tall if she were a foot, a towering figure and nearly as wide as the door. After a moment, I guessed it to be a woman. She was clad in spandex pants, which were tight enough to re-veal the dates on the coins in her pockets, had there been any, which I suspect there were not. Her hips were wide enough to nearly touch both sides of the doorway, and her rear end seemed to stretch into the yawning darkness of the room be-hind her. She was wearing a sweatshirt that said "Kill the noise! Turn up Jesus!" Her hair was clipped short, lathered tightly to her scalp in neat waves like the rippling rivers of a pond and dyed blond—which is why, I suspect, I had trouble guessing her gender at first. Overall, she was an impressive sight, for her face was gentle and pleasant, and not unattractive. She was a most bizarre amazon.

"Look at them," she said, nodding over my shoulder at the boys with the boom box who were approaching my car. "That's all they do. Piping garbage into their minds. What you want, mister? You a Jehovah Witness? We gave at the office."

"I'm the toy collector."

"Who?"

"The man who called about the train. From Pennsylvania."

She drew her head back and laughed, unbelieving, and by God, she seemed seven feet tall then, towering over me, her head thrown upward in laughter, giving me a clear view of an enormous mouth full of sparkling white teeth. She then looked at me again, took in my suit, my silver Benz parked behind me, which the youths had surrounded and were peering into its tinted glass windows.

"You came all the way here from Pennsylvania? For that old train?"

"Yes, I did," I said.

"You's a tad bit old for toys, ain't you?"

She motioned me inside. As we moved into the hallway, I heard the snarl of a dog and suddenly a huge pit bull burst out of a doorway and rushed me. "Buster!" she snapped. She stepped forward, picked him up by the collar, and tossed him into a bedroom, slamming the door tight. Behind the door, the dog howled. She led me back into the kitchen and motioned that I should sit.

"You sure you all right, mister? You got the right house?"

"Yes, I am," I said. I looked around and took in the kitchen.

I have a habit—call it professional instinct if you will—of sizing up a person's net worth at a glance. It's more ritual than anything else. I suppose this morbid curiosity is rooted in the fact that while most of my clients are worth millions, some toy collectors live like dogs. It's not my business, and God knows a lot of them live better than I do. But from what I could see, the Harts' entire estate, complete with interior house decorations, furniture, dog, home exterior paint job, and location, was worth about half the $90,000 I had in my briefcase.

The kitchen table where we sat was one of those giant wooden spools that hold telephone wire that crews carry to sites and abandon after the wire has been removed. Around it stood three folding chairs. The straw placemats on the table were chewed at the edges. The gas stove looked to be from the 1950s and was something you'd find in an antiques store in my part of Bucks County—as an antique. It required matches to light. A bare lightbulb hung from the ceiling. Dangling at the end of the light switch was a glow-in-the-dark crucifix of Jesus hanging off the cross with blood oozing out of his wounds. Pictures of Jesus in various states of repose and torture hung around the entire room: Jesus with his mother, Mary; Jesus being kicked; Jesus stuck on the cross; Jesus bleeding from his head and suffering every possible outrage.

She was seated with me at the table and got up to open the refrigerator, removing a large pie. "You want some sweet potato pie?" she asked.

"No, thank you," I said.

"Don't be trifling," she said. "It's bad to miss eating." She produced a butter knife, cut a large piece, and set the pie before me. "Bible says man got to eat and be merry. Unless you got a ram in the bush," she said. "You got a ram in the bush?"

"No, but I have a cat."

She eyed me warily. "This is a sanctified house," she said solemnly. "There ain't no cats in the bush." She said it as a kind of warning.

"I'm sorry. I've come to talk to your husband about the train."

"He ain't here. He's out working."

"Will he be home soon?"

"God knows."

"Where does he work?"

"Everywhere."

"Well, who does he work for?"

She looked at me oddly. "He works for the King of Kings, mister."

"Of course," I said.

"Jesus," she said. "Jesus is his boss. You got Jesus in your soul?"

I didn't want to tell her, but I'm a Jew who hasn't been to temple in fourteen years, not since my mother died. Rosh Hashanah and Yom Kippur sometimes make it onto my calendar. Once in a blue moon Hanukkah and Passover make the grade. Shavuot and Sukkoth, however, are more problematic. I mean, I sell toys. I need money. Who has time?

So instead of speaking out, I simply gave in and ate some pie to calm things. It tasted terrible.

"Wonderful pie," I said.

"Thank you, mister."

"So did your husband leave the train for me to see?"

"That thing?" she laughed. "Spurgeon be glad for you to have it."

"He will?"

She chuckled. "Men and their toys. Finish your pie first." She cut a piece for herself, gobbled it while I nibbled at mine, barely able to swallow.

My eyes watered with each bite. The pie tasted like mush and old goat cheese. I took a forkful and then another, wiping my eyes with my handkerchief.

"Spurgeon never did like toys," she said.

"Well, I'll relieve him of it. And pay him for it. I really want it. It's . . . I think it's worth quite a bit."

"Save your dimes, mister. Spurgeon called after you did and when I told him you called, he said you could have it."

I couldn't believe what I was hearing. "But I've come to buy it," I said. "Doesn't he want to discuss price?"

"He ain't interested. What you wanna buy it for anyway? You ain't even seen it."

"I'm a toy collector, and I'll pay a lot if it's what I think it is. I love old toys."

"Spurge said give it to you. I can't take no money if he said give it."

"Do you have any kids, Mrs. Hart?" I asked.

"Just one," she said. "Junior's off at choir practice." She went to the refrigerator, removed some milk, poured a generous amount into an old mayonnaise jar, and placed the glass on the table in front of me. "Have some buttermilk. It'll wash that pie down good."

"Mrs. Hart, I can't eat another bite. About that train set—"

She waved me off. "You ain't drunk your buttermilk, which I made fresh. Nor finished your pie. What I'm gonna do with all that?"

"I'm full, Mrs. Hart. Lovely pie. I'll take it home."

"It'll spoil. Can't go about wasting it. The Bible says Jesus told his Disciples, 'Gather up the leftover fragments so nothing's wasted.' That's John 6:12, sir. Gimme." She pulled the plate over to her and set to work on my piece, then grabbed my jar of milk and gurgled it down her throat in one impressive, mighty gulp.

"About the train," I asked timidly. "Where's it from?"

"It's just some old toy his grandma had or something," she said between mouthfuls of pie. "Spurgeon said take it, so take it."

"I have to pay you."

"He didn't say sell it. He said give it. Bible says, 'Don't say to your neighbor come back tomorrow and I'll give you what you need. Give it now.' Proverbs 3:28, I believe." And with that, she rose again, reached over atop the refrigerator, brought down a large shoebox, and set the box on the kitchen table.

How would you feel if someone set down a Rembrandt in front of you? Or if someone placed the riches of the ancient Egyptian pharaohs in your lap, or several bars of gold from the Mayan ruins, and then sat and ate sweet potato pie right in front of the thing, as if the riches of the world, just inches away, were nothing more than crumbs and buttermilk being chugged down their throat?

I have always favored African Americans. They have had their share of troubles, well documented. But at that moment, I could have strangled the woman. To show such disrespect for a valued artifact, a genuine piece of American history, was too much. I nearly blacked out with rage.

But then my excitement was overwhelming and I wanted to shout for joy as she pushed the box toward me with her elbow, so as to not drop her fork and drip a crumb of her precious sweet potato pie.

It took all my will to calmly reach out, pull the box close, open it, and gaze down upon my future.

"Might I have a glass of water?" I said.

"Surely," she said.

. . .

I INSPECTED THE TRAIN for an hour. It was in perfect condition. All three coaches, the coal car, and the engine. All of it, by God, kept in an old Thom McAn shoebox. A few bits of it were missing, mostly paint chipped and a few tiny pieces of piping off the coal car, but nothing that one of the great modern toy restorers of Austria or Belgium could not repaint or reproduce. Its tiny compartments, the engineer's cabin, the passenger car railings, were extraordinary, simply out of this world. The workmanship overall was exquisite, as if it had been made by a thousand tiny, thimble-sized engineers: perfectly crafted gauges, gadgets, switches, pipes, fittings, down to the tiniest detail. It was magical. Otherworldly. Immaculate. I felt faint as I examined it.

"I'm dreaming," I whispered to myself.

She looked at me, puzzled, chewing as she spoke. "Common sense is shy as rats in this world," she said. "That a soul would let a little toy have such power over 'em. Blessed God."

I barely heard. She was a fool and I was in love. I couldn't see her. Couldn't see anything but the train. I wanted it. I had to have it. My initial thought was to steal the train by offering them the increments of $9,000 I carried in my briefcase until I reached the $90,000 I had there. I discarded that idea. I decided to offer the $90,000 as a down payment.

"Do you have any idea what this is?" I managed to croak. My voice took a minute to come back.

"In this house, we care about souls, sir. The Word. Toys

don't count. You want your water? You ain't touched it. 'Cause if you're not thirsty, I'll have that, too. We don't waste in this house. How you like your gift?"

"I can't accept it as a gift," I said. "But would your husband sell it to me?"

"He don't want no money," she said. "Spurgeon said give it to you. How many times you gotta hear it?"

"I can't do that," I said. "It's valuable."

"You free, white, and over twenty-one, mister. Do what you want."

"I'll pay him. I insist. I'll pay him a lot."

She looked at me oddly. "What's the matter with you? That little ol' thing's just a worldly something. Spurgeon ain't no worldly man," she said proudly. "He's a man of God. He made a promise. The Bible says it: Ecclesiastes, fifth chapter, fourth verse: 'When you make a vow to God, do not delay fulfilling it; for he has no pleasure in fools.' God's first in Spurgeon's life," she declared. "Mine's too. You know Spurgeon's been running First Tabernacle out on Fulton Avenue in Brooklyn for twenty-six years this coming August."

"How nice. Couldn't your church use some money if you sold it?"

She thought a moment. "I reckon First Tabernacle could. That building's falling apart. And we need a new van. American made. But you got to talk to Spurgeon."

"Well, I will pay you enough for a van and to fix the church and even buy your family a car," I said.

"You talking crazy. Why would we take a car when the House of the Lord needs fixing?"

"You can do what you want with what I pay."

She eyed me. "Make sure you talk to Spurgeon, 'cause right now our phone is about to get cut off and Junior needs some new shoes. He eats enough for two people. Growing so fast I can't keep up with him. Why, he's twelve and he's bigger than me!"

Given her size, Junior must be so big they feed him with a harpoon.

"Let me tell you about this train," I said. "See this smokestack—"

"Mister," she was impatient now, "if it ain't got God's Kingdom in it, I ain't interested. Jesus, mister. Jesus! Put Jesus in your heart. Spurgeon is gonna try to save you when you meet him. Have you been saved?"

"Saved?"

"Got Jesus, mister?"

"Well, um. I do like him . . . but can we talk about this train? And the price?"

"It's nice of you to come all the way out here. But I got prayer meeting in half an hour. Spurgeon told me what to tell you. I done it. He said give it to you. Now you do what you think is best."

"I need to talk to him. Can I reach him today?"

"He's out at Rikers Island doing prison ministry."

That didn't seem safe. Even I have my limits as to where I'll go to talk about toys. "Tomorrow?" I asked.

"Prayer meeting from noon to seven."

"Friday?"

"Hour of Power Bible Study. He runs four classes."

"Saturday?"

"Church bingo in the morning, then feeding the homeless in the evening. Then his janitor job at Brooklyn College till two a.m., 'cause he's saving to send Junior to Disney World. Then his regular job at the night shift at the Domino Sugar factory in Williamsburg. From there he goes to the shelter on Kent Avenue and works with the homeless till noon. On Fridays he got a third job at a horrible club in Brooklyn someplace, sweeping the floor till four in the morning. But like I said, he wants to get Junior a ticket to Disney World."

"Doesn't he sleep?"

"You don't sleep when you got the calling."

"What about Saturday before church bingo? Bingo doesn't start at eight a.m. does it?"

"He's got prison ministry in Newark seven a.m. Saturdays. They need God in New Jersey, too."

"Sunday?"

She looked at me strangely. "Sunday's church day, mister."

"How can I see him, then?"

She rose from the table. "Don't you worry. Take the toy. I'll tell him you was here. If you want to give us a few dollars, go ahead, but you ain't got to. Spurgeon said take it. He was pretty clear about it."

I stared at my briefcase. Ninety thousand dollars and a release form, and I was rich for the rest of my life. Free of Bucks County. I could get rid of that drafty converted barn with its lousy heating system and field mice. No more pretending to be a professor for stupid clients willing to kill each other over hundred-year-old dolls made of porcelain and wood. No more being the only Jew in the room with no connection to anyone or anything. I would find a temple I liked. Hell, I would build a temple I liked. Even with attendant lawsuits, bad publicity, and more lawsuits—and a prize like this would draw more lawyers than dung draws flies—the worth of the train would cover me in retirement in Maui for the rest of my life. That was my dream. Maui. I could see it. I never thought it would happen.

But I couldn't stand it. I'm a dealer, a businessman, not a thief. I wanted the thing free and clear. Besides, the Reverend, not his wife, was the owner of the train. It had been passed down from his grandmother, she said. I needed the story behind it. A toy dealer is only as good as the story of his toys. That's what you use in part to sell the thing. It's a good part of the value. I needed that, too. The stories sell the product. Given the rarity of the asset, I needed that story badly.

"I'll wait for him, then. Here. If you don't mind."

"You can't do that," she said. "I got to go and you can't stay with Buster here. Not by yourself. That dog's crazy. Plus you want Junior to come home from choir practice and find a white man in a suit setting at the table and nobody explaining nothing to him? He'll be scared stiff. You wanna take it or not?"

As tempting as it was, I had to be aboveboard. "I can't. I have to get your husband's okay in writing. He has to sign a release."

She shrugged and stood up. "Suit yourself. I'm already late for prayer meeting. You wanna take some pie with you?"

I nodded out of courtesy. She wrapped another piece in a paper towel, handed it to me, and headed toward the door. To my horror, she left the train on the table.

Trying to hide my incredulousness, I chirped out, "Mrs. Hart. The train . . . it shouldn't be left on the table."

"Oh, you're right," she said. "Spurgeon is funny about this darned thing."

She picked up the world's rarest, most precious toy train set and dropped it back in the shoebox as if it were a pile of junk, then plopped the box atop her decrepit refrigerator, next to a box marked "Rat Poison."

"He had a little wood box that came with it at one time," she said. "Handmade. Nice little thing. It's around here somewhere. Junior keeps his Legos in it."

It was at that point that I had to restrain myself from grabbing her by the throat—assuming I could reach it—and cracking her head against the table. Toy boxes in mint condition are often nearly as valuable as the toy itself. In this case, the box could be worth God knows how much . . . many millions.

"Mrs. Hart, just so you know, this train is worth quite a bit of money," I repeated. "In fact—"

She cut me off and patted my hand patiently. "Mister, the only train I care about is the train to Kingdom Come. Jesus, mister! Come to Jesus! You ain't saved. I can tell. Don't worry. Spurgeon'll fix you."

She placed her hands on her hips. It was time for me to go.

"Can I call him tonight?" I asked.

"I told you our phone's getting cut off. Phone company's shutting it off today at five. That's what they said and they ain't fooling. We'll pay it next week and get it going again. He'll get back to you then. Don't worry."

"Isn't there any way of reaching him now?"

She shrugged. "Well, I suppose you could scoot over to the Domino plant if you want," she said. "He works the overnight shift."

"You sure I can catch him there?"

"Why not?" she said, ushering me to the door and out onto the front step. I glanced at my car, which was mercifully intact.

"His shift starts at eleven. Take care, mister. And you ought to check yourself. Running around after a silly little train. There's a bigger train coming for you. The big train, honey, bound for glory. You best be ready."

With that, she nudged me down the steps and closed the door.

. . .

THAT NIGHT, cloistered in a room at the Hilton on Sixth Avenue, I made a few careful inquiries by phone to three of my most important buyers, massively rich clients who try to outspend each other just for fun, frivolity, and ego. After spending several minutes convincing them that I was not joking and might in fact shortly be procuring, at great cost, the Under Graham Railroad Box Set that was once the property of General Robert E. Lee, their laughs and disbelief turned first to shocked silence, then to muted exuberance, and finally to bursts of fast figures, first murmured, then shouted. The initial offers began in millions—then tens of millions. The numbers made me sweat. I told them I'd get back to them and then hung up.

The Reverend's shift started at eleven. I was out of the hotel and heading for the Domino Sugar plant in Brooklyn by ten o'clock. I had changed and was dressed for battle, wearing a crisp white shirt, khakis, and—to complete the transformation—left the Benz at the hotel garage in favor of a rented car and driver. The briefcase was locked in my hotel room safe. The idea of pawning off 90K and a release to this man for the train set was, I decided, a bad idea. This man worked several jobs, was obviously intelligent, and, I suspected, would not part with this object easily. Despite what his wife said, I decided there was a game afoot, a long-winded game plan to coax more dollars out of me. There was no reason that train was sitting on the refrigerator with him telling his wife to give it to me other than he wanted it to bait me in some kind of way or draw me into some kind of trap.

I decided the Reverend was toying with me and gave up the idea of walking away with the train for a mere pittance. I was ready to bargain. The Reverend, profoundly clever operator that I knew he was, would not find a better toy dealer. I would convince him of that.

Instead of cash, I toted along a backpack bearing the Reverend's portfolio. The plastic binder had long ago been replaced by a hand-hewn leather-bound spiraled job with the name "The Reverend Spurgeon T. Hart" emblazoned in crisp, gold, roman letters, with gold braiding around the edges. The photo of the Under Graham Railroad Box Car Set was between two pieces of glass, covered with acid-free paper. I hadn't shown this wonderful piece of theater to his wife, saving it for what I expected would be a second go-round or perhaps a last-ditch attempt to lure the prospective client. This seemed an appropriate moment.

I arrived at the plant's front entrance with no small amount of fanfare, having given the plant owners the dazzle treatment before I left the hotel, a song-and-dance involving one of my customers, a bank branch president I called at home, at night, who in turn telephoned the CEO of the Domino Sugar Packing Company and made a few discreet comments about values, indexes, blue-chip stocks, and the kind of clients I represent. The rich have their own language, and it worked like magic.

When I arrived at the plant and emerged from the back seat of my shiny, hired Lincoln Town Car, I was promptly ushered inside by a sheepish-looking foreman to a long row of workers on an assembly line stamping sugar cubes out of huge sugar blocks.

"There's your guy," my guide said.

Rev. Spurgeon Hart, owner of the most valuable toy in the world and a millionaire in waiting, was stamping sugar cubes and stacking them in one-pound yellow boxes in a line with twenty-five other workers. He was rail thin, a foot and a half shorter than his wife, a light-skinned black fellow with long dangling arms and a tattered baseball cap that said "Jesus Is Coming." He wore a plain plaid shirt, a pair of yellow ragged polyester pants, and scuffed shoes.

The plant floor was busy, and over the hammering of the machinery the infernal racket of rap music was pounding in a boom box near the Reverend, property of a young man who worked across from him on the other side of the assembly line. Clearly, the music seemed to cause the Reverend no small amount of consternation, for he occasionally glanced at the boom box in irritation as he dumped sugar cubes into boxes and expertly placed them on the rack, where they were fed to another set of workers who crated them. The incessant boom of the irritating music, combined with the hammering of the assembly line machinery, was so loud I could barely hear myself think.

As I approached, the Reverend glanced up, saw me coming, and actually seemed to shrink inside himself. He began to work faster, as if by being busier it would make me disappear. He didn't wait for me to speak.

"I know who you are," he shouted over the din. "My wife told me you were coming. Can we talk tomorrow? I'm busy."

"I think what I have here is worth taking a break for," I said. I smiled and held up the cover of the portfolio with his name emblazoned in golden letters. I had spent several days putting it together and was quite proud of it. I held it high so he could see it. He glanced at it and grimaced.

"I told her to give you the train already," he shouted, pulling a stack of yellow sugar boxes off the rack and placing them into a carton.

"But we have to agree on a price."

He stopped packing for a moment and sighed heavily, stepping closer so I could hear him. "Meet me in the workers' cafeteria at two a.m.," he said grumpily. "We get a break then."

"Will they let me stay that long?"

"Foreman says you know the president or something like that," he grunted. "Ain't nobody gonna fool with you." Then he turned away and began stamping sugar cubes again.

I sat in the cafeteria a solid two hours, drinking coffee from an old coffee machine that charged fifty cents a cup. The sugar, though, was free. At 2 a.m. the assembly line machinery ground to a stop, the roar of the cranks died, and several weary workers tromped into the room, Rev. Hart among them.

He strode in with a distinct, pigeon-toed gait, which reminded me of a superb Negro baseball player I had once seen as a boy in 1947 play in Brooklyn at a Dodgers game with my father, who loved baseball.

He sat at the table across from me and without a word opened a brown paper bag and unfurled an egg salad sandwich and a piece of the appalling sweet potato pie. I noticed it was the same partially eaten piece that Mrs. Hart had left on her table that afternoon when she got up to leave; that is, after half devouring my piece, she gave the rest of it to him. He unwrapped it, grabbed the odorous thing with his fingers, and gulped it down in what I can only characterize as an act of unbelievable willpower, for whatever ingredients had been tossed into it seemed to have spawned by then, as it smelled horrible. He got rid of it quickly.

As he turned to his more appealing egg sandwich, several workers still streamed in, one of them the young man bearing a boom box, which he placed on an adjacent table and turned on, joined by three of his young friends. The infernal racket of rap music, full of pejorative curses and pornographic references, pounded across the room. The Reverend glanced at the radio, clearly irked, which gave me time to think of an opening line.

"Rev Hart, you walk just like Jackie Robinson," I said brightly.

He waved me off. "One minute," he said. He sat up, placed his palms upward, bowed his head, and prayed, drifting off into a kind of zone, murmuring to himself. His prayer, as best I could tell, started out sounding like a choo-choo train, slowly, softly, with several incantations to the Lord for forgiveness, apologizing for gulping his wife's pie down before giving thanks, holiness, help, blessings for this and that and so forth. He warmed to the task slowly at first, which took about a minute, and five minutes later was full out, preaching like a roaring diesel engine, eyes closed, gone, hollering at God for redemption, mercy, help, and forgiveness for his coworkers. He ended with a long, ranting tirade about devil music, making a few direct references to the roaring, cursing filth that was emerging from the nearby boom box, praying for cleansing and dimension and all sorts of business for those who listened to it, praying for the boom box and even its owner, a young African-American man he referred to by name.

This brought a chortle from the young fellow and his three coworkers, two men of African-American and one of Hispanic descent respectively, sitting with him eating their 2 a.m. meal, talking at the Reverend with genuine amusement and, dare I say, encouragement.

"G'wan, Rev."

"Git it, Rev."

"Preach, Rev! You the man!"

"Gracias, Rev."

"Mention me, Rev, mention me!"

Then they turned the box up a notch. The music boomed louder.

The Rev. Hart, still in prayer, ignored them. He was in his own world. He roared on a bit longer, delivering a litany about the blasphemy of the pornography and funk that wafted out of their boom box. For several minutes, man and boom box shouted at each other. It was a kind of war. And then the box won. The Rev. Hart sat in silence. And as a reward, the other side relaxed: The young man turned down the box to a decent volume.

The Reverend, sitting meditatively, opened his eyes. The spell was gone. Several older coworkers, mostly Dominicans and Haitians who had joined him in fitful prayer with their eyes shut, opened their eyes, too, and smiled at him. The room finally began to simmer down and eat.

"I can break their junk every time," the Reverend said, glancing at the four young men who were now busy eating. "They don't know what's good for 'em." Then he spoke to the young men directly. "Y'all don't know what's good for you. That music is devilment."

The young men grinned, amused.

"Right on, Rev," said one.

"You the man," said another. "Do your thing, baby."

This whole business took nearly fifteen minutes, and he had yet to speak to me. I was under the impression from the previous lunch break crew that he only had thirty minutes to eat. So I got right to it.

"About the train," I said.

He cut a nervous glance at his fellow workers, none of whom were now paying attention and who chatted among themselves. "Oh, that old thing," he said dismissively. "That's from my grandmother. She died when I was a boy. I never knew her well."

"Well, she left you quite a present." I produced the leather portfolio bearing his name in neat gold gloss trim. He barely glanced at it. I opened it to the picture. "Is this you?"

"Naw," he said, waving his hand. "That's my great-grandpa there. He got his money same way my pa did. Selling booze and cigarettes. Making money hand over fist selling evil, the devil keeping score," he said, biting into his egg sandwich.

"Reverend Hart, let me be clear here. That train is rare. It's quite valuable. I'd like to buy it."

He frowned, suddenly miserable. "For God's sake, go ahead then. Since you keep crowing about it, g'wan and buy it."

"Don't you want to know what I'll pay?"

"Whatever you say," he said miserably, looking away.

"It's probably worth . . . I'd say it has considerable value. Much more than you think."

He looked around nervously, then glanced at his watch and brightened. "Only three minutes left for meal break," he said gaily. "Factory rules. They're tight about mealtime breaks around here."

"Reverend, for what that toy is worth, you could buy this place, fire your boss, and have lunch all day."

A sudden, wild look crossed his face, then disappeared.

"Just do what you want with that thing," he said. "How much you wanna pay me for it? Whatever you say is fine. I'll take whatever you got."

I could stand it no longer. "Reverend Hart, do you realize what you're saying?"

I spoke louder than I wanted to, and several people sitting nearby glanced at us. He suddenly reached over and grabbed my arm with such force that I was nearly pulled across the table. The pallor of his yellow face seemed to darken. He leaned in close, whispering, his face drawn tight, and suddenly fierce and wild.

"Do what you want with it," he said. "I got a church to run. And a God to serve. And that devilment"—he pointed to the boom box—"is what I'm put on this earth to stop. That dumb train is just a silly earthly thing setting in my house gathering dust and bringing sin. You come all the way here to talk 'bout that thing? I already told you: Do what you want with it. Talk to my wife."

"But she told me to talk to you!"

He stared at me with such force, such severe purpose, his face crunched into outrage, his eyebrows furled into angry valleys meeting at his eyes, his thin mustache suddenly drawn around the corners of his mouth in roaring fury, that I became frightened. His whole sense of purpose seemed so deep and wretched that I felt panic.

He must have seen the fear in my face, because he released my arm and with what seemed a great effort cleared his face of the expression until it was again blank and docile.

"Just set it up so that Junior gets any money from it when me and my wife is gone," he said. "I don't want him to know about it till I'm gone. You'd be doing me a favor. And don't tell my wife what it's worth. Can you do that for me?"

I assured him I could.

"Then it's done," he said, standing up. "And I reckon there's a small piece in it for you, too, somehow, which I hope you enjoy. And take it with my blessing. Good day, mister. God bless you. I got to get back to work."

To make a long story short, I got the train.

And a few days later I sold it.

I am rich.

It drew so many millions to myself and to the good Rev that I . . . I am loath to state exact amounts, as Uncle Sam has developed a sudden interest in the hyper boost to my once-modest income, and my lawyers have their hands full. Suffice to say it was the biggest—and emptiest—commission I ever got in my life. I could have gotten many more millions had I sold the train on the open market, but the fact is, I have no children, and the Reverend wanted quiet. And frankly, how much money does one really need?

As it was, the buyer paid quite respectably—very respectably—for it, and he too wanted secrecy. He was one of my regulars, a billionaire from America's upper crust who was familiar with the train's story and wanted it kept quiet, in honor of General Lee and his beloved son and his beloved South. I'm told when he took possession of the train he put it on a private plane and flew it to Zurich, where it was placed in a private Swiss bank. It lives in a specially air-conditioned vault by itself. Every week, a worker wearing an all-white, special dust-clean suit, complete with mask and gloves, enters the vault and cleans the train and air brushes the entire vault.

The 15 percent commission set me up for life. That's what the Reverend insisted I take. It's above my usual 10 percent. The Reverend, of course, is set as well as any millionaire in New York City.

I never spoke to him again. Milton, my attorney friend in New York—he got so fat from this deal he retired—handled everything from the Reverend's end. The Reverend bought his wife a new stove, paid off his phone bill, and had the rest of the sale proceeds placed in a trust in his son's name. Even his wife doesn't know the value of the fund, which at the moment, according to Milton, brings in about four million a month toward little Junior's future, give or take a few hundred thousand. Every day the Reverend, who, as I understand it, has yet to buy that American-made van that his church so desperately needs, draws $45,000 in interest.

I supposed that would be the end of it. But I confess I could not understand it. I still can't. I am, after all, a man who sells more than toys. I sell stories. And the story of the Under Graham Railroad Box Car Set eluded me. It was confounding. The Reverend refused to tell me how he got it. He refused to talk about his grandmother or his family. That was the condition of the sale as well. That I never ask. I had to accept those terms, which afterwards I deemed simply unacceptable. It just clawed at me.

I suppose it was for that reason that several months after the sale was completed I called his house. The surface reason was that one of his funds had matured and needed his signature, though Milton could have easily processed the business without him. But it gave me a worthy excuse, since the Reverend refused to talk to Milton himself and only dealt with him through me when the deal was consummated.

I was happy to call him—delighted, in fact. To my surprise, his phone was shut off. My curiosity wore at me, and I began to drift toward his Queens neighborhood occasionally. I came up with the notion of actually buying the dream house in Maui I once wanted—I could afford it, after all—and the idea of flying to Hawaii out of JFK seemed suddenly attractive. Thus I found myself frequently driving four hours from Pennsylvania to Kennedy Airport, knowing the freeway passed the Reverend's house. I drove through the neighborhood several times, hoping to spot the Reverend by chance and broach the subject with him of how the train survived this long, how it made it to the North, who stole it from the general, and so forth. But to no avail. When that didn't work, I drove to Brooklyn and parked outside the Domino plant at night, hoping to catch him on the way in or out of the busy plant gate. But I could never spot him in the hundreds of workers who wandered by.

This is where I started to wonder: If he didn't know his grandmother, how did he know the story of the train? Perhaps he didn't. Perhaps it was all some kind of ruse, a game he played with himself? Or with me?

It was too much. After several months I gave up, decided to enjoy my newfound wealth, and almost forgot Reverend Hart.

Until last month.

I happened to be in Brooklyn. I was there to check out a collection in Greenpoint owned by an Orthodox Jew. The collection wasn't worth much, maybe a few hundred thousand, but the man planned to use the money to pay tuition for his daughter to attend New York University, and that's a big order these days. He was a nice fellow, an English teacher, and he really needed help, and I was glad to assist. I planned to meet him Friday morning, but I got hung up in traffic and didn't make it to his house in Brooklyn until nearly 7 p.m. Too late did I realize, awful Jew that I am, that it was Friday night, the beginning of the Jewish Sabbath. He couldn't see me. He couldn't touch a doorknob. Even if he could, he wouldn't be amenable to discussing anything as worldly as money. Or a toy. He wouldn't be available until probably Sunday.

I was disappointed and starving, and knowing I had a long drive back to Pennsylvania, I drove around Greenpoint looking for a place to eat. I stopped a passing pedestrian to ask about the whereabouts of a good diner and was directed to nearby Williamsburg. I found the street and diner in question, and as I sought a place to park, I noticed a crowd lining up to get into a corner bar across the street from the diner. The neon sign above the door said *"The Tonk: the funkiest, nastiest, skankiest, hip-hop and R'n'B club in New York City!"* Underneath that in smaller brightly lit script letters it read *"Tonight and every Friday night: Dr. Skank."*

I pulled my Mercedes-Benz, the newest top-of-the-line model—which I own now, by the way, no more leasing—up to a parking spot across the street from the club. I was fidgeting with the back-and-forth of wedging my car into a tight parking space when a familiar figure with a pigeon-toed gait wandered slowly right in front of my car. I almost hit him.

It was Reverend Hart. I noticed his walk immediately, along with the telltale ragged baseball cap with the Jesus admonition on it. There was no mistaking it.

He didn't notice me. He seemed to be in a kind of fog, walking slowly, deliberately, as if he were marching to his own death. He trudged sadly, as if in a trance, to the front of the line of clubgoers who were waiting to get into the club. He stepped up to the bouncer at the door, who saw him, nodded, and let him pass, and the Rev disappeared inside.

"That's impossible," I said aloud. Then I remembered his wife said that his weekend job was the worst of all. Working as a janitor at a horrible nightclub.

I quickly finished parking, crossed the street to the club, stood in line, bought a ticket, and went inside.

In the bar it was dark, smoky, loud, filled with flashing neon lights, pounding rap music noise, and wriggling bodies of young squirming girls and bulked-up young men dancing. It was clear that I would not find him in that crowd, and so I gave up, deciding to make for the door, convinced I'd made a mistake. He'd never be here. However, the room was so thick with wild young people, packed like sardines, I could not make my way back to the door. I was pushed in deeper, trapped in a wedge of humanity as the incessant sounds of rap music pounded the walls and bounced into the air amid the excited crowd of young squirming bodies. They moved like wild animals, dancing, laughing, smoking, sipping beer, guzzling alcohol. Onstage, four young men in headphones operated turntables, each playing theirs in turn. It was a kind of competition, creating a tremendous, booming racket that blasted out of giant speakers on each side of the stage, while in front of the turntables, a young man holding a microphone beseeched the crowd, admonishing the youngsters in the most graphic terms imaginable to be foul, dirty, nasty, filthy, and to dance the night away. He was followed immediately by another young man who took the microphone from him, then by another, and then a young woman, then another young man, and then another, each surrendering the stage to the next in turn, ranting and talking in various rhymes, trading quips—a nonstop litany of rhyming and fibbing, flattering, and heretical yelling. While I've never been partial to this bit of youngster foolishness, trapped as I was, I found myself forced to listen, and was stirred a bit by some of what I heard. The young men and women were telling stories, some funny, some touching, some ironic, stories about their lives, their poverty, their middle-class lives, the emptiness of their parents' wealth, the strife of their struggling

mothers, and all manner of things, far beyond the mere pornography and filth I'd associated with this music before. Indeed I was so taken by some of the stories that after a few
minutes I forgot where I was, for each of the young poets who
leaped onstage was better than their predecessor, and each
ended their stirring performance by reminding the audience
that an even greater presence was among them, The Great
One, Dr. Skank, who had started it all, The Originator of the
Original, The Anointed and the First, The Greatest Rapper of
All Time, was coming in just a few moments. The crowd buzzed
with anticipation each time his name was mentioned: Dr.
Skank.

The mention of the coming messiah was enough to jolt me
back to the reason I stood among those young hooligans, an
old man among children, for I too had a special person I was
coming to see. I looked around for several long minutes for the
Reverend, who I expected was pushing a broom in the back
somewhere or admonishing a poor young soul—there were
plenty of candidates there, to be sure. But he was nowhere in
sight. I decided to try to leave again. I'd had enough. This was,
after all, his life and his business. This was his war. Let him
fight it. He'd asked to be left alone. I would honor his request.

Just as I turned to fight my way to the exit, the music onstage quit and the stage lights dimmed, the flashing neon lights
ceased, and the dark room went quiet.

An excited announcer took the stage. "Y'all have been
cool," he said. "Y'all have been nice. So now, here's what you've

been waiting for: The Grandmaster of Dirty Ass Funk, The Mister Meister of Sweetness. The Funk Beast of the Infatuation. The Original Godfather of Rap. The One. The Only. The Grand Funkmaster and Stinkmeister. The Original Rapper of the Original Rap. The man who created hip-hop as we know it. Give it up y'all for The Doctor of *the Shit!* The Mister of the Mister. The Doctor of Historical Noise. Here he is. . . . *Dr. Skank!*"

The crowd roared. A lone spotlight hit center stage, and into it stepped Rev. Spurgeon Hart.

He was dressed in sparkling white tennis shoes, colored shoelaces, brand-new sweatshirt and sweatpants, and dark shades that covered half his face. He wore a brand-new baseball cap sideways, and a ragged T-shirt that said "Fuck you and everything you stand for."

He turned to the four DJs spinning records behind him and motioned. They began to whir up their machines, one at a time, as he pointed. He pointed at each, like a ground control flight director commanding fighter pilots to start their engines. One by one they cranked up, playing their music until they were in sync and roaring full blast. And only when they were at top volume, the sound shaking the walls, did the Reverend step to the microphone and begin—launching into a litany of nonstop cursing, roaring, funky, low-down, skuzzy, earth-scrapping, to-the-bone brilliant, rhyming lyrics that made the previous rappers before him seem like choirboys. His voice was unworldly. It sounded like sandpaper grinding on a gravelly road, yet smooth as a glass of water, both powerful and mighty, yet calm as the curve of an egg. The voice ripped through the room, the thunder of his words seeming to peel the wallpaper off the walls. The crowd went wild.

Looking back, I cannot recall every word the Reverend said, but the gist I will never forget.

His words had to do with history. He spoke of a nation of people with good hearts misled by men with bad souls. A system where men traded souls for cash and the most evil of them shouted the loudest and led the rest to sin: men who would be punished by God yet were revered by man; men ruling a world of underlings—slaves, Jews, Muslims, Arabs, Buddhists, Hindus, and Christians.

And amid this story was that of a little boy many years ago who had once owned a toy, who had done nothing wrong other than to live in a world where he suffered the punishment for crimes inflicted by generations before him. And the punishment of those whose sins had killed off this boy and his dreams before the boy even had a chance to live, before he had a chance to play with his toy, a simple train, which was more than a train, it was a weapon dressed as a train; the story of a boy dying in agony, an innocent child paying for generations of stolen trains, stolen cars, stolen land, stolen horses, stolen history, stolen people, arriving at a strange land inside a merchant ship, their innocence and freedom forever soiled, and then God's punishment for their captors, passed down for generations to their captors' innocent children, whose forefathers were fools stealing for today while leaving nothing for tomorrow, robbing their own young of their future, all of them, both captor and slave, suffering God's justice and inexplicable will, the punishment of a gigantic wrong gone awry for centuries, and the payment thereof of generations, whose clumsy attempts to try to right wrongs with war or halfhearted stumblings toward the right created even more pain and war. Suffering, all of it, greed, horror, a holocaust against decency causing unbearable agony. Pain upon pain upon pain. Suffering, all of it, because of some great wrong.

"You reap what you sow, you dog!" Mr. Skank roared as he wound it down, "and so it will be forever, you motherf—ers! Generation after generation. Till the end of time, you fucks! You men-bitches! Hooooo!" he shouted, releasing a torrent of vicious curse words that ricocheted across the room like machine gun bullets, yet from his mouth they sounded not like filth, but more like redemption. His filthiness cleared the air. His rage cleansed me even as I stood and listened. His rage washed the room clean.

I turned and left.

I never contacted him again. Why bother him? I'm set for life, and so is he. Because of him I get to move to Maui. And because of me he gets to be Rev. Spurgeon T. Hart, who could not afford to buy his wife a new car or send his son to Disney World, a poor preacher who holds down two jobs a week so that every Friday night he can be Dr. Skank the motherf—er, delivering true redemption to a small group of believers.

THE FIVE-CARAT
SOUL BOTTOM
BONE BAND

BUCK BOY

We was rehearsing over Mr. Woo's Grocery and Chinese Take-Out one day when the following happened:

We hear gunshots.

First we stop playing and hit the floor because in The Bottom you don't know who the good guy is. Then we hear Mr. Woo shouting downstairs and we run down and see him standing over Buck Boy Robinson.

Buck Boy be about seventeen years old, I guess. Don't matter now 'cause he laying on the floor dead as a doornail. Blood is everyplace. Buck Boy, dead as he was, still got a knife in one hand and a fistful of dollar bills in the other. His hand was clutching that money tight, like he never want to let it go.

Mr. Woo is a little old man who wear a yellow straw hat. Whether he's Chinese or Korean I don't know, but he let my

band rehearse upstairs over his store for free. He holding a
gun. He drop it like it's a firecracker and walk around in a little
circle, ringing his hands and talking in Chinese or whatever. I
couldn't understand a word.

Two cops come quick, chase everybody out the store, close
it down and take the gun from the floor. They leave us inside
because we are witnesses. The cop ask Mr. Woo what happened.

"He try to rob me," Mr. Woo say. He don't look too hot. His
face is pale and he look like somebody punched him in the
stomach. The cops have a heck of a time prying that money out
of Buck Boy's hand. Finally they get it out and hand it to Mr.
Woo, but the Chinese shake his head.

"Just get him out," he say. He don't look at Buck Boy when
he talk.

By this time the whole neighborhood show up, including
Buck Boy's sister Victoria, who be shouting and screaming outside Mr. Woo's store. The cops ask us questions but we really
didn't see nothing, so the cops call the black van to come get
Buck Boy. The van take its time to get there, but Buck Boy, he
ain't in no hurry now. So we sit there a half hour: me, Dex,
Goat, Bunny, Dirt, the cops, Mr. Woo, and Buck Boy. I seen
that Buck Boy was wearing a brand-new pair of white and purple sneakers.

Nobody around here liked Buck Boy too much. He always
be looking for trouble and he always be strung out on something what they call PCP or whatever that makes you lose your

mind. Drugs was his main line, but he'd steal anything. Steal a purse, steal the chrome off a car, steal a whole car. The worst he did was he stole our whole school bus two years ago when we was on it. He crashed it into a light pole on the Boulevard and bang us up pretty bad and run off. I don't think he went to jail for it.

So nobody cry too much when they carry Buck Boy from Mr. Woo's Grocery except for his sister Victoria. It's kind of sad, because his mother never pay him no mind from when he was a little boy, and I heard people say she is strung out on drugs herself. That whole Robinson family is bad news.

No sooner do they load Buck Boy into the van than television trucks come flying up. They come all the way from Morgantown, West Va., twenty-eight miles across the state line, even though we is Uniontown, Pa., a whole different state. The news don't care. News is news. And The Bottom is always good news for the news. 'Cause we mostly bad news. The reporters jump out and bust through the crowd like cops. Right behind them come Rev. Jenkins. He is the preacher of my church, Bright Hope Baptist. I read a story in the newspaper once that say ever since the 1980s, Rev. Jenkins has been the "community leader" of The Bottom. I don't know what that is, but it do seem like whenever there's a fresh-cooked chicken or a television camera around, Rev. Jenkins don't be far off. When people talk about how much they hate Rev. Jenkins, my ma says, "I don't hate his guts. He's full of my food."

Rev. Jenkins cover a lot of ground just standing in one place.

He's a big, fat man. I seen him undress at the pool one time, and it took me five minutes to see all of him. He got a slicked-back hairdo and he wearing one of his fine suits. He sports some of the most killing suits you ever seen. He's going with the pink pinstripe suit today, and when he bust through the crowd, people bounced off him like he was a beach ball. He hit the door of Mr. Woo's the same time the newsmen do, but Mr. Woo had locked it and pulled the shades down.

"Oh hell," Rev. Jenkins say. Then he starts talking loud about Buck Boy being shot to death, poor ol' Buck Boy, and it was a shame he was so young, and that he was tired of the foreigners always coming to The Bottom and starting up stores and treating the blacks like they're nobody after black folks spend all their money on them. And after a while he make it sound like Mr. Woo come all the way over from China or wherever just to shoot Buck Boy.

The newsmen kind of swill around and try to peek inside Mr. Woo's store. Then Rev. Jenkins say, "We're gonna do something about this. We need an investigation."

When he say that, the newsmen whip their heads up like a hunting dog who sniff a fox in the wind. They pull out their cameras and notebooks and turn on their tape gizmos and rush him.

"What kind of investigation?" one newsman ask. He got silver hair whipped up so much it look like cotton candy.

"A big investigation," Rev. Jenkins say. "Why, there shouldn't be no bigger investigation than this one. There should be a granddaddy investigation."

"You mean a grand jury investigation," one newsman say.

"Don't put words in my mouth!" Rev say. But then he is quiet a minute, and you can almost hear the machines in his mind clicking and spinning back and forth. He preach a fine sermon, but when he teach Sunday school I could read better than him and I'm only twelve. "You're right," he say. "We want the grandest jury investigation for all of it."

The reporters look at him and a couple of them laugh. That get Rev hot. He swell up inside his suit and it seem like the grease from his hair start to melt and spread and cover his face. "I'm saying that boy is a victim," he said. "That Korean had a gun. If that boy was white, would he be dead today? Would that Korean have shot him? Maybe he just went to get something to eat. Maybe the cops planted a weapon on him. Only God knows," he say, and he pull out a handkerchief to wipe his face, "because the cops ain't tellin'. But the truth is we tired of our children being gunned down like animals. We're tirrrrreed! We're gonna march!"

Rev. Jenkins can't read too good, but he sure got a way with words. This crowd getting warm now. "Yeahhh!" they say. "Let's march!"

"Is the march tomorrow?" a newslady holler out. She's a blond lady. I seen her on TV before. She look so good on television you want to kiss her, but in person she got so much powder on her face she look like a dustbag from a vacuum cleaner. On TV she looks young, but in person she look like she was born in the year of only God know. If she was two-faced, I think she could've used the other one. I was just so shocked to see her that way, but my friends Goat and Bunny was in love and can't take they eyes off her.

"There is no tomorrow for my people," the Rev say. "We will start right now. We will boycott this store. We will stand out here every single day and march and starve to death before we buy goods from a murderer. These foreigners treat us like second-class citizens. They shoot our children. They get minority loans from the government. We're sick of it. We ain't takin' NO MORE! We are FED UP! WE'RE GONNA MARCH!"

Now the crowd is fired up and newsmen are filming the whole thing. Everybody in this crowd I just about know, and they all know Mr. Woo ain't like the people from Sun Yung Restaurant three blocks down who put bulletproof glass over their counter and take your money and make sure not to touch your hand before they pass out the food to you and treat people from The Bottom like they ain't nobody, but everybody's laughing and watching Rev. Jenkins. He fun to watch when he get his wheels spinnin'. He really hot now.

"Ahhhh-haaaaa!" Rev. Jenkins say, "Ahhhhh hah! Tired! Lawd . . . a boy is dead . . . ," and he wipe his face with his handkerchief and start stuttering like he in church. "I knew this boy for years. He should have had a long life! What else did he have? He had no dreams! He had no hope! He had no aspirations! Ahh, but life! He had life! That's the one thing they couldn't take away from him, and now look. They took that away! Awwwwww! We are tired. We ain't takin' it!!"

"Yess!" say the crowd.

Rev. Jenkins point to Mr. Woo's store behind him. "We will march here tomorrow at this same time to see that this boy gets justice and this man gets driven outta here. And until he leaves we ain't quitting. We shall overcome. We shall overcome. We shall overcome! We SHALL-NOT-BE-MOVED!" and he shout them last words so loud one newsman with headphones yank them off.

The funny part is, if Buck Boy Robinson saw Rev. Jenkins in his fine pink suit walking down the Boulevard at night, he'd rob him down to his socks no problem. And Buck Boy would never protest for Rev. Jenkins if Rev. Jenkins was shot for holding up a store.

THE NEXT DAY The Bottom was jumping. Everybody and their brother show up. A bunch of white people come from town and from all the big towns around show up wearing T-shirts that say CARAO, which means Coalition Against Racism and something. The Guardian Angels like the kind they got in New York City come all the way from Pittsburgh, and more newsmen than I ever seen before. Fat newsmen. Old newsmen. Black newsmen. I even seen newsmen from China or Japan and look like Mr. Woo. They go all over the neighborhood asking about Buck Boy and Mr. Woo, except they don't call him Buck Boy no more. They call him Regis. I never knowed his real name was Regis.

Rev. Jenkins get a bunch of people walking around in a circle in front of Mr. Woo's store, but Mr. Woo was still closed. They marched anyway, singing "We Shall Overcome," and the TV cameras filmed it, but it wasn't too exciting. I didn't hardly know none of them protesters except Victoria Robinson and Rev. Jenkins. My whole band was there. The Five-Carat Soul Bottom Bone Band. Every member, even some of the old ones we threw out like Pig who don't never rehearse and Adam who they call Dirt who always smells funny. It was them two plus Bunny, Dex, Dex's brother Ray-Ray, Beanie, and Goat. We was in a fix. Our drums and guitars and Pig's saxophone was locked over Mr. Woo's store, 'cause he was holed up someplace tight and outta sight. We wanted our gear, but nobody was listening to us. They was busy selling beer and hot dogs to all them new people, the Guardian Angels and the CARAO T-shirt people and the white people from Morgantown and Pittsburgh and a few black folks I never seen before, not people from The Bottom. Not too many people from The Bottom who knew Buck Boy would march for him.

It wasn't more than forty people out there, but that night I see it on television and it looked like a real protest, with Rev. Jenkins out there leading hundreds of people, chanting and shouting and singing "We Shall Overcome" with Rev. Jenkins out front hollering and screaming. My mother watched it too and she laugh and say, "Hillary is a fool." Hillary is Rev. Jenkins's real name. My mother went to high school with him.

Next day The Bottom fill up with even more newsmen and protesters, and it's so many people swilling around on the Boulevard with new signs and more songs they stop traffic. They talking about burying Buck Boy soon, and the television people interview Buck Boy's mother who say she don't have no money to bury him. Next thing you know all sorts of money coming in. My sister Sissie knows Buck Boy's sister Victoria and Victoria told her that so much money come over the Robinsons' house that Mrs. Robinson needed three shoeboxes to put it in. She say one rich black man from Pittsburgh brung $1,200 cash to the house. Victoria said her mother bought a brand-new refrigerator plus a giant TV set and some new couches.

Buck Boy died on a Saturday. By Thursday The Bottom was still so full of newsmen knocking on doors that folks was running from them, so the newsmen started interviewing each other. Rev. Jenkins got his friend preachers to bring their churches from places out of town to keep the protest going, and more white folks like college students from Morgantown, West Va., showed up, yelling, "We're not taking it anymore!" They seem like nice people. I sure hope they leave The Bottom before dark.

They don't get around to burying Buck Boy till the following Monday because they was fussing over a place big enough for the service. First they planned to have it at the Gilbert Funeral Home on the Boulevard, but it only fits about seventy people. Then they move it to Mr. Wallace's funeral home on Simmons Avenue, but that got Rev. Jenkins upset. He say why not take it to his church, which holds four hundred people? They fuss about it and fuss about it even on TV and it make me a little sick. They fightin' over who can bury Buck Boy Robinson of all people. Nobody did nothing when Leonard Evans got shot in the back on Washington Avenue by that white cop for nothing, or Stella Brooks got raped by her father and he got away with it. But Buck Boy, who robbed a school bus and tried to rob Mr. Woo, he's a hero now.

The day of the funeral there must have been five hundred people packed inside Rev. Jenkins's Bright Hope Baptist Church and a ton of people outside who couldn't fit in shoving each other to get to the front where me and the rest of the band had camped out. They put me up front because I play the organ, but they didn't need me. They got a special organist all the way from Cleveland to play. Boy, he was something. He revved up the crowd good with them old songs. His was wearing the shiniest shoes you ever saw, and when he played he put his shiny shoes aside on a nice clean handkerchief on the floor next to the organ and played the organ pedals in his socks. And them socks didn't have nar hole in them.

Meanwhile, Rev. Jenkins was up front talking to the reporters from the pulpit till the last minute and he had a long time to talk to them because nobody had brought Buck Boy into the church yet.

Well, we just waited, everybody is standing around waiting, and waiting, and singing, and after a while the big-shot organ player from Cleveland he runned out of songs and had to get something to drink, and he walked off the organ, and now it's just people standing 'round. The body of Buck Boy is very late now, and finally we hear the crowd holler outside and we know Buck Boy's coming. Something about the noise the crowd made give me a very funny feeling, and when they brought Buck Boy I know why they hollered.

They had him in a pine box, and the first thing one of the newsmen say is, why that sure don't look like much of a casket. Then somebody laugh, and then somebody else laugh.

Buck Boy's sister and uncles and about a hundred cousins is up front and everyone is real quiet, just looking at that little box, with four little handles on it, no fancy-looking paint, nothing. You could see it was the lowest, cheapest casket come from out of Charlie's Bargain Store someplace. The funeral men carrying it set it down in front of the church and took off like they was ready to duck bullets.

Rev. Jenkins is looking around for somebody to open the casket, but nobody move. Finally he open it. Buck Boy look fine. Got a nice suit on, but that casket gotta go. Rev. Jenkins look around the front rows and ask for Buck Boy's mother, but she ain't there. I see Victoria Robinson standing there shrugging, so Rev. Jenkins got on the podium and sprint through his sermon like nothing's wrong, though he got one of them "We'll-get-to-this-later" looks on his face. Soon as it's over the funeral men come back and lift Buck Boy to the hearse while Rev. Jenkins march out of church in his robes hollering about the Gilbert Funeral Home and all the money they gave Mr. Gilbert for the funeral. There was about a hundred people following him and they was hot.

Mr. Gilbert's funeral home is right around the corner. Rev bang on the door and Mr. Gilbert open up and peek his head out. He see that mob and he don't open the door all the way. He's a spooky old man and he smell funny and he's always cranky, but his son Adam who they call Dirt plays guitar very good. Nobody but us wants Dirt in their band because he smells funny and everybody knows he works with dead people.

"I oughta skin you, Randy!" Rev. Jenkins say to Mr. Gilbert, and the crowd behind him raise up like they ready to trample Mr. Gilbert.

"It's not my fault," Mr. Gilbert say. "I can't bury nobody for free!"

"By God, we had four thousand dollars in donations for that boy," Rev. Jenkins snaps.

"Nobody gave me nothing," Mr. Gilbert say. "I swear to you, Hillary, I've had him in here more than a week and I didn't get a dime from nobody. No suit for him to wear, nothing. Didn't charge 'em for storage neither."

Rev. Jenkins, he turned and looked at Victoria Robinson,

who had marched over there and was standing right behind him. "My mother said she sent the money," Victoria say in a little voice, but she got a little jump in her voice and right then and there I knowed what happened.

Mr. Gilbert say to Victoria: "I tried to call your house but y'all ain't got no phone. I went by there but nobody answered the door and there were reporters all over. I went by a couple of times." And then he turn to Rev. Jenkins and say in a dry way: "I called you several times, too, Hillary, but you wouldn't return my calls either."

The Rev bite his lip and sway in his robes, then reach down and pull up his church robe to get at his pants pocket. "I'll pay for the suit and casket right now myself," he say.

"Nope," Mr. Gilbert say. "It's been paid for."

"By who?"

"Mr. Woo. He come by and paid me an hour ago. He gave me enough for a nice casket and a nice suit. I only had time to buy the suit. I didn't have time to order another box. And I didn't have no spares around here I could use in the meantime neither."

IT TOOK ALL AFTERNOON to sort out what happened at Mr. Gilbert's funeral home, for now everyone knowed Mrs. Robinson took all them donations and used them to buy televisions and couches and dope and whatever else. There was a lot of people in that crowd that wanted to find her and beat her brains out, but Rev. Jenkins said let it go. He told the newsmen to not say anything about it and a lot of them said they wouldn't but they did anyway. The Rev didn't care. He had his hands full keeping the folks from trying to fry Mrs. Robinson, and I think they would've gone no matter what if it wasn't for Victoria Robinson. That business tore her up and you could see it. She was only fourteen but she growed up right then and there. She really ain't so bad like the rest of them Robinsons.

After a while Rev. Jenkins say he had to go to the graveyard and say the last words over Buck Boy, so a bunch of us ride in the church van with him. Me, Mr. Gilbert, Victoria Robinson, my sister Sissie, Goat, Adam, Bunny, Dex and his brother Ray-Ray, just about the whole Five-Carat Soul Bottom Bone Band.

When we got to the graveyard it was almost dark outside and very quiet. The graveyard men had left the gate open, but there was nobody around and you almost couldn't see because there were no lights and it was getting dark and lonely with the wind blowing. Rev. Jenkins drove in on the paved road and said it suddenly occurred to him that he didn't know where to find Buck Boy's grave 'cause he'd rushed out of church before anybody could tell him where it was. But I knew, and I told him to keep driving around those little curvy roads till I told him to stop. When I saw Mr. Woo standing by himself on a little hillside with his yellow straw hat in his hand, I pointed and told Rev. Jenkins that's where Buck Boy is buried. And that's where he was.

RAY-RAY'S PICTURE BOX

There's five members in The Five-Carat Soul Bottom Bone Band: me, Goat, Beanie, Bunny, and Dex. Dex actually counts as one and a half when you include his little brother Ray-Ray. Ray-Ray ain't a full member. He's like a half member. He don't play nothing. He bangs on the cowbell and hoots and hollers mostly. He's more like a mascot. He's a brown-skinned boy with a clean, short haircut. He's only nine, two years younger than us, but he likes Kool and the Gang songs. Him and Dex is like night and day. Dex is serious and quiet and plays the guitar. Ray laughs and talks loud all the time. He likes to please. Ray-Ray will do anything for ice cream.

When we was little, Dex had to take care of Ray-Ray all the time. When they walked to school together, he'd tell Ray-Ray "Walk behind me," and Ray-Ray would walk a half block behind. I understand. I made my sister Sissie do the same thing when me and Dex went to school together. Sissie wouldn't bother with Ray-Ray. She'd walk a block ahead of him and make Ray-Ray walk another block behind her by himself, so he was actually two blocks back behind everybody. Of course, he'd get in all kinds of trouble being by himself, on account of his marbles wasn't all there. Like the time he got Hate Whistle mad. Hate Whistle's a drunk from The Bottom. His real name ain't Hate Whistle. His real name, somebody said, is Herbert. But mostly he's called Hate Whistle.

I never seen Hate Whistle take a drink. He's a happy drunk. He staggers around The Bottom all the time, smelling like whisky and laughing at nothing. Sometimes he plays baseball with us when we ain't got enough people and we don't mind because Hate Whistle's funny, plus nobody wants to play on our team, since we can't play nothing but music. Hate Whistle likes to dance on the sidewalk outside Mr. Woo's when we practice upstairs. Just look out the window and see him down there dancing in the street, he's just so happy and dancing around, and who don't like an audience?

The only thing about Hate Whistle is . . . well, you guessed it. Ray-Ray hit Hate Whistle's button one morning on the way to school. Me and Dex was walking to school that day and heard a lot of hollering and turned around and seen Hate Whistle chasing Ray-Ray around, so we had to go back and get Ray-Ray, and we was all late for school on account of Ray-Ray.

Dex said to me, "I didn't even know he could whistle." Then

he said to Ray-Ray, "From now on, just walk next to me and don't say nothing."

Ray-Ray done that, but he was never quiet on them walks to school. He was always asking questions to Dex. Ray-Ray asked a lot of smart questions for someone who's supposed to be not all the way there, like "Why do a bicycle have two wheels instead of five?" or "If Martin Luther King is dead, is we gonna be adopted?"

And Dex would say, "I don't know. Be quiet."

Sometimes Ray-Ray would complain, too. He'd say, "Dex, there's noise in my head. Can't you hear it?"

Dex would say, "It's the ocean, Ray-Ray."

"Where is the ocean?"

"It's far away, Ray-Ray."

"If I can hear it, why can't you?"

"I don't know, Ray-Ray."

Them two was raised by their daddy, Mr. Ernest. He was a short, heavyset man from down south. He never waved or talked too much to kids. Mr. Ernest was quiet like Dex. He went to work every day like clockwork, some kind of construction job because he always came home dirty, wearing concrete-type construction boots and a work hat. Dex said his daddy was from Alabama, but he never talked to me too much about him. His daddy was strict. I once went by Dex's house to pick up Dex for rehearsal and just before I turned in the gate I heard some talking on the side driveway and peeked over there and seen Dex outside talking to Mr. Ernest. I was too far off to hear what was said, but Dex said something to Mr. Ernest, and after he said it, Mr. Ernest grabbed Dex by the collar and slapped him across the face. Didn't say a word, just slapped him again and again, "slap, slap, slap," like that. Dex never cried or yelled. He stood there and took it.

I never did ask Dex what Mr. Ernest said or what it was about.

I never seen Dex's ma. I heard somebody say she worked at the post office in Falls Point. I never asked about her, 'cause it was kind of a secret, about Dex and Ray-Ray's mom. Whatever it was, it was probably gonna come out in The Bottom one way or the other anyhow. Dex being my best friend, I wasn't the type to ask him about that kind of personal thing. But one afternoon me, Ray-Ray, and Bunny was playing handball—it was mostly me and Bunny playing while Ray-Ray runned around laughing and fetching the ball for us—and after a while we set down to rest along the grate fence there and Bunny said, "Ray-Ray, where's your ma?"

"I don't know," Ray-Ray said, "but I got naked pictures of her."

Bunny's eyes got big. "Butt naked?" he said.

"Yep."

"Where at?"

"In a picture box in my basement."

Bunny plays sports good and fights the best on our block and he got the nicest house and the prettiest ma, so he's kind of the leader of The Five-Carat Soul Bottom Bone Band, even though he don't play guitar that good. Dex plays guitar way better than him. Bunny said to Ray-Ray, "If you bring me that picture box, I'll get you some ice cream."

Ray-Ray rocked from side to side when he talked, standing on one foot and then the other. He rocked from side to side a little bit, thinking, then looked at the sky and said, "Where's Dex?"

"Don't worry about him," Bunny said, "I'll get you a big ice cream cone if you bring me that box. What kind ice cream you like?"

That done it. Ray-Ray liked to please, and Bunny was leader of The Bottom Bone Band, and Ray-Ray loved himself some ice cream. "I like banilla," Ray-Ray said. He said everything that starts with a V as a B. Like "banilla" for vanilla, and "Bincent" for "Vincent."

"Vanilla it is."

Ray-Ray runned to his house and come back with a shoebox. He gave it to Bunny, who placed it on the ground along by the fence in the park and opened it up.

Whether it was really Ray-Ray and Dex's mom in them pictures, I don't know, for there was a lot of different women. I can't say really who it was, but when Bunny opened that box of pictures, my world kind of come apart. Nothing in my life put me ready to look at them pictures. It put girls in a whole new light. I never seen girls like that before. There was all types of girls, doing all kinds of things. Bunny flipped through 'em so fast and wild, he wouldn't hardly even let me get a look. He pushed through a few of 'em and finally tossed 'em in the box and stood up. "I'm gonna make me some money," he said.

"Where's my ice cream?" Ray-Ray said.

"I'mma get it for you."

Bunny headed out and we followed him to Mr. Johnson's grocery store on the Boulevard. Once we was inside there, Bunny drawed some money from his pocket—Bunny kept hisself some money, always had a quarter or fifty cents some kind of way—and brought Ray-Ray a giant vanilla ice cream cone. Then he said, "You go on home, Ray-Ray."

"What about the box?"

"I'll give it back in a little while."

"But I got to bring it home."

"Lemme make my money back first," Bunny said, and he headed off and me and Ray-Ray followed him along the Boulevard. But instead of turning back to our street, he crossed over the street and headed straight to the Cool Out Spot.

The Cool Out Spot in The Bottom was on the other side of the Boulevard behind some railroad tracks and bushes near an old soft drink factory that's been closed down for years. You can hide behind the bushes there and sit on an old wood fence near the old factory and drink beer without no grown-ups seeing you. That's where all the kids from The Bottom hung out, like The Six, boys from two blocks over who is our main competition in sports. The Six wasn't just six of 'em, by the way, it was a bunch of 'em. But they beat us in everything: baseball, football, Halloween fights, fistfights. They was older and cooler but they didn't have no band. But what they did have was Bo, Lightbulb, Chink, Junior, Amuneek—that was his real name, "I'm Unique"—Poogie, Toy Boy, and his older brother Tito. Tito was the leader of them Sixes. He wasn't too bad, but his little brother, Toy Boy, he was rough. All them Sixes was a little rough, but we got along okay. At the Cool Out Spot you was mostly safe from them anyway. It was kind of an agreement. No gangs from anyplace in The Bottom could beat up on you at the Cool Out Spot, so long as you had beer or brung soda or cakes or something to trade or share. It was a peace spot. Even some of the real bad ones that come around later, The Black Spades and The Seven Crowns—some of them was full-out bad—if you was at the Cool Out Spot it was mostly okay.

Bunny made a lot of friends that day. There was a bunch of pictures in that box, maybe fifty or a hundred—that shoebox was full to the top—and they all gathered around. Bunny announced he was selling the pictures, but mostly everyone was just looking. Somebody asked where he got the pictures and Bunny said, "Ray-Ray here said it was his ma," and Ray-Ray smiled. He was always trying to please. Some of 'em laughed, but not all of 'em. The Six knew Dex, and they knew Dex would stick up for hisself and was one of the few of our band that could actually really play sports. They stood around them pictures staring and passing 'em around except Tito, he took one look in that box and walked away and sat on the far end of the wooden fence and drunk his soda without saying nothing. But the rest of them Sixes and a couple of them Black Spade boys who was there, they runned through them pictures with their tongues hanging out. Bunny finally sold a few of them pictures for twenty-five cents apiece.

Ray-Ray was there licking on his ice cream cone the whole time, and dim as he was, he seen trouble. He wanted his picture box back and asked for it a couple of times, but them boys didn't bother with him. They kept sayin', "We'll give 'em back in a minute," flipping through the pictures. So Ray-Ray finally started towards home. Bunny looked up and seen him going and figured Dex would be coming next, so he closed up the box and said, "I got to go," and cut out after him. I stayed where I was, for I figured I was in trouble either way. I had got to thinking about Dex. Dex was my closest friend in The Bottom, and if Dex got mad I wouldn't have no close friends. Plus I never seen Dex mad. I think Dex never did get mad at me once that I could remember, but I seen his daddy mad, and that was enough for me.

I thought about this as I watched Bunny run after Ray-Ray, and I figured I'd better stay at the Cool Out Spot and let Bunny work that out, because it occurred to me by then that Bunny had took advantage of Ray-Ray in a bad way, and hot as them pictures was, I wasn't feeling so good about seeing 'em now. I figured if Dex came at me and I was at the Cool Out Spot, there was others that seen them pictures, and he'd figure it just wasn't worth it to fight all The Sixes and them two Black Spade gangsters that was standing around smoking cigarettes and drinking beer and sodas, and all of them seen the pictures too, so maybe he wouldn't blame me for nothing.

So I stood there trying to be cool and talking to Tito. Me and him always got along because Tito likes music and his aunt goes to my church and likes it when I play organ there.

Well, five minutes later, Dex and Ray-Ray turned the corner and come to the Cool Out Spot in a hurry. Bunny wasn't with 'em. Dex walked up to them boys crowding around their various pictures—I guess about five of 'em still had pictures in their hands they had bought, and some had already gone home with their pictures. He said, "Where's Bunny?"

Toy Boy spoke up. Toy Boy was a tall, thin, light-skinned boy. He was just as bad and stupid as his brother Tito was smart. Toy Boy wasn't worth two cents. He had bought one of them pictures and was holding it at his side when Dex come up. Toy Boy said, "He's gone," and started laughing. Dex stepped up to him, but Tito stepped between 'em and told Toy Boy, "Be quiet," and he said to Dex, "Bunny left out, Dex. He's gone."

"I want them pictures back," Dex said.

Toy Boy didn't want to give his picture back, and neither did the others. But Tito snatched the picture out of Toy's hand and then stepped over and snatched every picture out every one of them Sixes boys' hands and gived them back to Dex.

"Where's my money?" one of 'em said.

"Shut up," Tito said. Tito was the leader of The Sixes. None of them messed with him.

Dex took them pictures without a word, then spun on his heels and took Ray-Ray's hand and walked back to the block. I followed behind him. I knowed he was mad, so I said, "I ain't had nothing to do with it, Dex."

"Whyn't you come and get me?" he said.

"I didn't know where you was."

I followed him to Bunny's house, but Bunny wasn't there. We doubled back to the Boulevard towards Mr. Johnson's grocery store and sure enough, on the other side of the Boulevard, coming outta Mr. Johnson's store, come Bunny. He was holding a bunch of candy. Spending that money from them pictures he sold, I guess.

Dex crossed the Boulevard and went up to him. I was afraid he was gonna throw a punch and rock Bunny right there on the Boulevard, which wouldn't have been good. Bunny was bigger, plus he was a lefty. Lefties throw punches cockeyed. And Bunny can scrap. But Dex didn't throw. He didn't even look mad no more. He just held up the pictures in his hand that he got back from The Sixes and said, "You got about an hour to put that box back before my daddy gets home from work."

"What box?" Bunny said, for he didn't have the picture box on him. He had hid it someplace.

Dex said, "Tell you what, Bunny. Gimme the box back now and I won't say nothing to my daddy about it."

Bunny said, "I don't know what you're talking about. I gave it to Ray-Ray."

"No, he didn't," Ray-Ray said.

"He just can't remember," Bunny said. "You know how Ray-Ray is."

Dex stood there and blowed out his cheeks and waited a minute, thinking it over. He knew Ray-Ray don't lie. I lost a lot of respect for Bunny around that time. Then Bunny stepped to Ray-Ray and said, "Ray-Ray, you just don't remember. I gave it back to you, remember?" Ray-Ray looked mixed up. He shook his head and shifted from one foot to the other, while Bunny was sticking to his lie. Dex stood there a long time while Ray-Ray shifted from one foot to the other, nervous, looking at the sky. Dex weren't no punk, everybody knowed it, but Bunny was the leader of our group and fighting him was like treason almost. He directed everything. He had the best house. The most money. The best parents. His father had a good job wearing a suit and tie working in the downtown. Bunny was mighty big on our block. He was the roughest. Goat was bigger and faster, but Goat don't fight. Goat wouldn't hurt a fly. Bunny, on the other hand, when he was mad, he was dangerous.

Dex stood there for a moment thinking about it, then he said, "Okay," and he turned to Ray-Ray and said, "Let's go home," and they went back home, and I followed 'em along.

I don't know what all Bunny did later in life, for he left The Bottom when he turned seventeen and joined the Army and I never saw him no more. But that first mistake messed him up. He was never the same. All over a box of pictures. You never thought pictures of girls humping and sucking would make so much trouble.

. . .

THAT EVENING The Five-Carat Soul Bottom Bone Band rehearsed over Mr. Woo's like we done every night with Hate Whistle outside dancing and the customers from Mr. Woo's hollering, "Cut that crap!" like they always did. Bunny didn't come and neither did Dex or Ray-Ray or Pig who used to come with his sax but don't hardly come no more so we threw him out, so we didn't have no guitars or sax. It was just me, Goat, and Beanie—piano, drums, and bass—but we didn't hardly need no drums, for when Mr. Ernest stomped up them stairs with his concrete construction boots like two drum sets put together, the room got quiet. He come into the room with Dex and Ray-Ray behind him, both of them looking like maybe he whupped on 'em. By then Goat and Beanie knew about the pictures and everybody else in The Bottom did too, for Bunny had sold a bunch of them and the word had got around. Goat was closest to the door when Mr. Ernest walked in, and when he did, Mr. Ernest didn't have to say a word. He looked at Goat, who said: "I don't know nothing about no pictures, Mr. Ernest." Goat pointed at me. "Butter was there when Bunny took 'em to the Cool Out Spot."

Mr. Ernest turned to me, and I punked out right off. "Bunny done it on his own, Mr. Ernest," I choked out. "I was keeping an eye on Ray-Ray."

"Where is this Cool Out place?" Mr. Ernest asked.

"Not far," I said. "Just off the Boulevard."

"Show me."

I wanted to say Dex and Ray-Ray could show him, but there weren't no arguing with him. There wasn't nothing to do but take him there. Me, him, Dex, and Ray-Ray walked to the Cool Out Spot. While it wasn't but a few blocks, it seemed like the longest, worst walk in the world. Mr. Ernest didn't say a word to none of us. He didn't look mad, but he didn't look like Martin Luther King neither.

As we crossed the Boulevard, I was wondering what my ma was gonna do to me when she found out about me being around them pictures. I was more afraid of her than Mr. Ernest.

By the time we got to the Cool Out Spot it was almost night. The population around there always changed at night. That's when I noticed The Bottom was getting worse, by the way, when the Cool Out Spot started getting bad at night. In the old days, when I was eight and nine, it was just us and The Six and maybe one or two Black Spades, and we all come around and tell stories and trade candy and have fistfights about our baseball games and cut out. Then we got thirteen and fourteen and sometimes a few of us drunk beer to be cool, not a lot, just acting like we was drinking. But as we got to fifteen and sixteen, the badder kids from The Bottom had started coming around. Some of those was real gangs, with knives and karate nunchucks and even one or two who was supposed to have guns. The Black Spades, The Seven Crowns, even a few Five

Percenters, them types was older and rough. And they come around at night.

Most of The Six squad was gone except Toy Boy, Amuneek, and Bo. They was drinking beer with a few rough types I never seen. A lot of them setting there probably hadn't even seen Ray-Ray's picture box, now that I think on it, unless Toy Boy told 'em, of course. But they was a rough crew setting there, dressed all cool with dungaree jackets and clean white sneakers; a couple even had gangster drawings on their jean jackets. When Mr. Ernest walked up to 'em in his work shirt and construction boots, all dusty and dirtied up from his construction job, he looked bad. He looked like Hate Whistle, who was a drunk. He was just out of place.

He walked right up to 'em and said, "Good evening, fellers. Some outlaw here done took something that belong to me. And I want it back."

Well, he sounded like an old country bum when he said that, and a couple of them boys in their new jeans and clean white tennis shoes snickered when they heard him talking in his old down-south twang.

"We don't know nothing about it," one of 'em said.

"All right," he said. "I ain't gonna disrespect nobody here. Maybe y'all don't know nothing about it. But spread the word: I want it back. When I come home from work tomorrow, I want what's mine back in my house. Every single one of what was took. So whoever took it, put it back, and I won't trouble nobody further on it."

Well, standing there in them dirty work clothes, he looked like an old country bum talking to them young gangsters. Nobody said nothing, so he said, "All right then," and turned to leave.

Then Toy Boy piped up, "That box ain't 'round here nowhere." He showed his knucklehead side right then and there. Toy Boy's a dummy. If his older brother Tito had been there, he probably wouldn't have said nothing. But Tito wasn't there, and Toy Boy, well, he opened his big mouth wrong that day.

Mr. Ernest had already turned to go but when Toy spoke them words, Mr. Ernest turned around and said, "Who said it was a box?"

Well, that tied Toy Boy up, because nobody hadn't said nothing about no kind of box.

"Whatever it is," Toy Boy said, "I don't know nothing about it."

"How you know it was a box, boy?"

"Man, I don't know nothing 'bout some old pussy pictures!"

Toy was sitting on an old rail fence there when he said that. It was like an old ranch fence that you see in the western movies, except it was all tore up because of us sitting on it. Quick as you can tell it, Mr. Ernest stooped down, pulled a bottom rail off the fence, and rose up and swung it hard across Toy Boy's face in one motion. He hit him so hard the wood railing broke in half. One half flew in the street, the other half still lived in Mr. Ernest's hand.

Toy Boy dropped off the bench like a sack of flour, moaning and groaning and holding his head.

Them boys scattered like flies, everyone to the last except Amuneek and Bo, for they was The Six and stayed with their boy Toy till the end. They didn't move. Mr. Ernest walked up on Toy laying on the ground moaning in pain and stood over him with that piece of plank in his hand and I thought for a minute he might lean over and run the jagged end of that wooden stake right through him. You could see the wide shoulders and the muscles in his back. He wasn't screaming-hollering-mad, nothing like that. He looked just like he did in his driveway that time he slapped Dex about ten times across the face. He didn't look mad that day neither. Just downright dangerous. He stood over Toy and looked about to bust Toy's face apart. Then Ray-Ray called out: "Please, Daddy! I'm sorry! Please, Daddy! It's all my fault," like that, and Ray-Ray started crying.

That broke Mr. Ernest. He was standing over Toy with his back to Ray-Ray, and whatever fury come over him just hissed out his back like a balloon. He loosed the plank and let it drop to the ground. He turned away from Toy and said, "C'mon." He took Ray-Ray's hand and them two walked home, and me and Dex followed.

On the way home, me and Dex walked far behind them, and as we was walking, Dex leaned over to me and said, "I tried to tell Bunny."

"Maybe we can tell him tomorrow," I said.

"It's too late now," he said. "The train done left the station."

. . .

BUT IT WASN'T TOO LATE.

The next day Bunny got busy. He spent the whole day running around The Bottom, hustling around, buying back every single picture that he sold. He collected fourteen altogether. He had to pay triple for some of 'em, because some of them had heard about Mr. Ernest and knew Bunny was in a spot, so they got tough about the whole deal. Bo from The Six had bought two pictures and still had one that he hadn't given back to Tito, and he charged Bunny $1.50 for a picture he only paid twenty-five cents for. Another boy from The Seven Crowns gang lived up in Falls Point, and Bunny had to go all the way up there and pay him back nine dollars for a single picture, 'cause The Seven Crowns boy had paid a Black Spade kid two dollars for it, and *he* had bought it from Bunny for a quarter.

I don't know where Bunny got all that money from, probably from his daddy, but he paid 'em all. He got that done—bought back every single picture—and he gave Ray-Ray the picture box plus five dollars to put that box back in his house and tell Mr. Ernest he was sorry. Ray-Ray said he would, but Dex was standing there and he piped up, "You got to apologize your own self," he said. "Don't leave that to Ray-Ray."

"I want to say I'm sorry," Bunny said, "but I'm scared."

"I understand," Dex said, "but you got to leave Ray-Ray out of it."

Mr. Ernest got his box back and Bunny got off clean and never did apologize. Mr. Ernest never spoke to Bunny once about it neither, but the news about Mr. Ernest's nasty picture box traveled fast. That picture box was hot news in The Bottom, even among adults. It put a bad cloud on Dex and his family. Folks started muttering about him and his daddy, and his momma who nobody knew, and how neither Mr. Ernest nor his boys never went to church, and how Dex probably was a bad egg like his daddy. None of that was true, of course. Dex wasn't bad. Dex was different. Dex didn't like baseball or basketball like most of us. He liked ice hockey. He didn't like soul music like most of us. He liked rock and roll. He saved his money to see a white band called Edgar Winter's White Trash. He even played their records for me once and they was pretty good. Dex had his own thing. But that outburst with them pictures put a space between Dex's family and The Bottom. It caused a rift in the band, too. Bunny and Dex was never close after that, and Dex quit when he was fifteen, and then Mr. Ernest moved all of them over to Falls Point.

Falls Point ain't far, it's still part of The Bottom, so I'd see Dex in school or sometimes coming through. He had to walk past my part of The Bottom to get to the bus stop on the Boulevard, and one Saturday morning I saw him standing at the bus stop changing into a white shirt and tie and putting on a cop jacket that said "Security." I guess he didn't want nobody to see him wearing cop clothes. I went over and said, "What you guarding, Dex?"

"I got a job at an ice cream factory. Don't say nothing to nobody, Butter."

"I won't," I said. "I wish I had a job guarding ice cream."

Dex looked kind of sheepish. "I ain't guarding no ice cream," he said. "I guard the place where they make the cones."

"That's even better. I bet Ray-Ray likes that. How's he doing? I ain't seen him in a while."

"He ain't good. He's sick."

"In the hospital?"

"Naw. He's home."

"What's wrong with him?"

"Don't know. Got something wrong with his head. The doctor says something's growing up there."

"Like what? A brain?"

"Very funny, Butter. They got to operate when he gets older, to get it out, whatever it is."

That made me feel bad, joking like that, so a couple of days later I walked over to Dex's house in Falls Point and gave Dex my forty-five record of Sly and the Family Stone, which he's crazy about. He liked that, and give me a whole row of ice cream cones in a paper bag. Then he said, "You wanna see Ray-Ray? He's upstairs."

We went upstairs, and they had Ray-Ray in the bed, and when I seen him, I was surprised. I almost didn't recognize him. I hadn't seen him in like a year, and in that time he growed to nearly six feet. He used to be a skinny boy but now he was a tall teenager. He was sleeping under the covers when we come in, and when Dex tapped him he shook awake and seen me and said, "Butter!" He was happy to see me. So I reached in my bag and showed him all them cones Dex had gived me. I said, "You want one?"

"Naw," he said. "I eat 'em all the time." Then he looked at Dex. He looked a little fuzzy, squinting his eyes at Dex. He said, "There's a roaring in my ears, Dex. Just a roaring."

"That's the ocean, Ray-Ray."

"It's so loud, I can't stand it, Dex. Can you hear it?"

"Naw."

"Come closer, Dex. You can hear it. Lissen. It's roaring loud, Dex. Lissen to the ocean."

Ray-Ray reached up his arm, which I noticed was thin and weak looking, and he pulled Dex close to his ear. He put Dex's ear right on his ear. Like maybe he was hoping Dex could hear it, too.

"Can you hear it, Dex? Can you hear it?"

"Naw, Ray-Ray, I don't hear nothing."

Dex stayed like that, with his ear close to Ray-Ray's ear, right up on it, with Ray-Ray talking at him.

"Can you hear it, Dex? Can you hear it?"

3

BLUB

Blub is a mumbler. There's lots of folks in The Bottom who mumble bad, but Blub is the champion mumbler of The Bottom. He sounds like a bubble machine when he talks, "blub blub . . ." That's how he got his name.

Blub's a big boy for his age. He's two years younger than me—I'm fourteen and he's only twelve—but he looks older, being that he's tall and big. Blub don't have no brothers and sisters, and since he only live two doors from me, I used to translate for him when we was little, walking around The Bottom, taking care of our business and such. It was a good deal back in the day, because Blub would split his goods with me. We'd go into Mr. Johnson's grocery store and Blub would say, "Blub blub blub . . ."

Mr. Johnson would say, "What's Blub want?"

"He wants two Sugar Daddies and a pack of Now and Laters."

"All right, Blub."

We rolled like that for years, me and Blub. But when I started The Five-Carat Soul Bottom Bone Band with Goat and Dex and them, Blub couldn't play nothing, so I couldn't translate for him no more. He was on his own. But he still come around my house, mostly on account of my little sister Sissie. He was crazy about her.

One morning he come banging on my front door looking like somebody shot him. He was mumbling so fast I had to make him stop and start all over again three times before I understood him. Then I finally got it: "Thursday is dead!" he said. "Thursday died!"

Thursday is Sissie's cat.

"You lyin'," I said.

"Sho nuff."

"Show me," I said.

I followed him out to the Boulevard. When he got to the bus stop, he stopped there and pointed across the road, and sure enough old Thursday was dead on the other side of the road, cars and trucks rolling right over him. He was smashed flat, his black and white fur mashed like a checkerboard.

"You see it happen?"

"Naw. I was standing here at the bus stop waiting for Sissie to get off the bus from school, and I seen him."

Sissie was ten then, and she was animal crazy. She adopted

every kind of animal that ever wandered around The Bottom: raccoons, possums, mice, birds, dogs. She even pulled a lizard with red spots and two brown frogs from the canal that runs through The Bottom, and that canal is so dirty even Wooden Joe stopped fishing in it. They say Wooden Joe is Dome's father—Dome's a boy, by the way—and Wooden Joe would fish in a toilet bowl if he thought there was catfish in it.

"We got to move him before Sissie gets here," Blub said. "Her bus'll be here any minute."

I seen Thursday there, and he was gone, was my thoughts. I didn't feel too bad. Thursday didn't go far to die. He lived in the street and died in the street. He was a bum, really, perfect for The Bottom. He come 'round when he felt like it, then disappeared for weeks. He was about as popular as a can of tomatoes in The Bottom. Nobody liked him, not even other cats. Come to think of it, Thursday didn't have no friends in The Bottom except Sissie.

Neither did Blub. He was too shy for most people. His mother, Miss Rosa, she was shy, too. You'd see her coming and going to work every day, but that's about it. No big conversation from her. She ate Chinese takeout from Mr. Woo's almost every day. It showed too, for when she walked down the street next to Blub, she gave him a lot of shade. I don't know her exact size, but there was a whole lot of her. One time she got stuck in the bathtub and Blub had to call the fire company to come get her out. Soon as they left you could hear her hollering, "Earl! Earl! Git over here!" That was Blub's real name. She was always yelling at him. I could hear her through the window two doors away. That's one reason I think Blub spent so much time at my house.

The other reason was Sissie. They was good friends them two, mostly because Sissie was a tomboy. She liked animals more than people, which made Blub perfect, because Blub wasn't all the way human neither. He was part animal, in a way. He just wandered around, doing nothing, following anybody that come along, smiling about nothing, he dressed bad and smelled funny. But he would do anything for Sissie.

But I wouldn't. She was just my dumb sister. So when Blub said we got to move Thursday off the road, I said, "We ain't got to move him. He'll be mush by the time she gets off the bus."

"That ain't right," Blub said. "We got to bury him."

"Go 'head then."

Blub turned around and set out for home, and being that he was younger than me it shamed me a little, so I caught up to him and said, "All right, Blub. But you're picking him up."

We went home and got a shovel, came back, and I stood watch while Blub dodged traffic and scooped up Thursday, cars honking and drivers hollering at him. Blub got that thing off the ground about thirty seconds before Sissie's bus pulled up. We seen it coming a few blocks off and Blub was still holding that shovel full of guts and fur on the sidewalk, so I said, "Quick, let's throw him in a garbage can up the street."

"Sissie might see him," he said, and took off running back towards The Bottom.

I caught up to him after a couple of blocks, and when we turned the corner and now the bus stop was out of sight I said, "Let's take him behind Mr. Woo's. There's a dumpster back there."

"I ain't putting Sissie's cat in no dumpster," Blub announced. "We can bury him in your yard."

"You crazy? Sissie already got a graveyard full of dead animals back there. My ma ain't having that. How 'bout your yard?"

"No way," he said. "What about Thresher Park?"

"I ain't going in there," I said. Thresher Park was off limits. That's where knuckleheads like Bo, Chink, Lightbulb, Junior, and the rest of The Six gang from Mills Basin played basketball and smoked weed. Thresher Park was at the edge of The Bottom, near Mill Basin, the next town over. It's wasn't exactly their park. And it wasn't exactly our park. But them Sixes was nothing to fool with. We played baseball against them and fought them with eggs at Halloween. But they could get cranky sometimes and a little dangerous.

Blub started walking toward Thresher Park before I could stop him, holding that shovel full of poor old Thursday. I had to go then. I didn't want him thinking I was chicken-hearted.

Thresher Park used to be a nice park with a bunch of trees and benches back in the days when the steel plants was open. That's what my mother says. She said after the plants closed and the city didn't have no money, they came in and cut down all the trees except for one. It's a big old sycamore tree with peeling bark and big electric wires running through the top branches. There's a basketball court in the middle of the park, and a fence, and you have to walk past the basketball court to get to that tree.

Blub walked right in there with a shovel full of dead cat. He had growed pretty big by then, going on close to thirteen, and he didn't blink when he walked past the basketball court where The Six boys was playing. They looked over and saw Thursday in that shovel and stayed away.

Blub found a spot underneath the sycamore tree, cleared a bunch of bottles and dog crap, dug a deep hole, and buried what was left of Thursday. Then he took out a little pocket-knife and scratched Thursday's name onto the tree trunk. "Now we can tell Sissie," he said.

"I ain't telling her," I said. I didn't want to hear it. But Blub mumbled the whole story to her when she got home. She howled, of course. Then she followed Blub over to Thresher Park and he showed her where he buried Thursday and she howled some more. Blub felt so bad he pulled out his pocket-knife again and scratched her name beneath Thursday's in the tree. She said that made her feel better.

Then Blub said, "Can I scratch my name underneath yours?"

She didn't say nothing, which meant no. In them days, if a boy scratched his name under a girl's and wrote the plus sign to it, that meant they was boyfriend and girlfriend. The only thing Sissie liked back then was animals, of which Blub was one, but she more favored this light-skinned boy named Fingers. Fingers was a loser who was in juvenile jail for three months but he wrote Sissie a letter every day. Even though he was a rat, she liked him, which shows you how girls think: If you're nice and boring and bury their cats and all like Blub did, they can't be bothered. But go to jail for three months for stealing and keep 'em interested because you need fixing up and keep writing 'em notes from jail saying you gonna straighten up, why, they'll suffer any wrong.

So she told Blub, "Not right now. I'll think about it."

So Blub said, "Wanna get some ice cream from Mr. Johnson's?"

"Not this time," she said, and went home. That busted his bubble. I won't say it was the beginning of the end for old Blub. But something inside Blub knelt down and died that day. It was the end of something. I just don't know what it was.

TWO WEEKS LATER I come home from school, and who should I see setting on the front steps? I ran two doors away and fetched Blub. You should've seen his face when I showed him.

Thursday the cat was setting there, big as day with his evil self, licking his paws and kissing his own butt.

"It's a miracle," Blub mumbled.

"But we just buried him!" I said, and while I was talking Thursday got really deep into eating his own butt the way cats do, and I couldn't stand him all over again. "It's too bad we buried the wrong cat," I said.

"Who cares?" Blub said. "Sissie'll be so happy."

He sat on my front steps all afternoon waiting for Sissie to get home from school. Meanwhile Thursday, his old raggedy self, ducked under the front stairs and went to sleep.

Sissie was so happy when she saw Thursday she gived Blub a hug, and this time let him take her to Mr. Johnson's for ice cream.

The next week Blub got some money someplace and bought a can of real cat food and knocked on the door. He gave it to Sissie saying, "This is for Thursday. Wanna get some more ice cream from Mr. Johnson's?"

But Sissie had gotten another letter from Fingers by then. Every time she got a letter from that idiot, she got all weepy. She took the food from Blub but didn't do nothing else with him.

It went on like that all summer, Blub trying to be nice to Sissie's evil cat, and her ignoring him. Then Fingers got out of juvenile a few weeks early and showed up with a new dungaree jacket and a new Afro, and that was it. Sissie followed him around like a puppy. She cut Blub loose. She told him, "Fingers brought Thursday a new collar."

That done it. Blub drifted off then. I got busy with The Five-Carat Soul Bottom Bone Band around that time and lost track of him that summer, because we had a gig coming up. Of course, the gig was four months away, but a gig is a gig, so we was rehearsing hard and smoking a little weed and drinking a little Thunderbird wine, and rehearsing some more, 'cause that's what you do in a street band when you about to go to high school. You get ready for gigs. It don't matter that gigs mostly never happen. That's not the point. A gig is a gig. Blub couldn't hang around when we rehearsed over top of Mr. Woo's restaurant anyway, because his mother showed up there too much and she wouldn't do nothing but drag him home. Plus, he was like my little brother. Who wants your mumbling little brother around when you're jamming with your buddies and being cool? So I'd send him off.

I didn't see him much then. Sometimes I'd see him going back and forth to Mr. Woo's to pick up takeout for his ma. Sometimes from my room I'd hear her hollering, "Earl! Git over here!" But I just plain forgot about him, and before I knew it, the summer was over.

That fall I saw him at Mr. Johnson's store and he was wearing a brand-new leather jacket. I asked him, "Where you get that jacket?"

"Friend at school," he mumbled. I didn't know Blub had any other friends.

"What school?" I asked, because he wasn't in my school. I had just started high school myself.

"I'm actually not in school yet," he said. "But they're putting me in a special school. Where they teach you how to speak right and get jobs and stuff."

"Where's the school?"

"I dunno. I'm waiting for the papers to come."

His story sounded funny, but I didn't think nothing of it. I had my own problems and lost track of him.

I was standing at the bus stop on the way to school one morning not long after when Sissie came up to me with a funny look on her face and said, "You hear about Blub?"

"No."

She handed me a newspaper. I saw Blub's picture and another guy's picture. Underneath his picture I saw his real name and the word "Murder."

I said, "Blub is dead?"

She didn't say nothing. The bus came and she got on it while I sat there, reading. I couldn't believe it.

Blub and another kid had got arrested for killing two people. A black man and his wife. The newspaper said Blub and his buddy broke into the house, clobbered the couple with pipes, bound them, tied them up, robbed them, and killed them both. There was a two-year-old baby girl in the house, too. When the cops got there, they found the baby girl alive, on her dead mother's chest on the bed. The father had been duct-taped and drowned in the bathtub.

I thought it was a mistake. I couldn't move for a long time after I read it. I just sat there on the bench. By the time I looked up, the last school bus was long gone, so I got up and walked home.

When I walked in the house my ma said, "What happened?"

and I showed her the paper. She was so shocked she had to sit down a minute. She said, "That can't be right."

"They got the wrong man," I said.

Suddenly, sitting at the table, she got mad at me and slammed the paper down on the table. "He ain't no man!" she said.

"Yes he is," I said. "Blub's a young man. The paper says he's seventeen. I thought he was only fourteen. He musta got left back a few times and didn't tell me. But he's a young man."

"I don't give a tinker's damn what the paper says," she yelled. "He's no man! He's a boy! Just a stupid, silly boy! And so are you! Get up! Git to school!"

"What'd I do?"

"Get your ass to school!" she said. "Earl's in jail. And you'll go there too if you fool around with the wrong people. Get out! Get to school! Right now! Or I'll warm your toasters right here with my switch! You think you're too old for it? You wanna see?"

She was being stupid, so I was glad to cut out.

When Sissie got home from school later, she asked me to find out what happened. I asked around, but nobody knew nothing. I couldn't call the police because who's dumb enough to ask them? I went to Blub's house and knocked on his mother's door, but Miss Rosa wouldn't answer.

I told Sissie, "Nobody knows nothing. Forget about it." She was upset, but she was getting like my ma then, turning thirteen and trying to act cool and grown-up about men and all. She sucked her teeth. "The boys 'round here ain't worth two cents," she said, and went outside and sat on the stoop with Thursday in her lap.

There was not one soul from The Bottom who knew what happened. So what I know of it came from what the newspapers said. It was a nice religious couple that got kilt. The man was a minister. He had hired Blub and his friend to do some work in his house and they had an argument about money. What it was exactly about who knows, but the case was pretty bad against Blub and his buddy. The paper said they was both there and the cops had fingerprints and all kinds of proof. I asked all over The Bottom about the other guy that Blub was with, but there wasn't one soul from The Bottom who knew him. Somebody said Blub met him in that new school he went to.

Fall came, and I forgot about it. Then the case came to court and Blub was in the newspaper all over again. He was more famous now in The Bottom than he ever was when he lived here. All kinds of people came up to me and asked, "What happened to Blub?" I wanted to say, "You wasn't interested before," but what was the point? He and his new buddy was gonna cook together.

Well, come time for the trial, I couldn't stand it. I like to read, but I didn't read none of it in the paper. Even so, I still heard some of the bad parts, because that kind of news gets around in The Bottom. Folks talked about how the man who died had struggled in his bathtub, and how somebody strong must've had to hold him down, and how his wife was suffocated and maybe died after her husband was killed. Whoever did that evil a big strong devil, they said, and didn't you notice how Blub had got so big and strong?

It was just too much. Blub was a big boy. But evil . . . I couldn't deal with it, so I blocked it out. Thank God for The Five-Carat Soul Bottom Bone Band, because while we do not have many gigs, we can jam, and music keeps your mind right, especially when Goat plays drums. He's what you call a basher. You can't think about nothing once he's finished crashing cymbals in your ears.

All that bashing helped me forget Blub, until my ma got a call from the courthouse from a man who said he was Blub's lawyer. "We need your son to testify," he said.

"Absolutely not," she said. "He ain't had nothing to do with it. He's an organ player in church."

"All the better," the man said. "This is the sentencing phase. Earl's already been found guilty of double murder. He's likely to get the death sentence. He says your son knew him. Maybe something your son says could change things for him a little. So he won't go to the electric chair."

"We can't help," my ma said. She hung up the phone and walked away, cussing and hollering. "Why's he calling here?" she shouted, talking to the whole house now. "This ain't my business! The only thing we can do for Blub is pray for him."

But then that night Mother Miles, who is the mother deacon of Bright Hope Baptist Church, she come by and I heard her talking to my ma in the kitchen. Mother Miles said she knowed Blub's mother, Miss Rosa, and I heard her telling my ma that

Miss Rosa never done no wrong, how Miss Rosa worked all her life, and how Miss Rosa didn't know nothing about raising kids. It was the father that did all the raising, Mother Miles said, and when he runned off, why, there it is. So my ma said she'd think about it, and the next morning she got me out of bed and asked me do I wanna go down to court and testify for Blub.

"Yes, I will do it for Blub."

"If you go down there and tell any lies to make it easy on him, you will suck sorrow in this house," she said.

"Why would I lie?"

"You better not. 'Cause two people are dead. And Earl was in that house. That's the truth of it. And don't bring your sister. I already had one convict writing letters here. One's enough."

THEY HAD PUT BLUB and his new buddy at separate tables in the courtroom. Blub had on a brand-new suit. He looked nervous and scared. When I saw that new buddy of his, I knew then what had happened. He was a squat, thick, mean-looking devil. He never moved in the court. He looked straight ahead. Blub had got hisself into some real deep water, was my thoughts. He looked out of his mind scared.

They was setting before an old black judge, a jury, and three lawyers—one for Blub, one for his friend, and one for the courtroom. That courtroom was full on one side with people who knowed the couple that was dead. On the other side was

just me, Miss Rosa, and Rev. Jenkins, who come to speak for
Blub. Nobody had come for Blub's new friend.

So they done a little of this and that, a lot of thees and
therefores and what all they do in court, and finally called me
up to testify. I sat there with my heart banging on my chest
'cause I had never done no wrong to be on nobody's court
stand before. But I done my best. First Blub's lawyer talked to
me nice. And I told him the story of how I knowed Blub all his
life, and how he looked up to me, and how his mother yelled at
him a lot. I said no matter what, I couldn't believe Blub could
kill nobody.

Then the other lawyer from the court got up and tried to
make me into a fool. He told me about how the dead man had
been tied up, and his wife tied up, and both of them murdered
so bad, and their kid left alone who was two years old, and the
poor kid don't have no parents now, and how would I feel if
somebody done that to my ma and dad and left my sister to die?

I said, "Mister, I have never known my dad. And Blub would
never do that to my ma. Or nobody else."

He got mad and said, "How do you know? Was you in that
house when those people was murdered?"

I said, "I was not," and then I told the story of Thursday the
cat. And how Blub had found the cat dead on the Boulevard.
And how Blub was all upset and came and got me, and made
me bury the cat with him over in Thresher Park, and scratched
the cat's name in the old sycamore tree. And how he broke the
news to Sissie, and how he didn't want Sissie to see her dead

cat. And then I told him how happy Blub was when he saw Thursday was alive.

And the lawyer said what does that got to do with anything? And I said well, I don't know what happened in that house, mister, but I guess if there was a little kid left alive in there, it was probably because Blub was there, because Blub wouldn't let nobody hurt no kid. Blub wouldn't hurt a fly. He just follows people around, I said. He ain't got a lot of friends. He just follows people around.

Rev. Jenkins, he testified too. He's a troublemaker but he did speak up for Blub. And Blub's mother, Miss Rosa, testified. She mostly sat in the witness stand and busted into tears. After it was done, I never wanted to see Blub no more, not even that day. But they told me to stick around when the jury left the room. They might need me again. They said it wouldn't take long.

It didn't neither. The jury came back in a couple of hours. First they announced their verdict on the other kid, Blub's new friend. They asked him to stand up. The judge read the verdict from a piece of paper, which said "death penalty." He made each juror, one at a time, stand up and actually say the word "death" out loud. He said it was the law. They done it. Each one. Some of them had tears in their eyes when they done it. But not all of 'em. Blub's friend didn't make a sound nor sweat it when they called it out on him neither. Didn't move a muscle till he was told to sit again, which he did.

Then Blub was asked to stand. He got up shaking and sweating. And I remember thinking, *This is all going too fast for me.* Seem like just yesterday me and Blub was at Mr. Johnson's grocery store ordering Now and Laters with me translating for him, and now Blub's standing before a judge, about to . . . I couldn't deal with it. I looked at him shaking and sweating, and seen how big he'd grown in jail, just a tall, good-looking man. And I wished then that Sissie could see him now, see how Blub had grown, how big and tall and slim he got, handsome in his suit, like a movie star. She had begged me to sneak her to the trial, but I kept my word to my ma. "You ain't never gonna see him again," I told her, "so you ought best forget him."

The jury sent over a note to the judge, and he called the lawyers over to him, and the lawyers talked with him for a while. Then the jury sent over a second note, and the judge read that. And then the jury sent over a third note, and the judge wrote down something on a piece of paper, and then he read from the piece of paper in his hand.

The judge said this man is gonna get forty years to life.

When I got home, I told my ma what happened and she said, "Don't tell your sister," but of course Sissie dragged every bit of it outta me. She was quiet for a few days afterwards, and then we just rolled on. Winter came, and then spring, and high school came, and The Five-Carat Soul Bottom Bone Band kept rehearsing, and just like that Blub was gone from The Bottom.

Myself, I tried to forget him. When I had to walk past his house, I'd circle the block and go the long way. When I seen his mother going back and forth to work and ordering food from Mr. Woo's, I'd avoid her, or sometimes I'd wave, but she hardly seen me and kept walking. And then after a while things got back to like they always were. And they went along normal again for a while—until Thursday the cat vanished.

He just never came back one day. We was used to that. Sometimes he'd disappear for days, even weeks at a time. That was normal. But this time he just never came back. Sissie put out food for him and called and called and watched out for him through the window, but the food stayed there. A month passed. Two months. Three months. Then the snow came, and after that I figured he was gone for good and forgot all about him, till one afternoon that cold winter I was coming home from rehearsal in the snow and passed by Thresher Park and seen Sissie in there at the sycamore tree in the middle of the park scratching away at the tree trunk.

I seen her from the sidewalk, at a distance, through the fence, and backed off and waited by the fence out of sight till she was done with whatever she was doing. When she left I went up to the tree and seen where Blub had scratched Thursday's name, then scratched her name underneath Thursday's name to make her feel better.

And now she had scratched Blub's name under hers, with a plus sign on it.

THURSDAY THE CAT

+

SISSIE

+

BLUB

4

GOAT

When I was little, I used to look out my window and see a little boy running behind a man on a bicycle every morning. I seen that boy running behind that bike every day before I even knew him, just some crazy boy running behind a man pedaling a bicycle. He'd run behind the man all the way to the corner, and when the man got to the dirt road that runned up the hill and out of The Bottom going towards downtown, that boy would stop running and watch him ride off, then turn and run to school. That's my friend Goat. He plays drums in The Five-Carat Soul Bottom Bone Band. The man on the bicycle is his daddy, who everybody calls Mr. Popcorn.

Goat is a dark-skinned boy who walks pigeon-toed and laughs all the time and likes to make jokes. He's a pretty good drummer for somebody who's twelve, but he plays too fast. Everything Goat does is fast. He talks fast. He eats fast. But mostly he runs fast. He's the fastest kid in all The Bottom. Everybody knows Goat got speed. I think he got it from running after his daddy all the time.

I don't know why they call his daddy Mr. Popcorn, for I have never seen him eat no popcorn. Goat told me his daddy's real name is Irving Evans. He's a little, chocolate-skinned man with shiny eyes and a big smile. Mr. Popcorn works way downtown in a yard where there's big oil trucks that say "Waste Oil" on the side. He rides his bike to work every day, and he works them pedals on that thing good and keeps it moving. It's a dandy bike. It's red and blue with stingray handlebars on it and a banana seat. It's put together from a bunch of different bike parts from Mr. Popcorn's yard. He got a ton of junk in that yard. Bricks, bike parts, tires, and real chickens. He even had a goat in there once—a real goat, which is how Goat got his nickname, for he used to have to feed it—but the city made him get rid of it. That whole family is country.

Mr. Popcorn got three boys: Minnie Jug, Tory, and Goat, and they is all fast. Minnie Jug is the oldest. He's like a bigger, meaner Goat. He stole my bike once and it would've ended up in Mr. Popcorn's junkyard until Goat told me, "I seen my brother Minnie Jug riding your bike." I ran out and caught Minnie Jug on it and he said, "Oh I just borrowed it," and he gived it back to me along with a dime so I wouldn't tell my mother. Minnie Jug played baseball with us sometimes. He could hit that ball a mile too, but he quit when he was a teenager and got too old.

Next come Tory. Tory likes girls and cigarettes. We used to call him "half boy, half man," 'cause Tory had a mustache and beard when he was only twelve—or said he was twelve. He was in my same class but I ain't seen him in a while. They say he's in Job Corps, which is like jail except all the kids ain't bad. I asked Goat once, "Where's Tory?" and Goat just shrugged and said, "Tory messed up," which makes me think Tory ain't in no Job Corps after all.

Goat is the youngest of the three. He ain't like his big brothers. He don't steal. He don't fight. He don't chase girls. He ain't never mad. He just runs. I never seen nobody run like Goat. It's like a different person climb into him when he runs. He leans forward and gets low and just flies along like a diesel train.

Everybody knows Goat is fast. People from all around The Bottom come to race him. He raced Bunny's daddy last summer and beat him and he was only eleven. Bunny's daddy got mad and said, "Gimme a half a block head start next time and if you win, I'll give you twenty dollars. But if you lose, you pay me a dollar."

"I ain't got no dollar," Goat said. But Goat gave him a head start anyway and took his money. One of The Sixes, a boy named Junior, came around once and said, "I can beat Goat." Junior's sixteen and plays football in high school. He's a quiet, light-skinned boy with big, thick leg muscles. When The Six beat us at something, Junior's one of them that does it the most.

Last Halloween when they beat us in our yearly egg fight, Junior ran me down and hit me with an egg so hard it felt like a bullet. Well, Junior raced Goat and got beat, too.

Last spring Goat got famous. They had a big track meet out in Falls Point, with the white kids and everything, and they threw Goat in there and he beat everybody in the city in the hundred-yard dash except for one guy. He didn't even have sneakers. He borrowed Dex's sneakers. Only problem was he didn't have no birth certificate, so they threw out his win. Our school didn't have no track coach, we just had Miss McIntyre. She teaches English, and she saw Goat running around the schoolyard and said, "That boy's fast," and when she heard about a track meet over in Falls Point she put him in her car and drove him over there to race in it. After he came in second place they asked Miss McIntyre, "Where's his birth certificate?" and Miss McIntyre said, "I don't have no birth certificate for him," so he didn't get no medal because they couldn't prove he was twelve.

Goat was disappointed and told Miss McIntyre he wasn't going back to run no more. But Miss McIntyre said, "Go home and get your birth certificate. We'll have it the next time."

"There ain't gonna be no next time," Goat said.

"Why?"

"My ma ain't got no birth certificate," Goat said.

"We'll see about that," she said.

Miss McIntyre's a nice lady, but she don't know nothing about The Bottom. She's young and brown-skinned. She wears nice dresses and has nice glasses and a button nose that's so cute. Sometimes when I fall asleep at night I think about Miss McIntyre. She does her hair in an Afro like Cicely Tyson, that famous actress I seen on TV once, or Angela Davis, who I don't know exactly who she is but they say she's got guts and ain't scared of white people. One time my sister Sissie asked Miss McIntyre, "Where's your perm?" and Miss McIntyre gived her a book with a picture of a lady named Harriet Tubman who freed the slaves or some such kind of thing. Sissie looked at the picture and said, "She ain't got no perm neither," and Miss McIntyre got mad.

Miss McIntyre couldn't get it out of her head about Goat not getting his medal and not having his birth certificate. She kept bothering him about bringing it in and he kept saying "I forgot," so one day she said, "I'm gonna write your mother a note."

"Write all you want. It ain't gonna do no good," Goat said.

"Why not?" she said.

"She ain't worrying about no birth certificate," Goat said.

"I'll take care of it."

I don't know where Miss McIntyre live, but she sure don't live in The Bottom, because that very weekend she came to The Bottom and drove right through our baseball field.

It ain't a real field. We call it The Triangle. It's actually three dirt streets that come together at the bottom of a hill where you first enter The Bottom. The Triangle is perfect for baseball, but it's also the only entrance to The Bottom if you driving. Most cars roar through there because the drivers is either from The

Bottom and wanna get home—or they ain't from The Bottom and wanna get home in one piece.

Miss McIntyre creeped through there at ten miles an hour. In a shiny little red car, on a hot Saturday, with her pretty little purse on the passenger seat next to her and the window open so somebody could reach in there and snatch it. We was playing The Six when she come through, and she bumped right over home plate where they was and stopped.

All them Sixes stared at her when she stopped, setting there in her little red car wearing one of her nice school dresses, squinting through the windshield looking for addresses—there ain't none in The Bottom—with her side window wide open, basically begging somebody, anybody, to snatch her purse off that seat and make themself some money. I think they was so surprised to see someone so stupid come through there it froze 'em. Them Sixes—Tito, Toy Boy, Junior, Lightbulb—stood there holding their bats with their eyes popping out their heads as she sat there a minute.

Then quick as you can tell it, she was on the move again, roaring off home plate. She turned one way, then the other, backed up once, then rolled over the pitcher's mound where Bunny was standing holding the ball—she almost hit him—then kept going past him and rumbled over second base where Dex was, then bumped past me at shortstop, then finally drove out to left field where Goat was.

The left field of The Triangle ain't really no left field. It's really Parsons Road. It's a pretty far distance from home plate.

But that's where The Six mostly clobber the ball when we pitch it to them. That's why we put Goat out there. He runs down their gigantic home runs and catches 'em for outs. But he gets bored out there sometimes and stands around daydreaming, staring up at the sky.

He was doing just that when Miss McIntyre drove past him. She was squinting with her glasses, swiveling her head back and forth looking for addresses, and had just about passed him when he glanced in the car—then done a double take, when he seen who it was.

He stared as she passed, and when her car reached the corner of Parsons and turn left towards his house, he dropped his glove and said, "I gotta go," and took off towards home.

That ended the game right there. We can't beat them without Goat. Plus it started a fight. Each team switched gloves when they took the field because not everybody had a glove, and Goat was using Lightbulb's glove. He had it in his hand when Miss McIntyre drove past and he threw Lightbulb's glove to the ground and ran off. Lightbulb saw Goat running and said, "One of you girls better bring my glove," and Bunny who was pitching for us said, "Get your own glove, caveman," and we laughed, and them Sixes charged, which meant we had to show them Sixes who's boss. We did what The Five-Carat Soul Bottom Bone Band does best. We scattered quick.

Bunny and Beanie and the rest of them made it safe to Bunny's house, while me and Dex took off for Mrs. Wilson's yard to cut through and catch up with Goat. We had never seen no teacher in The Bottom before, especially not one so pretty like Miss McIntyre. We loved us some Miss McIntyre.

We got there just in time to see Goat beat Miss McIntyre to his house. Goat acted like he ain't seen her and zipped inside the front door and slammed it behind him just as she pulled up. By the time she parked and got out and walked through all them bike parts and weeds and chickens to knock at the front door, that house seemed quiet as a mouse.

My cousin Herbert lives two doors away from Goat and his family ain't never home. So me and Dex crouched behind the steps at Cousin Herbert's house to listen in and see what would happen.

Miss McIntyre knocked at the door. Nobody come, so she knocked again louder. Finally a voice hollered out, "We gave at the office!" That was Goat talking, trying to sound like a grown-up.

"I need to speak to you, Seymour," Miss McIntyre said.

Me and Dex laughed. It was funny to hear Goat's real name spoke in The Bottom.

"Ain't nobody here but us chickens," Goat said.

Well, that just got Miss McIntyre stirred up. She banged at the door harder this time and then finally the door cracked opened and Goat's mother, Mrs. Shays, peeped out the side of it.

I don't know Mrs. Shays well, but I seen her a lot when my grandma died because she works in the cafeteria at the old Carver Hospital. She's a tall, brown lady who keeps her hair neat permed and got a wide nose. She peeked out the side of the door with her eyes and said, "What he done did now?"

"Are you Seymour's mother?" Miss McIntyre asked.

"If you mean is I the someone who teaches him not to brush his teeth and clean his nose out in public, yes, I am his mother," Mrs. Shays said. "But if you from social services and come out here fending and proving and pretending you know everything, which must be a terrible strain on a person, then I ain't nobody."

"So you are his mother, then?" Miss McIntyre said.

"If it look like buzzard and smell like buzzard, miss, it ain't catfish."

"Does that mean you his mother?"

"Is you social services or not?"

"Course not!" Miss McIntyre said. "I am his teacher."

"Well, whatever he done wrong, I'll straighten him out," Mrs. Shays said, and she slammed the door shut.

Miss McIntyre banged on the door again. Nobody opened it, so she hollered out, "Seymour's done nothing wrong."

Mrs. Shays wouldn't open the door. But she hollered from inside, "If he ain't done no wrong, stop banging at my door."

"I need to talk to you."

"You hurting my door, miss. I paid for it. Git along, please."

"This is about a scholarship!"

"A what?"

"Money!"

That done it. The door cracked open. Mrs. Shays stood

there with her cafeteria uniform on. There wasn't no screen door, just some steps leading up to it, so when Mrs. Shays opened the door full, she was standing above Miss McIntyre like a giant. Behind her the house was dark. Goat's people don't have electric most times. Mostly they light their house with candles and flashlights, but nobody makes fun of them 'cause Mr. Popcorn ain't the only one in The Bottom who can't pay his electric.

"Miss, he didn't meant to steal no scholarship," Mrs. Shays said. "You ain't got to get him arrested. I already told you I'll clear him of it. No need to call no police."

It occurred to me then that Mrs. Shays didn't know what a scholarship was. Miss McIntyre said: "He didn't steal a scholarship. He needs one."

"Well, I can't afford it, whatever it is."

"It's a free education," Miss McIntyre said. Then she explained about how Goat was the second fastest runner in the whole city and should get a medal for that track meet he did in Falls Point and maybe could get into a special high school for free college because he ran so fast.

Mrs. Shays lightened up now, listening. Then she said, "You say he can get all that on account of him running?"

"Yes. He runs very fast."

"Well, he probably got that from his daddy," Mrs. Shays said.

"Was he fast, too?" Miss McIntyre said.

Mrs. Shays sighed. "That man got feets of clay now, miss. Why you poking 'round in my business? What's in it for you?"

"Nothing. I just need his birth certificate so he can run in track meets here in the city."

"Why can't he do that now?"

"They need to know his age. From his birth certificate."

"Why would my boy lie about his age?"

"Miss Shays, there's several coaches from some good high schools looking at him."

"If they so high and mighty, why can't they get his birth paper?"

"They're not his mother. Only his mother can do that."

"Miss, you yelling down an empty hole. I ain't got no birth papers for him. I'm his mother. He's my son. That's all. I got no birth papers for him."

"You get them from where he was born."

"That would be Kentucky."

"They have colleges in Kentucky, too," Miss McIntyre said brightly. "I bet they'd love a boy like Seymour on one of their college teams."

"I wouldn't send him to Kentucky for all the lollipops in the world," Mrs. Shays said. "I ain't never going back there."

"You don't have to go there. Just write a letter to the state. The state keeps all the hospital birth records."

"Seymour wasn't born in no hospital," Mrs. Shays said. "He was born in a house."

That made us laugh. Dex blurted out, "Goat was hatched like an egg." By now we had parked our butts on the stoop of my cousin Herbert's house in full view of them so we could hear it all. Then we looked at the door and seen Goat peeking behind his mother's dress. He seen us laughing and when he seen that, he come out from behind his ma and said, "Miss McIntyre, I don't want no scholarship."

"That's crazy," Miss McIntyre said. "Don't you want to go to a good school?"

"No."

"What you wanna do then?"

"I wanna get a bike and ride to work like my daddy."

Well, that got Mrs. Shays hot. She turned around and slapped Goat right across the back of his head. Pow! "Boy, I'll drop your britches and warm your two little toasters right here."

"I don't wanna—"

"Quiet!" she said. She turned to Miss McIntyre. "What's that birth paper called again?"

"A birth certificate. You write a letter to the state or the county. And they'll send it to you," Miss McIntyre said.

"Even if he was born in a house?"

"Yes. They file records somewhere."

"Ain't nobody filed nothing for me in Kentucky. I picked cotton. That's all the filing I was doing. I filed cotton in a bag."

"It's state law."

"To pick cotton?"

"No. To file birth certificates. They have to do it. You just write them and ask them and they'll send to the proper county records birthing office or the census office, and the county will find it."

Mrs. Shays sighed. "That sounds awful complicated," she said.

"Don't you want him to go to college?"

"Sure I do," Mrs. Shays said. "But writing letters to counties and all, I don't know about them things. Plus we're talking Kentucky. This is Fayette County, Pennsylvania, miss. White folks mostly follows the laws up here. In Kentucky, white folks got all the mojo and say-so. They won't give me the time of day down there."

"It's a simple letter. Takes ten minutes to write."

"I got too many problems to set about writing some old letters," Mrs. Shays said.

"What kind of problems would stop you from getting your boy a good education?" Miss McIntyre asked.

Later on, I think Miss McIntyre was sorry she asked that. She was a young thing and didn't know. Only a fool would ask somebody in The Bottom to spill their guts about their troubles unless they got a year to set and listen.

Mrs. Shays started right in. "Well, Popcorn was hauling lumber down in Mason County . . . ," and on and on she went, and before long it was dark, and poor Miss McIntyre was sitting out there on Goat's front steps in her pretty little dress, barefoot now, 'cause she'd taken her high heels off, and by then three hours had passed and Goat had got bored and cut out for the soft drink factory with Dex to see if they could scare up some empty bottles to sell, while I sat there alone on my cousin's steps listening because I like Miss McIntyre.

I sat there a long time, hoping Miss McIntyre or Goat's mom would at least notice me and say hello or feel sorry for me and wave me over and offer me a glass of water or something, because I was so thirsty I'd'a been happy to drink some of that nasty chittlin-smelling water they probably drink in Goat's house, but they never done that. Mrs. Shays talked the whole time, and after a while she come out the door and sat next to Miss McIntyre on the steps, still spilling her guts. She told Miss McIntyre about how Goat's dad, Mr. Popcorn, married her back in Mason County when she was seventeen and rode her around on his bike handlebars when they was young and happy, but after they got up here to Uniontown, Pa., and The Bottom and he got laid off at the steel mill, he rode his bike home from work every night from Monday to Thursday and don't look at her twice and every Friday he gets dead drunk like clockwork and she has to throw him out the house and how he comes back on his bike every Sunday saying he's sorry and promises to change and she lets him in again, and how he been doing the same bit for years while she can't pay the light bill and can't get Goat no new sneakers or dungarees or nothing.

And I got to thinking about Goat, how he really never did have nothing and how raggedy he always dressed, being poorer than most folks in The Bottom who make fun of him for being country when they is altogether pretty country themselves. I heard more than I wanted to hear.

Miss McIntyre listened the whole time and didn't say hardly nothing but "uh huh, uh huh," and once in a while she offered little suggestions and stuff, and I could tell by the look on her face that she got more than she bargained for. But she was hanging in there until the story got worse when Mrs. Shays started talking about how Tory got put in jail for robbery and when I heard that I said to myself, "I *knew* he wasn't in no Job Corps," and then finally Mrs. Shays busted into tears and said: "The Army wants my boy. They want my boy to join up and I don't know what to do. He's my best boy."

"Seymour?"

"No. Minnie Jug."

"Who's Minnie Jug?"

"Sylvester's his name. They call him Minnie Jug. My oldest boy. He's nineteen. The Army wants him. They sent him a letter. Wanting to send him to Vietnam. That's where Mrs. Cruz's boy got killed. And Ellie Boyer's son, too. Both of 'em dead over there. Killed fighting some white man's war. Now they want my son, too." She boo hooed some more.

Miss McIntyre sat quiet for a minute and then said, "I'd like to see that letter from the Army. You have it?"

"No."

"Where is it?"

"Minnie Jug got it. But it ain't no use, miss," Mrs. Shays said. "I can't read no way. I know a few wee old letters and can write my name, but that's it. That's why I can't get no birth paper for Seymour. And I can't write the Army to ask about my son. I'm in a hard position." Then she boo hooed a little more.

Miss McIntyre didn't say a word for a good while. She

coughed once or twice, then drew a handkerchief from her pretty little purse and gave it to Mrs. Shays, who wiped her face. Then she said, "You should've told me that first. That would've saved us some time. Just because you can't read doesn't mean you're not smart. You're a bright woman."

"When you have been spit on," Mrs. Shays said, "it don't matter much what else you think you know."

"What about your husband?"

"He can't read neither. And even if he could, he ain't no real help to me. I thank you for trying to help my boy, miss. But Seymour ain't right for no scholarship no how. I put him in God's hands."

With that, she got up and turned to go in the house, opened the door and stepped inside.

Miss McIntyre said, "There's alternatives, you know."

Mrs. Shays turned around. "You got a good heart, young lady. But if you fool around with us colored folks here in The Bottom, you'll end up dwelling in sadness. I know how to handle my boys. And Popcorn, too."

Miss McIntyre nodded and rose up and put her shoes on, then looked around. It was dark all around The Bottom now. Pitch-black, 'cause there's no streetlights, but up the hill past The Triangle you could see the lights of downtown Uniontown far off, the tall buildings all lit up and looking rich and happy.

"Get that letter from the Army and send it to school with Seymour," Miss McIntyre said. "And tell Seymour the name of the town where you had him when he was born."

"I don't think that Seymour knows how to write it," Mrs. Shays said.

"He can write all right," Miss McIntyre said. "And he can spell, too. Because I taught him."

Then she got in her car and drove off.

Mrs. Shays watched Miss McIntyre's taillights till they vanished, and still kept staring long after they was gone, just looking into the dark. Then she glanced over and seen me staring, setting on my cousin Herbert's stoop, then went inside her house, which was dark now, lit by candles inside, like it most always was.

MAYSVILLE. THAT'S THE NAME of the town where Goat was born. Miss McIntyre found it out after Goat brung that name to school on a piece of paper. She got busy with him and kept him after school and they wrote to Maysville, Kentucky, and they sent Goat's birth certificate right to Miss McIntyre at school. Miss McIntyre took that birth paper the day she got it straight down to Falls Point where Goat should've got that medal. She showed it to the people over there and said, "I told you he was only twelve." They still didn't give Goat no medal, but one of them white coaches down there from one of them big white high schools said, "I'll take that kid onto my track team right now."

But he had to wait till the school year was over when Goat could be in high school, so Goat stayed in school with us. That coach wanted Goat so bad he let Goat practice with his track team anyway and showed Goat some things about running the hundred-yard dash. And Goat took them things the coach showed him and runned for our school. He was the only member of the George Washington Carver Middle School track team. He didn't have no real track shoes, just some old basketball sneakers he got from someplace, and he didn't have no real track uniform neither. Miss McIntyre was his coach. She coached him by getting him a uniform from the school basketball team and he runned in that. That was all the coaching he got. And he tore 'em up all over the city and in Fayette County, too.

He became a star. Well, as much a star as The Bottom seen, for we never had too much in the way of stars, unless you count Rev. Jenkins, who gets in the news by starting as much trouble as he stops, or the time somebody in the church stole all the Christmas club money and a cop came in to investigate it and the church secretary, Mrs. Friday, was showing him where the hiding place was in the church basement and she fell down the basement stairs and broke her leg and knocked over a kerosene heater, which started a fire down there and the cop picked her up on his back and brung her out. That don't seem heroic really, unless you know that Mrs. Friday weighed about four hundred pounds. And the cop weighed two hundred pounds. So that was six hundred pounds altogether that he lifted and brung up the stairs. That was a white cop, too, and when Mrs. Friday got well she told everybody what happened and the newspapers got hold of it and made a big deal about it and that church put so much chicken and punch in that cop and all his friends when they came around off-duty one Saturday afternoon nobody knowed who was who, for somebody from the church had spiked the punch with moonshine and everybody knew it, and the whole bunch of 'em was staggering around drunk and playing cards and telling lies, until Mrs. Friday's husband threw up and said if they'da thrown his smooth Georgia white lightning in the punch instead of Mr. Johnson's old South Carolina hootch, which ain't nothing but gasoline, nobody would'a got sick off it, and the cops said, "Don't say no more," and they left.

But wasn't too many star kids from The Bottom, mostly because the kids from The Bottom don't get far enough in school to stay in sports, or they move away, or they end up working jobs or go to jail by the time they is old enough to really get some kind of scholarship. And that included Minnie Jug.

He was working a job down at the same waste oil place as his daddy when Goat asked him about that letter to join the Army, for Minnie Jug was the one who had it, not his mother, 'cause Minnie Jug could read, and his ma and pa couldn't.

At first Minnie Jug wouldn't give it to Goat. Minnie Jug is more serious than Goat. He don't laugh as much. He's bigger and taller and could've been good in sports, for he is cut something serious with muscles. But he's kind of hard. He told Goat, "I ain't showing no letter to no teacher."

But a funny thing happened to Goat after he got that birth certificate, something bigger than even winning track meets and all. He started getting something he never had before. He got confidence. He started reading books Miss McIntyre got him about other people in track, like a white man named Glenn Cunningham who they said would never walk because his legs was burned up in a fire, but he ran anyway and became a world champion. And Tommie Smith, a black man who broke the world record in the Olympics and raised his fist for black people on the medal stand. Goat got interested in them things.

So when Minnie Jug said, "I ain't showing no letter to no teacher," Goat stayed on him and said, "Why you wanna go to the Army and make Momma all worried up?" He stayed on him so much Minnie Jug gave him the letter and Goat brung it in to Miss McIntyre.

I was in class that day, for Goat walked to school with me and Dex most mornings after he runned behind Mr. Popcorn and seen him off to work, and when we walked to school he showed us the letter from the Army. It wasn't nothing much to look at. It was just a little letter that said "Sylvester Shays so and so" and a bunch of numbers and such.

When he gave it to Miss McIntyre she read it, and Goat watched her close.

"Well, it says he's one ninety-eight," she said. "It doesn't mean he has to go into the Army. It means he has a chance—a good chance—that they might call him up for service. But they haven't yet. So go back and tell your ma we're gonna try some things. But I need to write for all the birth certificates of all your brothers."

"I ain't got but two. Minnie Jug and Tory."

"All right. Tell her I'm gonna write and get those."

Goat done that, and Mrs. Shays agreed, for Miss McIntyre wrote the letters and Mrs. Shays signed them. So Miss McIntyre sent them letters off to Kentucky, and while we was waiting for them birth certificates to come back, Goat kept winning. He cooked like that the next few weeks, getting better and better, winning all the time. He growed into a star in Uniontown, beating boys from all the high schools in town. By the time the spring came around, he was the best in all Fayette County, and now they was talking about making him run up in Pittsburgh, the big city. Racing the big boys. A boy from The Bottom. Unbelievable. And when they had that same big track meet in Falls Point that next winter, the place where it all started, he runned again against that one guy who beat him before in the hundred-yard dash and beat the pants off that guy. And this time, they did give Goat a medal.

I was there when he runned that race. He was so excited after that race he didn't know what to do. It was a small race for him, really. By then he was beating lots of faster boys. But that's where it all started, and he wanted a lot of us to see it. His ma wasn't there, of course. Neither was his daddy. They was too busy working. But me and Dex seen it, and Miss McIntyre, because she drove us there in her little red car and took us out for ice cream afterwards. Then after ice cream she drove us home to The Bottom and dropped us off at The Triangle, that very place where she had once drove through and stopped our game. Goat had was so excited to show his ma his medal he had one foot out the door before Miss McIntyre even stopped the car. "You ought to come see my ma," he said to Miss McIntyre.

"That's okay," she said. "Tell your ma I'll write her a note soon. You can show it to her."

"Whyn't you come see her now? She's probably home from work."

But Miss McIntyre had a funny look on her face. "No, Seymour, it's fine. Tell her I . . . I have some more information about your brother Minnie Jug."

"Is it bad news?"

"No, Seymour, actually it's . . . it's good news. But you go home. I'll send her a note soon."

So Goat got out and runned home. Then me and Dex got out and Dex vanished to his house—but I lingered. I seen something in Miss McIntyre's face that worried me, so I headed around the corner, doubled back, and stood behind a pole in the dark to watch her leave, just to make sure she was safe getting out The Bottom.

But she didn't leave. She sat there at the wheel of her car in the middle of The Triangle, staring into the dark. Then she done a U-turn and pointed the car towards the hill that led out towards the city. Then she stopped again, staring out. The car didn't move. It sat there, the motor purring. Her glasses was the only thing I could see in the dark, reflecting off the dashboard lights, and them glasses didn't move. Seemed like she was thinking about something. Finally she put the car in gear and drove up the hill and was gone.

I watched her taillights go, wishing I could've gone with her, for I started feeling love for that woman at that time, a real love, and it was the first time. Thing is, when somebody's thinking about love in The Bottom, mostly nothing good comes of it. Love comes and goes, they say. But understanding? In The Bottom, understanding don't come easy. It comes hard. And it don't never feel good neither.

AT THE END OF SCHOOL the next day, Miss McIntyre called me aside after the bell had rung to finish the day and said, "Stay here."

I said, "I got to walk Sissie home."

"Dex and Seymour can walk her home." She told them and they done it.

After everybody left, she said, "I need you to do something for me."

She was sitting at her desk and I walked over. She reached inside a drawer and gived me a fat envelope. "Take this over to Mrs. Shays and give it to her."

I said, "What is it?"

"It's called none of your business."

"Is it about Minnie Jug? He got to fight in the Army now?"

"Just give it to her. If she asks you to read it to her, read it."

"Why me?"

"'Cause you're the best reader in this class. And you're a nosybody."

"What'd I do wrong?"

"Listening to other people's conversations is what you did wrong. Just give her this letter."

"What is it?"

"It's about Sylvester."

"Who's that?"

"Minnie Jug. Don't give it to him. This is for his mother. Not him."

"She's Goat's ma, too. Can't Goat give it to her?"

Miss McIntyre, for the first time ever, looked a little confused. "It's a favor to Goat too, okay?"

"Why I got to do Goat's business, Miss McIntyre?"

She looked at me stern. "'Cause you're so concerned about everybody's business."

"I didn't mean nothing that day you was at Goat's."

"Then why'd you sit there three hours listening to me and Mrs. Shays?"

"I just . . ."

I didn't know what to say. I wanted to say, "I sat there 'cause I loves you, Miss McIntyre. And I want you to take me out of The Bottom and make me your son. And then later on I can be your husband and live downtown in the city where the lights are bright. And we can drive your nice red car. And when I go to sleep at night I can wake up and see you first thing in the morning, the way I see you in my dreams at night, looking so pretty with your glasses off." But all them thoughts made me scared. Me and her alone in the room after school suddenly didn't seem like so much fun. She was staring at me, setting close to me at her desk, all bothered and serious, and I could smell her perfume and see her makeup and all, and them big brown eyes behind them pretty glasses was looking on, and that cute little button nose and all the rest of her right there, and I could see she was bothered about something inside, and that got me plain scared of the whole deal.

"I would take it myself," she said, "but . . . I'm in too deep now as it is."

"You done something wrong?" I asked.

"Course not!" she said. She thought a moment, then said: "Tell you what. Take it to her job at the hospital. Tell her it's from me. Tell her she needs to find someone who's not in her family to read it to her. Can you do that?"

"Yes."

"And can you promise me not to breathe a word of this to anyone? Though I know that's probably not gonna work." She sighed.

She seemed to be saying that last part to herself more than me. She looked so sad and pretty then, it was all I could do not to leap up and declare: "It's all right, Miss McIntyre, I can protect you. I won't tell a soul, I swear. It's me and you against the whole world now, no matter what, and I will do anything including jump out this window into the ocean before I tell a soul." But I didn't do nothing but nod and say, "Okay."

"That's good," she said. "And for your trouble—and for keeping it a secret—I'll give you two whole dollars."

She leaned over at her desk and opened a drawer to give me them double dollars, which gived me a chance to peek at some other doubles, them two brown bunnies paired up beneath her blouse, knocking about as she fumbled for her purse, that same pretty purse that sat in the seat of her car as she drove past The Triangle that day just before last summer. I ain't worth two cents, is what I thought to myself, for this is the very thing they be hollering about in church. I had a fit with myself, standing there watching her knockers. But she wasn't paying me no mind. She had opened the purse and pulled out her wallet and was fumbling around through it, and that's the last I seen of her that day, for by the time she had flipped through the tiny papers and books and matches and little papers and got to the crumpled dollar bills in that wallet and was holding them up in her hand, I was out the door. I had snatched the thick letter envelope off the desk and was gone.

MY GRANDMA DIED at the old Carver Hospital, so I know it pretty good. I know the cafeteria exactly where Mrs. Shays worked, 'cause me and my sister Sissie was in there a bunch of times with my ma while she sat at a table sobbing and carrying on during my grandma's last days. Mrs. Shays was nice to my ma then. She brung her coffee and said nice things and sat down and prayed for my ma and my grandma and all. My ma likes Mrs. Shays.

I found Mrs. Shays where she always is, serving food behind the counter at the buffet line where people bring their trays to get food. I got in line, and when I reached her she nodded hello and I stuck my face over the counter and whispered in a low voice, "I got to talk to you a minute, Mrs. Shays. About Miss McIntyre."

She said, "Wait a minute till I get a break," and gived me a piece of cake. I sat in the cafeteria and waited till she was clear.

She came over to the table and sat down and looked at me a long minute. Finally she said, "Do I need to talk to your ma about you being a busybody and poking your nose in other people's business?"

"No, Mrs. Shays," I said. "And I'm sorry. I just wanted to see Miss McIntyre."

"Don't you see her enough?"

"Yes, ma'am, I seen her today in school. She said to give you this."

I handed her the letter.

She took the envelope and opened it up and pulled out the pages. She held the pages upside down first, then turned them the right way, then glanced around the room to make sure no one was watching. Finally she said, "You know this don't mean nothing to me, Butter."

"Miss McIntyre said to tell you 'Get somebody to read this who ain't no relation to you.'"

"What's it about?"

"She said it's about Goat and Minnie Jug."

"You sure?"

"Yes, ma'am."

She glanced around the room. "Okay," she said. "I'll give you a dollar to read it to me. I get paid Thursday. That's in two days."

"Mrs. Shays, I thank you for it, but I don't want your money. I already stuck my nose too far into you and Miss McIntyre's business now. If my mother finds out, she'll whip on me so bad no amount of dollars is gonna help me. I won't do it no more. I learned my lesson. I swear to God."

She smiled a little bit. "Most of us has a desire to mind other folks' business," she said. "That's the child in you, Butter, not the man. But every child has to learn grown-up things in some form or fashion. So I guess this is your time, for I needs to know what's in here. I got ten minutes before I got to get back to work. Can you read all these pages in ten minutes?"

She handed me the pages. I looked 'em over.

"I think so," I said.

"G'wan, then."

So I did.

The first was a letter Miss McIntyre had wrote to the Army saying that, according to the law, if the Army wants to draft a boy who is the oldest boy in the house and his ma is a widow and that boy is the breadwinner and caretaker and all helping his ma, then rule 7a, clause B or whatever, that boy couldn't be drafted no kind of way, 'cause he got to help his ma who's a widow. She had wrote the letter and signed it as Mrs. Shays, and the Army wrote back to her and said "we agree" and would review it and so on and so forth, but it looked like Minnie Jug was in the clear.

"So my boy Minnie Jug is safe then," Mrs. Shays said.

I didn't say nothing, for that letter from the Army had said, "If the ma is a widow." Mrs. Shays wasn't no widow. Popcorn was her husband. But I already seen she was a lot smarter than me even if she couldn't read a lick, so I didn't say nothing.

Then she buried her face in her hands silently, choked a little bit, clearing her throat, then pulled her face back up high, looked into the palm of her hands, and said, "Now read the other."

I opened the second letter.

"It's birth certificates," I said. "Four altogether."

"Read all the names," she said.

So I read 'em. The first was Goat's. It said Seymour Shays. Daddy named Irving Evans. Ma was Ruth Shays.

The second was Minnie Jug's birth certificate. Same daddy and momma. Irving Evans, daddy. Ruth Shays, momma.

The third was Tory. Same thing.

And then there was a fourth: Irving Evans.

I said, "This last one—" then cut myself short, for I seen somthing was wrong.

I read it close, then checked the dates. It wasn't no mistake. They was all brothers: Minnie Jug, Tory, Goat—and Irving Evans, the oldest—all born a couple of years apart. On Irving

Evans's birth certificate, the father wasn't no Shays. It said "colored." The space for "mother" was marked "Ruth Shays."

All brothers. Or half brothers. Or something like that.

And Goat had told me that his daddy Mr. Popcorn's real name was Irving Evans.

Mrs. Shays was looking at me as I looked at the papers. "Does it look proper?" she said.

"Yes, ma'am, it looks proper," I said.

"Good."

I gived her back the paper and went home. Maybe it was a mistake, I thought. Maybe Irving Evans was a little Irving Evans and his real daddy was a big Irving Evans someplace else.

Or maybe the white folks put Mrs. Shays's name on that birth certificate because one colored looks like another in Kentucky.

Maybe Irving Evans wasn't Mr. Popcorn. Maybe Irving Evans died someplace and nobody brung him up on account of how he died.

Later on, I thought to do the math and figure out who was who. But then I figured that's probably what Miss McIntyre already done, which is why she didn't want to see Mrs. Shays herself.

I thought about that all the way home, about how Goat spent every morning for the past ten years running behind Mr. Popcorn while Mr. Popcorn rode his bike to work, running next to his brother who was also his father and his brother at the same time. And maybe that's what made Goat run so fast.

FATHER ABE

Here they come!"

Eighteen little colored children, tiny tufts of life, peeked their faces out the doorway of a ruined arms factory and made their way into the sunshine of a glorious Richmond, Va., afternoon. As they emerged in line, holding hands, forty-three Negro soldiers, members of the 32nd Pennsylvania Colored Infantry Regiment, dressed in tattered Union Blue, stopped and leaned on their shovels to watch. They'd spent this morning as they did yesterday morning, and the one before that and the one before that, digging a trench around the ruins of the Tredegar Gun and Ammunition Factory, which they had helped destroy the month before, along with most of Richmond, the capital of the Confederacy. Several weeks had passed since they'd taken this town. The war was nearly over but not quite. No one was quite sure. Nobody told them anything. There were still things to do, but where to do them, and how to do them, and when to do them, they had no idea. Their orders were to dig, and when they stopped, to dig, and dig again.

And dig they did. For nine days the soldiers dug, with only one distraction. Each day around noon, the men, thirsty and hot, exhausted from digging, would stop to lean on their shovels and admire the day's one form of entertainment, a daily ritual: Each day eighteen orphaned Negro children, aged five to thirteen years, emerged in the gorgeous Virginia afternoon sun from the ruins of the factory and paraded past, marching out in double file to follow their caretaker, Sister Coles, on a daily trek to the Freedman's Bureau about four miles up the road, for a meal of hard tack and biscuits.

The soldiers enjoyed watching the kids. Each day they gathered in small groups to swab their faces with handkerchiefs and guess the origins of each Negro child as the orphans marched by.

"That big one there, he's a Georgia Negro," a brigade cannoneer remarked. "See that wide head? That's how they look."

"Naw," another soldier offered, "that's a Sea Island boy. See them wide feet? Them's fishermen's feet, I'd reckon. South Carolina. Low Country."

"He ain't Low Country," the cannoneer snorted. "He's from Maryland. That boy's daddy is a waterman. That's where his feet come from. Watermen got the biggest feet."

A portly rifleman stepped between the two and said gaily,

"I wouldn't bet a smooth dollar on none of y'all guesses," he said. "But that one there," he pointed. "I know who his daddy is." He called out. "Hey Abe Lincoln! Hey boy!"

At the end of the line the last child, a tiny, mixed-race boy, looked up. Abraham Henry Lincoln, aged five, his soft skin the color of creamed coffee, the sun bouncing off his curly hair and light eyes, gaped in awe at the muscled, tall, smiling men leaning on their shovels. He waved and smiled shyly, showing several missing front teeth, prompting a burst of laughter and woofing.

"Boy, when you gonna grow some teeth!"

"Son, them gums is ripe enough for butter beans!"

"Keep your mouth closed, boy, less'n flies get in there!"

"Hey Abe," the cannoneer called out. "Want an apple?"

Little Abe Lincoln stopped short, dropping the hand of the kid in front of him, lingering, as the rest of the kids marched ahead in twos. He stood shyly for a moment, then slowly crossed the road as the line of kids drew away.

"Where you from, boy?" the cannoneer asked. "We got a bet going."

"Where's my apple?" he asked.

"Lemme see now," the cannoneer said, searching his pockets. "I just had it . . ."

Little Abe Lincoln watched anxiously as the cannoneer, bereft of apples and any other food, searched his pockets.

"Aw, leave 'em be, Pete," the sergeant said. His name was Big Nate, a tall, serious man from Alabama. He patted Little

Abe Lincoln on the head. "G'wan, boy. Catch up to the rest, before Sister Coles comes back and puts a cat's tail on ya. I'll might fetch you a real apple tomorrow."

"Where you gonna get it from?" the cannoneer sneered.

Nate ignored him and nodded at Abe. "G'wan ahead, boy."

Little Abe turned to hustle to catch up with the line of children, which had nearly reached the corner of the battle-torn street of ravaged homes and storefronts. The child had nearly caught up to the others when suddenly the cannoneer shouted out, "By the way, your daddy's coming tomorrow!"

Abe stopped short as the line of children moved away, turned the corner, and disappeared out of sight. He trotted back.

"You know my daddy?" Little Abe said. He stared up at the cannoneer, a portly soldier named Vernon, who seemed as tall as a tree and as wide as a house.

"Course I do! It's Father Abe hisself," he said, with a wink at the others.

Little Abe Lincoln stood alone now. The line of kids had vanished.

"How you know he's my pa?" he asked.

"He got the same name, don't he?" the cannoneer said. "*He's* Abe Lincoln. *You* Abe Lincoln. Put two and two together, boy. He's a big man, y'know, your pa."

"You know him?"

"Why, everybody knows Abe Lincoln, son! He's the biggest white man in the world. He lives in the biggest white house you ever seen. Got land yonder far as your eyes can see. Got more money than the King of France. And he's coming tomorrow! Right here to Richmond!"

"He is?"

"Surely! Heard that from a mule skinn—"

"That's enough, Vernon," the sergeant, Big Nate, said.

The cannoneer glanced at his fellow soldiers, whose smiles had disappeared.

"I'm just funning him, Nate," he said.

Nate turned toward Little Abe and knelt down. Abe saw the big man's gentle eyes focus on him.

"Now, son—" and suddenly Little Abe felt himself being snatched in the air and the world was upside down. He found himself seeing the sergeant sideways. Sister Coles had grasped him and snatched him in the air. Her strong arm held him on her hip like a sack of meal. She glared at Big Nate.

"How'd you like that soup I made for y'all last week, Mr. Nate?" she asked.

"I liked it fine, Sister Coles," Big Nate said.

"Good. Because I peed in it."

The soldiers laughed as Sister Coles turned away, holding Abe Lincoln under her hip like a pig suckling, moving down the road fast, as if her speed would ease the great pain that she knew had ached Little Abe all five years of his life, from the moment he could recognize himself. That he was named after a man he never saw, a father that never was nor ever would be. And that at age five, he still had no idea who Abraham Lincoln was.

. . .

THAT NIGHT, A LONE OWL stood guard atop the peak of the shelled-out roof of the destroyed north wing of the abandoned Tregador Gun Factory. Beneath a twilight sky and shattered rooftop, Sister Coles's orphans lay on makeshift straw mattresses serving as beds, underneath tables that once held lathes, tools, and machine presses and now served as roofs during the rain, inside a factory workshop that had once powered a mighty nation to war against itself. Their hissing, chattering voices lifted into the night air, through the gaping roof and up into the night as they discussed matters of life, their whispers carried aloft by the wind into the sky, where every dream seemed possible and the echoes of past pain and lost parents vanished into the promise of tomorrow's coming.

"When my daddy comes to get me," said one eight-year-old, "he's gonna make me a feather bed."

"My mamma promised me she's gonna bring me a pocket full of sugar candy when she comes back," bragged a seven-year-old girl.

"Oh hush!" snorted Solomon, the oldest among them, a wise old man of thirteen. "Ain't nobody comin for y'all. When Mamma Coles gets tired of you, you gonna have to shift for yourself. Y'all ain't got no mas or pas. You got no place to go. Git that through your heads."

There was a raw silence. Then a rustling. From the end of

the room, a tiny voice piped up. "I got a pa," Little Abe Lincoln said proudly.

"No you don't," Solomon said.

"Yes I do. I got a pa, and he's a great, big white man. He lives in a great, big white house. He's got more land over yonder than you've ever seen."

Solomon cackled. "Abe Lincoln ain't your pa, stupid. You ain't even got a name. Abe's the name somebody throwed at you when they found you on the road someplace. Your real name's No-Pa."

A burst of laughter covered the room, echoing off the walls and into the sky above.

Little Abe Lincoln felt his face flushing hot. "That's a lie, Solomon. I got a pa, and he's coming to get me tomorrow!"

"Who said?"

"Soldier said it."

More howling and guffaws.

"Abe Lincoln ain't your pa, cheese face," Solomon said through his laughter.

"Yes he is!"

"No he ain't!"

"Yes he is! And when he comes tomorrow, he's gonna bust your face and—!"

A sudden opening of the door silenced the room. The kids flopped on their backs onto their straw beds. Sister Coles, holding a lantern, walked into the silence, her bare feet slapping against the wooden floor. She swept a lantern light up and down the aisle of mattresses and makeshift beds.

"Next one I hear talking in here'll get it from my switch something scandalous," she said.

She stood in the middle of the floor, staring around as a cone of silence enveloped the room. She then counted eighteen heads as she did every night. All eighteen in place. Then she turned on her heel and left, closing the door behind her.

The next morning, at dawn, when she came to wake the children to milk the single cow in the yard, she counted seventeen heads. There was one missing. Little Abe Lincoln was gone.

TWO CANNON BATTERY SNOUTS peered into the night sky like devil's eyes. Behind the pitched tents and dead fires, the 9th Louisiana Colored Infantry Regiment slept. Somewhere in the camp's darkness, a harmonica sounded wearily. It was 4 a.m. at the corner of Walker and Greal Streets, and it might as well have been 4 a.m. all over the world, for the men of the 9th Louisiana Colored Infantry slept the sleep of dead men. They had arrived three hours previous, fresh from a terrible skirmish in nearby Petersburg, led by a bungling Union commander whose idiocy and cowardice had sawed off whatever edge of strength and goodwill they had left. The fight, against the desperate 14th Virginian Greys, white farmers and mule

skinners like themselves, men of grit and guts who were simi-
larly exhausted, was a disorderly, wild, scandalous, useless mess,
which deteriorated from cannons to rifles to bayonets to stones
to fists—the whole bit of it just at war's end, too. They were
exhausted. They wanted no more of it.

In the eerie darkness, a lone sentry named Settles, smoking
a pipe near the edge of camp, noticed a possum slip into a ditch
covered by old planking near the road, which some soldier had
obviously used as shelter to cover himself as he slept. He trained
his rifle on the ditch, thinking he had scored his own private
dinner. Then, out of both greed and deference to his exhausted,
sleeping colleagues, he yanked out his bayonet, placed it on the
tip of his rifle, and rose to score his meal in silence.

He crossed the road, picked up a large stone, gently set it on
one end of the ditch to plug it, then crept stealthily back to the
other end. He stood over the ditch on the planking and raised
the bayonet in the air, readying to stab the creature as it scampered out the only exit. Then he stomped down heavily onto
the plank with his boot.

He heard the creature wriggling down the ditch, but it
fooled him, for it was bigger than he thought and wiggled so
hard it rumbled the plank a bit. Settles, startled, stepped off
the plank just as the rodent scampered out the end of the ditch
and rose on two feet like a man, facing him like a ghost, causing him to backpedal, trip on a stone, lose his balance, and
fall on his rear end with a shout, dropping his loaded musket

to the ground, which discharged on its own with a resounding bang, blasting a precious musket ball into the woods behind him.

The camp leapt to life. Fires were doused. Grunts were heard. The clattering of pots and pans. Men rushed from every direction, half dressed, rifles in hand, some dressed in rebel gear they'd recently procured. They found the sentry Settles standing over Little Abe, the kid crouched into a ball, his hands held over his ears, his tiny face scrunched in agony, with the sentry standing over him.

A colored sergeant stepped forward. "What's going on, Settles?"

Settles, rattled, blew a whoosh of air out of puffed-up cheeks. "I damn near killed him, Sergeant. He come out this here ditch. Damn fool . . ."

The sergeant, a huge, friendly-faced Negro, rubbed the sleep out of his eyes, stooped down, and scooped up the child with big, muscled arms, picking up Little Abe like he was an infant. He sat on the large pipe with the kid in his lap as the other soldiers crowded in. "What you doin' here, boy?"

"I'm looking for my pa," he said.

"Who's your pa? He got a name?"

"Abe Lincoln."

The men burst out laughing. Several clapped Little Abe on the back.

"Father Abe? That's a good choice, boy."

"I'd give five whole dollars to see Father Abe, chile."

"Best man in the world, your pa! God bless him!"

The sergeant frowned. He took a lantern from a fellow soldier and held it to the boy's face. Now they could see him clearly. The white features. The curly hair. The brown skin. "Gosh," one soldier said. "He's a regular buckaroo."

More laughter. The sergeant grew serious. "Be quiet," he said. He sighed and looked around. "Anybody know this child?"

"He might be from that gun factory over yonder on Taylor Road," said one soldier. "Heard a colored woman started an orphanage over there. The Pennsylvania Thirty-Second's digging ditches 'round it."

"Well, we gonna stay clear of that," the sergeant said. "We ain't digging no ditches." He nodded at the sentry. "Settles, get a mule and a wagon and take this boy back to the gun fact—"

"Naw!" Little Abe grasped the sergeant's chest and arms. "I want my pa."

"Son, he ain't here."

"Where is he?"

"I don't know."

"He's coming tomorrow!"

"Well, you'll see him tomorrow then."

"Ain't no Abes here?" the boy asked.

"We got three or four Abes here," the sergeant said. "In fact that's my name, Abe. But I'm Abe Porter. Not Abe Lincoln."

"You my pa?"

"Course not," the sergeant said hotly.

This prompted a round of laughter and wry comments from the men standing behind the sergeant.

"I knowed you was a hot one, Sarge."

"Hey Sarge, you got a ready-made family . . ."

"Sarge got a busy noodle, don't he? And I thought he was a preacher!"

"Hush that!" the sergeant barked. He looked around, serious. "Hush up. Nothing funny in it. Nothing funny at all. Boy's got nobody in the world."

The men fell silent.

"Who gave you that name, boy?" he asked.

"I don't know," Little Abe said.

More soft chuckles, interrupted by an abrupt rustling sound heard in the bushes. A lantern was seen moving toward them in the trees. The lantern emerged from the foliage, illuminating a white face. The men straightened, turned, and saluted as a white captain stepped toward them. The sergeant stood up, holding the child.

"What's wrong, Sergeant?" the captain asked.

"Nothing, sir," the sergeant said. "Settles found this child here wandering 'round."

The captain shone his light on the boy's face. More men had gathered by now, and for the first time they all could see Little Abe Henry Lincoln clearly. Their eyes widened in surprise at the coffee-colored face and the curly hair.

"Get him back where he belongs," the captain said. "We just got word that the president is coming here. In four hours!

President Abraham Lincoln himself!" He was clearly excited, breathing deeply but trying to maintain the dignity of his rank.

The men gaped at each other in silent surprise as the captain peered at them, then down at the brown bundle in the sergeant's arms. He turned to Settles.

"Settles, roust up the camp right now so we can clean this place up and move at dawn." To the sergeant he said, "Sergeant Porter, take a detail over to Walker and Greal, straighten up our cannons and mule skinners. Get 'em cleaned up. Hurry up."

"What about the child?" the sergeant said, holding Little Abe.

"Settles can take the contraband back when he's done rousting the camp," the captain said.

The word "contraband" hung in the air a moment, like a barber's razor blade that slowly turns in the air, drifting toward a trusting customer's neck. The captain appeared not to notice.

"Git movin'," he said. "We got three hours till daylight." He disappeared into the brush and the darkness of the camp again.

The men stood around the sergeant, who still held the boy. Settles stepped forward and the sergeant spoke to Little Abe as he handed him over.

"Well, child, the captain says you got to go now."

"I don't wanna!"

"Well, you gotta."

"No!"

"Don't cling on me, little feller. I ain't the Abe you want. I got no family and don't want nar, not in slavery time, no sir.

G'wan now. Stop clinging on me. Don't make me git tough on you, fella. G'wan with Settles here. Settles, take this boy off me! . . . C'mon, child, easy now. Stop all that fussing. Settles, help me out here, would ya? Lissen, boy, Settles here'll take good care of you. Leggo me, would ya, please? Quit that crying now, child . . ."

AFTER A FEW MINUTES, the child quieted down, but he would not be wrested from Sergeant Porter. Porter glumly sent Settles to fetch a mule and wagon for the trip back to the orphanage while he sat on the edge of the ditch with Little Abe in his lap. A few of the men drifted off, but several remained, kneeling in a semicircle around the boy held by the man seated in the ditch.

"I wanna go with you," Little Abe said.

"You can't go where I'm going."

"Why not?"

"Well . . . where I'm going, they ain't got no children."

"Where's that?"

"Lafayette Parish, Louisiana."

"I'll be the first child there!"

The sergeant stared at Little Abe. "You'll live a life of sorrow and pity in my home country, son."

"Then why you taking me there?"

"I ain't said I was taking you no place!"

"How come you live there if they ain't got no children? And

if you bring some, why can they tell you, big as you is, not to? Ain't you Abe Lincoln?"

"I'm Abe Porter!"

"Don't you live in a great big white house? Ain't you got more land over yonder than I've ever seen?"

"I ain't got nar house. Nor land."

"What you got?"

"Freedom, son."

"What's that?"

The sergeant looked around. A couple of men cursed and drifted back toward camp across the road. But several remained, watching silently, their tired faces grim.

"If you have to ask," Porter said sheepishly, "I don't know."

"Does it mean," little Abe piped up, "that nobody can tell you what to do?"

"Well . . . maybe."

"And you can come and go as you please?"

"I suppose so," the sergeant said miserably.

"That's what I'd like for myself," Little Abe announced, satisfied. "To come and go where I please. And nobody telling me what to do. Let's go to Louisiana."

"I can't just up and go, boy."

"Why not?"

"I got to pay my dues first. Freedom ain't free, son. You got to fight for it."

"When do the fight end?"

"It's just about ending now, I reckon."

"So freedom's here?"

"Well . . . not quite yet."

"When it comes, how you'll know it?"

Sergeant Porter seemed confused. "Know what?"

"When freedom comes. How'll you know?"

"How . . . ?" Porter stammered. He looked around at the men. Several more drifted away and now only a few were standing around. The clop of a mule's footsteps could be heard, then a mule and wagon, silhouetted against the campfires of the bivouacked camp, appeared on the nearby road. Settles dismounted from the wagon and walked over to the ditch.

"One mule and wagon ready, Sergeant," he said.

Porter looked up and down the road. Then glanced in the direction of the thickets toward the camp, where the captain had disappeared to. The faintest glimmer of sunlight could be seen now. There were only six men squatting around Porter now, including Settles, all silhouettes in the dawn.

Porter stared down into the ditch. He seemed lost in thought. Finally he spoke, staring down at the ditch. "I done preached to y'all the best I know how these past years. And we still among the living, ain't we, thanks to God's grace."

He sighed softly, then added, "But not all of us."

He looked up, shifting the child in his lap, his gaze moved to the camp behind them, his eyes shining, his features slowly becoming visible in the growing light.

"Something's been digging at me ever since they told us this war is winding down," he said. "I come to thinking. About Yancy Miles, and Irving Gooden, and Linwood Sims, God rest their souls. I come to wonder about their deliverance, and about what God wants. Not for them. For us, who has fought under other men's rulings and is not yet gone from labor to reward. Who among us is gonna remember them? Yancy, with his cussing self, and Linwood, who could sing so good, and Irving and his brother Zeke, and all the rest of the colored who's deadened in these fields. The white folks'll know theirs, won't they? They'll write songs for 'em, and raise flags for 'em, and put 'em up in books the way they know how. But ain't nobody but God gonna give more than a handful of feed to the ones of us who died out here fighting for our freedom. And what is that anyway? This child here knows more about it than I do."

He stood up, holding the boy. "Let God's truth roll according to circumstance. If I'm gonna swing, it won't be for nothing. I won't hold it against none of y'all should you turn me in to the captain. I reckon you'd be doing me a favor, for I'd rather hang from the gallows than torture myself for the rest of my life by selling lies and confusion to children, like I just done to this here child, fool that I am."

He said to Settles, "Hold him for a minute." To Little Abe, he said, "You wait here with Settles. I'll be back shortly." He handed the boy to Settles, turned, and marched toward the camp across the road.

Settles, Little Abe, and the other four men watched Sergeant Porter cross the road and disappear into the camp, now illuminated by campfires.

"He's taking me back to Louisiana?" Little Abe asked.

Settles found himself holding the boy so tight to his chest that the little fella was laboring to draw air. He loosened his grip so Little Abe could breathe. "If he do, he's walking there on his elbows."

"What's that mean?"

With one hand, Settles shifted the boy and pressed Little Abe's head to his shoulder so that the boy's face stuck out over his back and his mouth was close to the boy's ear. "Don't say one more blessed word, child. Nothing. If you do, I'll put you over my knee and warm them two little biscuits on your backside myself."

"What I done wrong?"

"What'd I say! Be quiet! Whatever you said to him, don't say it to me, for God's sake, less'n you'll have me in as much trouble as him."

THE NEXT MORNING, the 9th Louisiana Colored Infantry Regiment stood in proud formation, their cannons and mule skinners assembled in a tight straight solid line for nearly a mile, their uniforms, though dirty, buttoned and ordered properly, the brass buttons and broadsword handles of their commanders glistening in the sun, as Abe Lincoln himself turned the corner of Walker and Greal. The president walked with a small entourage of men and officers, he being the tallest of them, moving in a stately manner, like a tower among small cottages, his face pockmarked by grief and struggle, holding the hand of his son Tad. He nodded at the troops as he moved slowly down the road, occasionally tipping his hat and smiling. In ten days he would be dead, slain by an assassin's bullet, surrendered to history.

But for the 9th Louisiana Colored Infantry, it was the proudest, most electrifying moment of their lives, one they would, to a man, never forget. Thus, few among them noticed that among their 120 troops, 14 cannons, 11 wagons, and 45 mule skinners who stood in tight formation to greet the Republic's sixteenth president there was one missing Union Army mule, one missing Union Army wagon, several barrels of Union Army supplies, and one unpaid Union Army soldier named Sergeant Abe Porter, who at that moment was making tracks north with a boy named Little Abe, rolling that Army mule at a double trot as fast as it could go, man and boy bound for the North and the long wait for the arrival of freedom and all that it represented, whatever it was, whenever it was, and however it was bound to come.

THE MOANING BENCH

The Gatekeeper strode briskly into the room, slamming the door behind him. He seated himself behind a mahogany desk with an angry grunt. He was short, stout, and clad in a long, tattered dark green robe. His facial features, if there was a face there at all, were hidden deep beneath the folds of a hood. His dark hands, thick, calloused, gnarled, and deeply veined, were clenched in anger. His fingers, topped by long nails, were curled together in outrage. His chest rose and fell in short huffs and puffs. It had been a long day.

He snatched the notepad on his desk and stared at it. Facing him on a narrow bench, five people in blue terrycloth robes sat, watching him nervously. From behind the door he entered came a sudden, wretched, agonizing human scream, then silence, followed by another blood-curdling howl, this one worse than the first, then silence again. The hooded figure at the desk seemed not to notice: He was busy with his pad, scratching notes.

When he was done, he put down his pen and took in his nervous audience seated on the bench, their backs against an unadorned white wall in the otherwise empty room. He cleared his throat, started to speak, and was interrupted by a sudden yelp from behind the door again, which caused a couple of the bench sitters to jump. He waved an impatient claw in the air.

"Oh please," he said. "Don't get all cracked up. They only work here. You oughta hear the customers."

He tossed the notepad onto the desk and got up, pacing in front of them. He hated mix-ups like these. Now he had to go through the trouble of explaining, and even worse, listening. He was so tired of listening.

His threw his hands into the air as he paced, the words flying out of his mouth into the barren room like hot coals.

"Your fat rear ends are parked on what we call The Moaning Bench," he snapped. "You're there because at your last conscious moment, just before you quit paying taxes for good, someone was not sure. That someone," he said matter-of-factly, "is my boss. Or thinks He is."

He cleared his throat and coughed. "Anyhow, that's a personnel issue and no concern of yours."

A howl emanated from the doorway behind him and suddenly quit, as if the howler were choked off. The five benchwarmers shifted again.

The Gatekeeper snapped: "Sit still. You can't open your yakking holes till I clear you. After I clear you, you can beg all you want. But keep the bleating and pleading to a minimum, please. 'Cause I'm in a fucking mood."

He sat down again, furious. He was sick of the gig, sick of the same play, day after day, the same human desire to keep living. For what? He liked it better when his packages came clean. Banished. That was perfect.

"Since you're borderline cases, there are other factors involved," he said. "But I don't feel like explaining all that today. Besides, most all of you are gonna end up behind that door anyway." He nodded behind him, where another howl was heard.

"Did I mention the furnace was acting up?" he said with a yawn. "Something 'bout the blower burning slow."

He watched as they shifted in discomfort again.

"Don't worry. That thing'll still take the edge off."

He chuckled at his own joke and flipped pages on the pad, reviewing his notes again. Finally with another yawn, he stretched, sat up, and said cheerily: "All righty then! Let's get going. State your case one at a time. And don't take all day. I been hearing shitty excuses since the ancient Druids."

He pointed to the man at the far end of the bench. The white-haired, elderly gentleman, who wore a tailored gray suit under his terrycloth robe, felt himself released. The man burst into voice. "My name—"

"Stand up," The Gatekeeper directed.

The man tried to stand, but he was trembling badly and couldn't manage it. The Gatekeeper impatiently pointed a finger and the man rose off the bench and floated, his feet several inches off the floor, until The Gatekeeper curled his finger away and the man plopped unceremoniously, like a sack of potatoes, back onto the bench.

He popped to his feet, trembling, his terrycloth robe opened showing his suit, now wrinkled, his face damp with perspiration. He yanked a handkerchief from his vest pocket and wiped his brow as he spoke. "I'm Ed Tannenbau—"

"*Ed, Ed who peed the bed. Peed till he was seven. Then he dropped dead,*" The Gatekeeper whined. "That's your sister's ditty, remember, Ed? But you didn't drop dead, did you, Ed?"

"I did not!"

"Did not what?"

"Pee the bed till I was seven," Tannenbaum said.

"Oh goody. A liar," The Gatekeeper snorted. "You might as well throw out those vacation folders, buddy. We got plenty of room for you here. Sit down."

"But what about arguing my case?" Tannenbaum asked.

"You got no case. And you peed the bed till you were eight, by the way."

"You said we could."

"What? Pee the bed?"

"No, argue the case—"

"Not till we're clear about who peed the bed, Ed."

"Oh, for Chrissake, I peed the bed, okay? But I deserve my chance to argue my case."

"All right. Go ahead, Mr. Ed-Who-Peed-the-Bed. C'mon. Speak up! Snap-snap! Chop-chop! Hit it. What'd you do in life, Ed-Who-Peed-the-Bed?"

Ed cleared his throat. "I was a realtor."

"Strike two, ya lying lawyer."

"Well, technically I'm not a lawyer since I haven't practiced—"

"You low-down, pee-filled, yellow-bellied, sap-sucking dog!" The Gatekeeper roared. "You almond-headed, two-faced, small-nutted professor of push-'em-around! How dare you come into my house and lie with such ease? Only *I* can lie in my house, sir! Should I decide."

Tannenbaum reddened. "What I meant about me being a lawyer is—"

"What? Not true? Say it, counsel!" Two bright, glowing pings of light suddenly appeared beneath The Gatekeeper's hood, eyeballs shining like tiny lightbulbs.

Tannenbaum was silent.

"Now I TOLD you I'm in a FUCKING MOOD, sir! You wanna wake up as a fly in a spiderweb? Or be a bird sucked into the engine of a 747? I could squash you like my ass-cheeks squash a fart. You want that?"

"Course not."

"Then get with it. Shush the nonsense. State your case, Ed.

The private stuff, please. The crime. The punishment. The redemption. One, two, three, go."

"I can't think of anything . . ."

"It's the lying I love!" The Gatekeeper said to the others gleefully. "You sorry-ass, Pull-Yourself-Up-by-the-Bootstraps, Mr. Salute-the-Flag, One-Nation-Under-God individual asshole. Punk! Chump! You waffle-faced, lowdown ratbutt-sniffer! And you're wondering why you're here! What about those whores in Tibet? You ever think about their children?"

"I was actually there to climb Mount Everest to raise money for charity."

"Right. And I quit selling oil wells yesterday. You're going to the smoking section, brother."

"Serving time?"

"No. You'll be smoked like cigarettes. Again and again. By the same Tibetan guides that you screwed. You and the rest of those do-gooder assholes who climbed Mount Everest over the years, leaving your garbage and corpses while you went to find yourselves on your spiritual path. Here's the scene, Ed: A bunch of do-gooders climb Mount Everest. One of them dies on the mountain. The rest can't get him down. Guess what? His corpse stays there. And if he's one of mine, guess who's got to haul up there to claim his soul? Assholes. What's wrong with people today?"

"I wasn't part of that. My expedition didn't—"

The Gatekeeper pointed a long, jagged finger at Tannenbaum, who rose into the air again like a piece of paper caught in the wind, slammed against the wall, and slid up and down like a volume slide knob, up, then flopped onto the moaning bench, where he curled into a ball, feet on the floor, face in his lap, fists balled upon his forehead.

The next person stood. She was a handsome, middle-aged woman with brown shoulder-length hair. Beneath her robe she wore a frumpy nightgown that reached her ankles.

"What's the matter, Patty Bross? You left your drawers with Santa Claus?"

Bross shot an embarrassed glance at the others on the bench, then drew the robe closer around her. "The least you could've done was let me die with my clothes on," she snapped.

"Excuse me? Were you teaching Sunday school when I yanked your pale, cellulite-loaded, pot-bellied ass up here? C'mon, Miss Sweet Meat! You were eighteen miles from home, banging skins with a Dixieland drummer! Dixieland. I hate that crap. Devil's music, my ass! Myself, I prefer rap."

He waved a hand and a torrent of horrid, filthy, expletive-filled rap blasted into the room at a deafening volume. Patty covered her ears in agony, while The Gatekeeper nodded and grooved with the music, his hooded head jouncing, moving his hands to the beat.

"Turn it down!" Patty pleaded.

He waved a hand and just as suddenly the music was gone, and the room was silent.

The Gatekeeper's hand disappeared into the dark folds of the hood. The outline of his hand rubbing a dark jaw could be seen beneath his shroud. "You got a problem, miss. It says here that your little hot box, according to my notes"—he regarded his notepad—"over the course of two years has been made available to every man in Cincinnati with a ding-dong who drinks Budweiser." He put the pad down. "And everybody," he said wryly, "drinks Bud."

"My mom died," Bross said. "I was lost."

"Now you're found, you stinker! And you're blaming your ma. Jeez! Take a load off!" He motioned with his finger and a powerful force slammed Patty into her seat.

The next candidate rose and removed his robe, revealing a heavyset white man clad in a plaid shirt, overalls, and a construction helmet. His face, arms, and hands were covered with black coal dust. His clothing fit him loosely, and a short, heavy spade and other miscellaneous digging tools dangled from his work belt.

"Did anyone say you could take my robe off?" The Gatekeeper asked.

"I got my own clothes," the man said.

"Well, Wayne Goines, you won't be needing 'em soon. You got plenty of friends here. And they all chug beer and got double chins just like you. Probably 'cause they spent their lives humping their cousins while they saluted the American flag. Bunch of hootenanny idiots, you types, with your tears in your beers and guns in your pockets, howling to the moon about your civil rights being kicked around. The poor white man."

The Gatekeeper mimicked a child's voice: "*Nobody knows me. Nobody cares 'bout me. Boo hoo. I'm the poor white man.* State your case, honky."

Goines stared at him grimly. "Fuck you."

"Be careful, stranger."

"What for? The game's up. I didn't sling black rock for thirty-four years to hear you beat up on everything I hold dear. Wiggle your fingers and make all the magic you want. I had fun." He added wistfully, "I could've used a motorcycle, though."

The Gatekeeper stood up from his desk and paced behind it for a long moment before saying anything else.

"Funny you should say that," he said. "There's some second thoughts about you, Mr. Goines." He folded his hands beneath his cloak. "On one hand, you didn't hurt anyone. On the other hand, you bought your ticket here."

"Meaning?"

"You drank and smoked."

"So what? I could afford it."

"What about porking that sixteen-year-old girl from Grundy?"

"I was nineteen. And she said she was twenty-five."

"And looked thirty-five," The Gatekeeper said. "Oldest-looking sixteen-year-old I ever saw. She had so many wrinkles, she needed pressing. Then again, I'm talking to a man whose wife has a thicker mustache than he does."

Goines's face reddened under the black soot. "I'll thank you to keep your filthy mouth off my wife. She's a good Christian. The Lord sits in her judgment. And mine, too."

"Ohhh, the Lord," The Gatekeeper said airily. "Is He nearby? Where is He?"

Before Goines could reply, The Gatekeeper pointed his finger at Goines's neck and Goines began to choke. The others watched, horrified, as Goines grabbed his neck and was slammed against the white wall behind the bench, his feet kicking, straining to breathe, choking, as The Gatekeeper's finger, an invisible force, slid Goines up the wall, Goines's feet kicking as he rose, his back pinned to the wall as if magnetized to it.

"Where'd He go?" The Gatekeeper said calmly. "Did He stop off for bread? Did He step outside to shake out the rug? Where? Show me where He is, Goines, and I'll turn you loose."

Goines desperately clawed at his neck, trying to breathe, kicking at the wall with his boots as he tried to free himself from the force that was strangling him. His face went red, then purple, then blue, then his kicks slowed. His struggles grew weaker and his hands fell to his sides.

The Gatekeeper retracted his finger into his sleeve, and Goines gasped for air as he crumpled into a breathless heap on the bench.

The Gatekeeper yawned. "All right, let's finish up." He snatched the notepad from the desk, regarded the list, and glanced at the bench. "You last two I'll clear at the same time. But I warn you: Beg one at a time. Ladies first."

A little girl stood up and removed her robe to reveal a patterned dress. She said, "I'm Heather Gallini and I'm twelve years old and—" The Gatekeeper cut her off and held his hand up. "Wait! School lesson number one, sulky poo! When Mama says, 'Honey, NEVER cross the highway in front of an eighteen-wheeler, 'do you . . . a) listen to Ma, or b) act like a little stinker and take a ch—"

"Stinker? Stinker!? What's the matter with you, man!" The person behind the voice, the last man on the bench, stood up.

He was a boxer, a huge, young, glistening brown man clearly in his prime, resplendent in white trunks and white ankle-high tennis shoes, with fur balls at the tips of the shoelaces. He was tall and broad, with wide shoulders and muscular biceps tapering down to steel-like wrists and forearms, his huge hands covered by red leather boxing gloves. His right eye was slightly puffed, his body was greased and slick. Sweat ran down his chest and back in rivulets, as if he'd been dipped into a pool.

"Stinker," he snapped. "Brother, you oughta have your mouth scrubbed out with soap. Calling kids names like that." He stood, put his hands on his hips, and stalked around in a small circle. "Shoot."

"You," The Gatekeeper said.

"That's right, baby. You know me. Everybody knows me. I'm Rachman Babatunde. Father of four, man of one, son of the seventh son of the seventh son," he said. He took a step back and began to shadowbox, bobbing up and down, sending blazing lefts and rights into thin air.

"You ought to sit, son," The Gatekeeper said. "The fight's over."

"My eye it's over," Rachman said, still shadowboxing. "I was whupping Blue Higgins and the world saw it. I had him. The fight was mine."

"He knocked you down in the seventh."

"I was whupping Blue and the world saw it, brother," he repeated. "*You* put me here, not him," Rachman said, bouncing on his toes as he shadowboxed.

"It says here"—The Gatekeeper regarded his pad—"that two out of the three judges had him ahead on points."

"You can buy a judge in New York for fifteen hundred dollars," Rachman said. "Plus, Blue can't hit that hard." He continued shadowboxing, spinning lefts and rights and whistling into thin air, feinting his head from side to side and sending lefts and rights whooshing past. "I'm so fast!" he whispered. "So fast. I'm so fast it's wrong. I'm faster than Superman. I'm so fast I make darkness run and hide. I'm faster than the truth. I'm faster than light. Everyone's scared o' me." He whispered, hissing to himself, *"Too fast! Too sweet! Oh, they all got plans till they see me. Then they get hit and ain't got no more plans. 'Cause I knocks 'em out."*

He turned to Heather, who was standing next to him. He

playfully swung a few punches at her. "I knock out kids, too," he chortled. He towered over the youngster like a giant over a flower. Then, as if an afterthought, he placed his huge forearms under her armpits, picked her up, and set her down on the bench. He thumbed her nose playfully with his glove. "I don't make no exceptions," he said. "Be careful 'round me, little girl. I'm a bad man." Then he stuck out his tongue at her. She stared up at him a moment, then giggled.

He turned to The Gatekeeper. "You ought to be ashamed of yourself. Scaring little kids with them tricks. I got an aunt who can put two horse hairs in a glass of milk and turn you into a snake in two days."

"That'd be interesting, at least," The Gatekeeper said. But Rachman ignored him. He stepped back and began to shadow-box again, skipping and dancing on his toes in a circle, feinting his head and stabbing his hands in the air. "Sissy!" he hissed, whispering, repeating to himself. "Sissy! Scaring children who ain't got no free choice! Some men in this world need a good spanking!"

"Are you really that fighter, Rock Man?" Patty asked.

"*Rack*-man, lady, not *Rock*-man. *Rack*, like clothes rack," he said, bouncing on his toes. "Speaking of clothes, you need some before you talk to me. That raggedy robe you got looks rented."

Her face reddened. "What do you expect? You know what this is?"

"Don't care, miss. I'm the greatest! Rachman Babatunde. Don't forget my name. Tell all your friends," he said again as he sent a flurry of fists whipping just past his own nose.

Goines sat up, recovering. "Ain't this a mess! I know you, son. I saw your first fight against that English fella. What was his name . . . Landey? He knocked you down."

"I got lazy," Rachman said. "Bob Lanker. I knocked him out in the third. I would've put him out in the first, but his wife was there. I predicted the third anyway. All my fight predictions is true."

The Gatekeeper said, "I can predict what will happen to you quite soon."

"Oh, I'm 'bout full up with you blabbing everywhere like it's a day's work," Rachman said. "You said you wanted the truth down here? Well, here it is. I'm so pretty. And I am the greatest. And you so ugly, you ain't. I bet that face of yours is so ugly, you oughta be cremated."

"An apt choice of words."

"Before you do your magic on me," Rachman said, still shadowboxing, "just give me five more minutes so I can put Blue Higgins to sleep and shock the world."

"Why would I do that?"

"So you can see the shock on Blue's face. He's ugly as you. Bring him here so I can whup him again."

The Gatekeeper chuckled. "I'm going to enjoy you here."

"If I got to stare at your ugly mug for eternity, I'll knock your green teeth out just so I can eat breakfast. You ugly enough to keep ants out of a picnic, mister. No wonder you wear a hood. And that's just the front. I bet the back of your neck looks like a pack of hot dogs."

Goines laughed as Rachman began shadowboxing again. Goines dug into his pocket, fumbling around, pulling out a blackened pencil and a piece of paper. "My youngest boy's got a picture of you hanging on his wall. Can you sign this here?"

Rachman stopped shadowboxing, obediently took the paper, grasped the pencil in the thumb of his glove, and whipped it across the page. As he did, the pencil and paper suddenly disappeared.

"That was momentarily amusing, but the fun's over," The Gatekeeper said.

Rachman shrugged and began shadowboxing again, but Goines placed his hands on his hips and barked at The Gatekeeper. "That pencil didn't belong to you," he said.

"Everything here belongs to me."

"I bought that pencil and paid for it and Rachman here was writing his name for my boy."

"Would you like your pencil back?" The Gatekeeper asked.

"I would."

"I can park it in your intestines."

"Pay him no mind," Rachman snorted, still moving. "He ain't real. Not even the devil is stupid enough to disrespect Rachman." He zinged a left that barely missed The Gatekeeper's face. "Ain't that right, lumpface?"

"Amusing," The Gatekeeper said again.

"I'm more'n' that, brother man. I'm your worst nightmare. I got a left that'll make you cry and right that'll make you die. Wanna go a few? Without your little tricks?"

"Why should I?"

"Take that robe off and fight, you devil you. Pull that hood off. Lordy, that mug of yours must look bad as a snake bite. You so ugly you keep your eyes closed when you kiss your wife—so you won't see her suffer."

"Enough!" Tannenbaum stood up. "This is madness." Tannenbaum spoke to The Gatekeeper. "Can we work out something?"

"Sit down," The Gatekeeper said.

Rachman ignored them both. He seemed inside himself, dancing from left to right, spitting, pacing a little from side to side, then dancing on his toes again, fists up, sweating, pounding hot, firing punches into the air, stoked up, swinging left crosses and right hooks, fighting an imaginary opponent and muttering to himself: "I am the greatest. No man on earth can whup me. No devil can whup me. I am the greatest! The greatest in the galaxy! Why? Because it's so. Because nobody can whup me. Nobody in the world!"

"Time to end this nonsense," The Gatekeeper said. He pointed his finger at Rachman as he'd done with the others, to slam him against the wall, choke off his breathing, humiliate and redress him.

Nothing happened.

Rachman continued shadowboxing, swinging lefts and

rights, talking to himself, murmuring. "He's just a bunch of old card tricks. They don't work on me. 'Cause I'm the greatest . . .'"

He snickered and turned his back to The Gatekeeper, shadowboxing the wall now, ducking, dodging, whistling punches into the air. He glanced at the others seated on the bench. They were staring at something behind him, their eyes wide in shock.

He turned and found himself glaring at The Gatekeeper, who had pulled his hood off to reveal his face: the grim countenance of Blue Higgins, his lips the color of cooked veal, his eyebrows furrowed in anger, wearing The Gatekeeper's robe.

"Blue, why are you here?" Rachman cried.

"I'm not Blue," he said, speaking in The Gatekeeper's voice. "I'm the accumulated sum of all evil knowledge that lives inside each of you."

"You sound like one of them people that goes to them peace conferences," Rachman said. "You can't be Blue. 'Cause Blue wouldn't know words like that if they walked into a room dressed like an elephant. He didn't finish third grade, y'know. So you the same devil then?"

"Course I am."

"Who's managing you?"

"Why do I need a manager?" The Gatekeeper said. "Can't I let the earth go for one month? And be the sum of all your fears?"

"If I'da knowed my fears was that ugly, I'da sued 'em."

"I'm gonna enjoy punching a hole in your face, Rachman, then setting fire to it."

"You can try, but after I whup you, I want outta here."

"Fair enough. I like a challenge."

"What about the rest?"

"Them, too. If they want it."

"No!" Tannenbaum rose, sweaty and flustered. "This is ridiculous."

"Oh, sit down," The Gatekeeper said. "Choose one or the other. You choose the winner, you get to pick your destiny. Myself, I like my chances. This is wonderful fun."

He removed his green robe, and now the others saw him in full. He was splendid. Short, brown, and massive. His body gleamed, his stomach muscles were tightly knotted, his thighs were thick, his chest was broad and solid, broader than Rachman's. His shoulders were round and huge, larger than Rachman's as well. He was a densely packaged fighting machine.

"We on?" he asked.

"Fool!" Rachman chortled. He stepped in to fight, but Tannenbaum stepped between them. "I don't want to bet. Judge me on my own. I gave to charity. I threw fund-raisers."

"Sit down on your rump right now or I'll remove it and you'll be taking a dump outta your mouth for eternity," Blue snapped. Tannenbaum sat.

Blue spoke to the four seated. "Pick one of us. Your fighter wins, you go with him."

Tannenbaum sat with his face in his hands. Patty and Wayne Goines stared at one another. "The child's too young to gamble," Patty said.

"We'll pick for her," Goines said. He nodded at Rachman. "My bet's on Rachman here. So's the kid's."

Blue looked at Patty. "You?"

She frowned and pointed to Rachman.

Tannenbaum seemed to have trouble deciding. He placed his chin on the wall and stared at the ceiling, his eyelids twitched up and down.

"This is a dream," he moaned. "A bad dream."

"Come on, ding dong, we ain't got all day," Goines said.

"I . . . pick the boxer."

"We're both boxers," Blue said.

"You ain't no boxer," Rachman snapped. "You a fraud. A devilment. Whupping you won't take very long. But what about the promoters?"

"What?" Blue asked. He seemed confused.

"The promoters," Rachman said. "You can't have a fight without promoters. And the boxing ring. And the press. And all the people. You can't have a fight without all the people."

"We have an audience," Blue said, and without warning he swung a left hook that caught Rachman flush in the face and nearly dropped him.

"Blue . . . you cheatin' dog . . . ," Rachman said, staggering backwards.

Blue laughed. He charged the stunned Rachman, who brought his hands up reflexively to guard his kidneys as Blue swung a long left hook. Rachman blocked it, stepped back, and sent a flurry of blazing lefts and rights at the head of Blue, whose head snapped back like a whip before he drew out of range.

The two fighters circled now, just out of range of each other, as the onlookers watched, two giant men breathing and huffing in the odd silence that cloaked the room. Blue stepped in and hammered Rachman's midsection. Rachman clenched him to slow him down, the two fighters hugging and resting.

"C'mon, boy," Rachman snorted. "Is that all you got? I pity the fool that cheats Rachman. I pity him." He shoved Blue off, danced right, left, skipping on his toes, and peppered Blue several times with lefts and rights, then danced out of range as Blue, slower and stronger, plodded after him, looking deadly furious and frustrated.

The fight went on and on. There was no stopping, no resting. Rachman sent screaming lefts followed by searing rights that caught Blue across the forehead. Blue wobbled slightly, and countered with thunderous right crosses that caught Rachman flush and nearly spun him around.

Rachman never seemed to tire. "Is that all?" Rachman said gleefully after several vicious exchanges. "Quit love-tappin' me, Blue! You can't hurt me. I'm too fast!" He stepped back to counter Blue's attacks, danced on his toes, and sent a series of rat-tat-tat super-speed left and right jabs that connected with Blue's face, forehead, and midsection.

Blue, plodding, powerful but slowed, tried to counter with driving lefts and rights, but Rachman danced out of range, zinging him with several hard right hands before Blue responded with a hard left. The two fighters clenched, exhausted now, hugging and resting. As they clenched, Rachman whispered in Blue's ear again, "That all you got, Blue? You hit like a girl."

Blue roared in rage and stepped back to fight again. As he did, Rachman sent a right to Blue's head that staggered him backwards. A welt appeared on Blue's face, just above his eye. Another hit and the two clenched in exhaustion again.

"You're cut, Blue," Rachman snorted as they clenched. "Quit now while you ahead. You better stop. I know your wife's watching. You wanna lose in front of your wife?"

Blue, furious, pushed back, swung a left hook that Rachman swatted away like it was a slap and countered with a thundering right hand that smashed the welt on Blue's eye and popped it wide open, sending specks of blood and flesh flying.

"Ho, ho!" Goines shouted.

Blue wobbled now, hurt, his knees slightly bent, and grasped on to Rachman to stay standing. As Blue leaned in, Rachman continued his chatter into Blue's ear. "Quit while you can, Blue. Why you wanna come all the way down here to hell to fight me, Blue? You coulda got your ass-whupping on top of the world. Don't you know me?"

"Yes, I know you!" Blue said suddenly. "I do know you. That's the point!"

He stood back, pushing off a hard-breathing Rachman, and

sent a crushing right—a powerful punch that moved with such swiftness and power that it seemed unearthly, catching the beautiful fighter right in the jaw.

This time it was Rachman who wobbled: His eyes rolled toward the ceiling, his hands fell. He leaned forward and crashed into Blue, fell into him. It was clear that the only thing that kept him standing was Blue himself.

Blue, holding him up, smiled over his shoulder to the seated audience, who watched, mouths agape. "You see, Rachman," he said. "I know who you are! Everyone's afraid here!"

Rachman, exhausted, his face resting on Blue's shoulder, suddenly clenched Blue tight, hugged him, held him close like a lover, and whispered something in Blue's ear that the others could not hear.

"What?" Blue said, shocked.

In that moment, Rachman pushed Blue away and lunged at him with renewed strength and power, as if he'd been running on batteries and were suddenly plugged into an electric outlet. He swung a lightning left that caught Blue's midriff, a right into the ribs, and another tomahawk right, this one to the jaw, which brought a groan from Blue's lips and sent him crashing face-first to the floor.

Just like that, it was done.

The four hopped up, surrounding Rachman. "Champ, champ!" Goines crowed, pounding Rachman's back. "When we get back, I'm gonna buy you a drink, son. I'll get you incapacitated. We're gonna liquor up till we get sponged."

"Don't drink," Rachman said, panting. He seemed troubled. He gasped for breath as he looked down at the fallen figure of Blue. "That certainly ain't like Blue Higgins, going down so easy."

Goines, exuberant, ignored him. "Well, he's out, and we're gonna go on a toot and a tear when we—" His words were lost in a sudden roar of howling wind as the door behind the mahogany desk suddenly flew open. A fierce hot wind swirled into the room.

The four watched in horror as Rachman, his face etched in surprise, was lifted from their circle into the air, flown across the room on his back, and zipped through the open door, which slammed behind him firmly.

The four stared after him in shocked silence.

Blue Higgins sat up, strode to the desk, picked up his cloak, put it on, and drew the hood over his face again. He sat, coughed, tapped his chest and cleared his throat, regaining his composure. Once again his hands were shriveled and gnarled; once again the face invisible. The Gatekeeper was back.

"Well, all riggghty then!" he said, with his old enthusiasm. He yawned loudly and said, "Y'all can go now."

"Where?" Goines said.

"Home. That was the arrangement," The Gatekeeper said. "One has to go so the others might be spared. The whole Jesus bit, really. Happens once in a while, even down here. One dies so the rest might be spared, all that jazz. Fact is, we only really wanted him all along."

"What?"

"Process it any way you like, Mr. Goines."

"We're free?" Goines said.

"If you call it that, yes. You'll be back, of course."

"But he beat you fair and square," Goines said. "You said we'd all go if he won."

"Oh, we throw back the little fish and keep the big ones, Mr. Goines. That's our motto down here. Now go home, get drunk, and forget all about it, Mr. American flag. What's it to you? You're going home to get a motorcycle. You won't remember a bit of this anyway. Now take a seat on the bench and I'll put you back. Hurry up before I change my mind."

"Wait a minute."

"Don't be stupid. Sit on the moaning bench so I can get you home. You gotta be seated on the bench to travel."

Goines stood. "I won't. The man won fair and square. Knowing he was fighting for me might've given him some extra strength."

"If you feel that strongly, put your foot in the road the other way," The Gatekeeper said, nodding to the door.

Goines hesitated. "You ain't playing fair."

"It's my house. My rules."

"Your rules ain't right. Jesus already paid for my life with his. One's enough."

"My understanding," The Gatekeeper said, "is that the late Rachman was Muslim."

"I don't care if he was an ostrich. I never did much like his loud talking," Goines said. "But I earned my way here, not him. And me owing him or anybody for my ticket outta here, that bothers me."

"You won't remember."

"Maybe not. But even if I was to forget like you say, the idea that somebody gave something to me that I couldn't pay for will likely find someplace inside me to live. That's how evil works. That's how *you* work. Giving out free crap. Cheap goods. Cheap thrills. Cheating good men and women outta what they won with blood and guts by papering 'em to death with crap and rules. The man won. That's a fact. So I'm staying."

"You sure?"

"Course." Goines blew his cheeks out. "God will take care of my wife and boy. And since you was all fuss and fuzz about him being Muslim," he said, "God lives in him same place he lives in me. Every God"—he tapped his chest over his heart— "lives here." He strode to the door and grabbed the handle.

The Gatekeeper shrugged and turned to the others. "Any other customers?"

Heather, the girl, rose without a word, strode to the door, and took Goines's hand. Patty, standing with her arms folded, sighed. "My husband won't want me when I'm old and wrinkled anyway." She frowned at The Gatekeeper. "And that Dixieland drummer's wriggling worm was worth the trouble." She walked over to the door and took little Heather's hand.

Tannenbaum had taken a seat on the bench alone. His gilded handkerchief lay on the ground. His right eye twitched nervously. He couldn't stop the trembling in his hands. He seemed to have lost control. Slowly, he rose. He wobbled nervously toward the others. "May God forgive me," he said, "for not trusting anything but my own selfish needs."

He grasped Patty's hand. Now all four were in a line. Without a word, Goines opened the door, and one by one, the four stepped inside.

PANDEMONIUM AT the Felt Forum at Madison Square Garden in New York City. Eighteen thousand screaming fans charged the ring to get a better view. They had just witnessed one of the greatest fights in boxing history. A seventh-round knockout. Clean. Rachman Babatunde, floored by a thunderous left in round seven from Blue Higgins, rose at the nine count, fought unconscious on his feet for a full minute and fifty-three seconds, then, unbelievably, recovered enough to knock Blue out in the last seconds of the same round, to gain his first-ever heavyweight championship title.

And now with the fight finished, physicians and attendants were rushing the ring, gathering around the fallen body of Higgins, knocked to unconsciousness by the greatest right hand the boxing world had ever seen. Higgins, who until tonight was the most fearsome fighter in boxing, was finished. His boxing career was now behind him.

They gathered around Blue Higgins, revived him with smelling salts, lifted him up and helped him stagger out of the ring and into boxing history. Meanwhile, Rachman Babatunde, the father of four and man of one, son of the seventh son of the seventh son, the loudmouth and newly crowned world champion, pranced around the ring, relishing the pandemonium, gloating, his arms raised, screaming at the television cameras: "I told you! I'm the greatest! The baddest! No man alive can whup me! Didn't I tell you!? I shocked the world!"

After several moments of wild frenzy, Rachman, who was prancing around the Forum's boxing ring filled with cops, handlers, ringside onlookers, and photographers, with his gloves tied and looped over his shoulders, slid his giant frame through the ropes, jumped down onto the arena floor, and started up the aisle toward the locker room. The entourage of trainers, cops, reporters, and tuxedos followed him like a flock of birds, a swarm of excited, shoving, laughing humanity.

Several rows up the aisle, the champ stopped short and the cacophony of humanity that followed him stalled. The people behind Rachman tried to press forward, but Rachman had already slid into the seats away from the aisle, leaving the entourage and cops to stare in surprise as he bumped past startled fans who grasped and touched his sweaty body as he squeezed past them, making his way to four seats in the middle of the row.

A cop assigned to the security detail grabbed Rachman's trainer by the arm. "What's he doin'?" the cop asked.

"Losing his mind," his manager said.

"What's that mean?" the cop asked.

"It's okay. It'll pass."

They watched as Rachman stopped in the middle of the row, facing four people who now stood, staring at the champ in awe. They were a middle-aged woman in a tweed fur jacket, a wide-eyed girl in a freshly ironed cotton dress, a straight-backed businessman in a suit and tie, and a man in a flannel cotton shirt holding a beer.

Rachman eyed them. He seemed puzzled for a moment and suddenly shy. "I don't know why I came over to see you," he said.

"We won these seats in a radio contest," the man in the flannel shirt said proudly. "Flights paid. Hotel. Expensive seats. Everything. And now you come to say hello! What a day!"

"Strange day," Rachman said slowly. "I had a strange dream this afternoon. Then I woke up." He glanced around the arena at the crowds, which had recovered from his detour and were now running at them.

He spoke to the man in the plaid shirt. "I shocked 'em, didn't I?"

"Sure did."

There was an awkward silence as the four people stared in awe and the fighter stared back at them. The entourage behind him began to squeeze into the aisle now, bumping through the seats to catch up to the champ. They pressed forward, surrounding the little group, watching the champ, who was suddenly strangely subdued.

"You said it was a radio contest?" he asked the man in the flannel shirt as he pulled his gloves from around his neck.

"Sure was," the man said.

"Well, I don't know nothing about no radio contest," Rachman said. Silently and without ceremony, he removed his boxing gloves from around his neck and handed them to the man.

"What's this for?"

"Wasn't I pretty? Tell me I was pretty."

"You was pretty," the man said.

"Tell me I'm the greatest."

"Yes, sir. You are the greatest. But can I ask you a question?"

"Surely can."

"What makes you great?"

Rachman reached over and grabbed the man and put him in a bear hug. He whispered into his ear. Then he turned away.

"I'm the greatest!" he said, shouting as he made his way back to the aisle. The huge swarming group of hangers-on that followed him reversed direction, laughing and high-fiving as they made their way to the top of the auditorium where the exits were.

The four watched Rachman make his way to the top of the auditorium, and as they did, the woman standing next to the man in the flannel shirt turned to him and asked, "What did he say?"

"He said he loved Blue. He said he loved the evil in Blue. He loves the evil in all people. Because in loving their evil, he loves the evil in himself enough to surrender it to God, who washes it clean. He's loving what God made, is what he said."

"That's what makes him great?"

"No. That's what makes him, him."

They watched as Rachman made his way to the exits, and above the cacophony, the yelling and shouting, above the roar of the crowd, the four could still hear his voice, and it seemed to come from outside him and inside their own chests, pushing inside their own veins, kicking through their feet and into the wide space of their own inner souls, ears, and hearts.

"I'm the greatest!"

THE CHRISTMAS DANCE

Herb was sitting with the old Judge in Sylvia's soul food joint in Harlem munching a plate of fried green tomatoes when the Judge spotted a stooped, elderly Puerto Rican wearing a post office uniform standing in line holding a tray of food.

"This is your lucky day," the Judge said to Herb.

"Carlos!" he called out. He motioned the man over.

The old man glanced up from his tray, saw the Judge, and threw his eyes toward the ceiling as if to say "Oh God." He paid for his food and shuffled over reluctantly, taking a seat.

"What'd I do wrong, Judge?"

"Want you to meet a man from Columbia University," the Judge said proudly. He nodded at young Herb sitting at the table. "Herb here's doing a report on the black soldiers who fought in World War Two."

"There was black soldiers in World War Two?" Carlos said.

The Judge laughed and winked at Herb. "This is the guy you wanna talk to," he said.

Herb was a slim, enthusiastic young fellow dressed in a black T-shirt, jeans, and a baseball cap, brimming with innocence. He shook Carlos's hand, which felt like a wet, damp rag. "Actually, I'm doing my thesis on the Ninety-Second Division," Herb said proudly. "They fought the Germans in Italy. I'm doing an oral history as part of my Ph.D. Trying to spread the light of history on the Buffalo Soldiers. Frankly, it's thirty years after the war and people know as little about the Ninety-Second today as they did in 1945."

"Why's that?" Carlos asked.

"You kidding, right? Because it was an all-black division."

"Well, there it is," Carlos said. "All blacks. Puerto Ricans had nothing to do with it." He turned to the Judge. "Judge, how come they don't serve plantains here? Puerto Ricans walk in and outta here all day and all Sylvia serves is collards and chicken. What's wrong with black beans and rice?"

"So what did you do in the Ninety-Second?" Herb asked.

"Engineer," Carlos said, not looking at him. He spoke to the Judge again, his mouth full of collard greens. "Judge, whyn't you speak to Maddy the cook? I think she boils these collards in gunpowder. She don't believe in salt. *Se sabe como mierda.*" He sucked his teeth and grabbed the saltshaker, flicking salt onto his plate. Herb noticed a big clump of a collard green had stuck to Carlos's front gold tooth.

"What kind of engineer?" Herb asked.

Carlos glanced at Herb, then looked away. "I blew things up."

"Wow. Like what?"

"Balloons mostly," Carlos said. "Balloon brigade. I blew up all the balloons. Red ones. Yellow ones. I pumped air into 'em. By hand mostly. Man, them things went high."

The Judge stifled a smile as Carlos shifted his irritated gaze from Herb back to the Judge. "So what's the number today, Judge?"

The Judge took a bite of liver and said, "I just missed it."

"You said that last week," Carlos said.

"No kidding. Missed it by one. I'm gonna change my picking strategy from here on out."

"What's it now?"

"I play my wife's birthday and my daughter's birthday. How 'bout you?"

"I play the grid."

Herb watched a checkered darkness slip across the Judge's face. The Judge's smile vanished and a weary, dark misery flashed into his eyes for a second, then it was gone, and his smile returned. The Judge was a man of eternal optimism. He said softly, "Drinking don't help you forget, Carlos."

"I don't drink to forget, Judge," Carlos said. "I drink to remember—all the good things in my life. So far, I can think of two. One is a girl from the first grade. The other I can't recall."

With that he stood up, left the tray at the table, and departed.

"He didn't finish his food," Herb said, watching him leave.

The Judge smiled again. He reached for his fork and dug into his fried green tomatoes. He was a bright, sunny man, always enthusiastic, a man of boundless optimism. He forked his food into his mouth and glanced at Carlos's back as he disappeared out the door. "You oughta see him dance," he said gaily. "Carlos is a great dancer."

AFTER CARLOS LEFT, the Judge clammed up. Before Carlos arrived at Sylvia's that day, the Judge was an open book, just the kind of veteran soldier Herb was looking for: cordial, fun, brimming with humorous stories about the colored boys fighting the Germans in Italy's cold Apennine Mountains, laughing as they dodged German .88 shells. It was so pitiful you had to laugh, the Judge said. He described the colored soldiers sitting around, bored, cold, warming their hands over a fire, laughing at some joke about a baby boy who was so ugly that his ma diapered the wrong end—then *woo-woo-woo*—the terrifying scramble as the whir of an .88 incoming rent the air, the men leaping into terrified action, grabbing for some gun they forgot to load, or sprinting over to the artillery guns to pump shells towards Germans labeled "Special Delivery from Harlem for Hitler." It was all light, funny, colorful stuff. But when Carlos left, the Judge grew silent and pensive, and he departed soon after Carlos, promising to meet Herb again the next week.

But the next week came and the Judge begged off, saying he had a doctor's appointment for his leg, which had been injured in the war and required him to walk with a cane. The next week he had a dentist's appointment. The next week a cold. Then a funeral for a cousin. Then a trial, even though the old Judge was retired. Finally the Judge stopped picking up the phone altogether.

After three weeks of desperate calling, Herb finally got the Judge on the line. The Judge seemed diffident. Oh yeah, he mumbled, we were getting some work done on that paper of yours, weren't we? Well, you probably got enough. I gave you all I had, son. That was a long time ago. I don't remember too much more. I wasn't a judge then, see, I was just little ol' Walter Booker from Harlem. The war wasn't nothing like the movies you see anyway, mostly just lying around and marching and feeding the Italians, that sort of thing. I'm afraid that's pretty much my story. But there were other guys who were there who might be around. I'll find some other guys for you to talk to. Then he hung up and was gone. He never picked up his phone again.

Herb was stuck. He'd been researching the story of the 92nd for two years. The Judge had been a gold mine, remembering names, places, numbers. Now the gold mine was closed and his Ph.D. was in jeopardy.

Winter turned to spring. Graduation was coming. With three weeks before his thesis was due, Herb went to see his professor.

"I hit a brick wall," he admitted. "My live sources have dried up. Most of these guys are dead."

"Find the written accounts," the professor said.

"There's not much there," Herb said. "Very few books. Most of the records of that division were destroyed in a fire at the Army's records storage facility in St. Louis. Most of the soldiers are dead. These two, the Judge and Carlos, are alive and they were there. But they won't talk about it."

"You say the Army files were destroyed in a fire? The Army doesn't make copies of files?"

"Not in our library they don't."

The professor smirked. "What kind of Ph.D. candidate looks for Army records in a civilian library?"

Herb did some legwork. He borrowed a car from his roommate and drove down to the Library of Congress, then to the Fort Myer Post Library near Washington, D.C. Finally he struck gold at the Army War College in Carlisle, Pa. The summary of the 92nd Division listed the men in each company roster. Among those listed on the roster of the 366th Regiment were Carlos Lopez and Walter Booker. Herb pored through the list of major battles for each regiment during the Italian campaign. The 366th Regiment was barely mentioned, with the exception of a "skirmish" noted by the report with an indexed reference. Herb looked up the reference, which turned out to be an additional report by Army intelligence added a year later, which reexamined the "skirmish" because of an unusually high American casualty rate. The report revealed a surprise Christmas Day 1944 attack by the Germans against American forces stationed in the Serchio Valley near Florence—in concert with the more famous German attack at the Battle of the Bulge. Herb read the report with deep interest:

> The surprise counterattack by the German forces occurred on Christmas Day 1944, in concert with the attack in the Ardennes region in Belgium and Luxembourg on the Western Front. As they did in Belgium, the Germans attacked a weakly defended section of the Allied line and caught the Allied forces in Italy completely off guard. The Germans achieved this total surprise due to a combination of Allied overconfidence, preoccupation with Allied offensive plans, and poor aerial reconnaissance.
>
> At approximately 0500 hours, the 67th SS Panzer climbed the Lama di Sotto Ridge and overran three companies of the 366th Regiment, comprised of 200 American soldiers, thinly spread out over a five-mile defensive line in the Serchio Valley at 1,400 feet. American forces were outnumbered three to one. Fighting was house to house, some of it hand to hand.

Herb looked at the roster of the three companies attacked in the German assault: Companies C, B, and F of the 366th Regiment. He ran his finger down the page of the roster of the companies. Among those in Company F were Carlos Lopez and Walter Booker.

He read the casualty report on Company F. It did not say much. But the numbers did. Seventy soldiers went out to meet the German assault. Seventeen returned. The rest were casualties. And it said nothing about a balloon brigade.

"A skirmish," Herb muttered. "Some skirmish."

HE CLOSED THE REPORT and left the library. No mention of specifics. So the company was mostly destroyed, he thought. But nothing else on Carlos or Walter. No specifics on the battle at all. No gold stars or Purple Hearts. No idea what they did. What were they hiding? Did they do something wrong?

Herb went back to New York, his curiosity now piqued. He called the Judge every day. No response. He went to Sylvia's six times in a six-day period. No Judge. In desperation, he wrote to a New York Italian association asking about the attack in the Serchio Valley, pulling the name of a town he'd seen mentioned in the reports: Sommocolonia. As luck would have it, a volunteer civilian at the Italian association had a brother who was a partisan and fought with the Buffalo Soldiers at Sommocolonia. She gave him the address of her brother and two Italian partisans who had also fought in the area. Herb wrote to all three, pleading for information.

Two weeks later, at 3 a.m., the phone rang in Herb's East Harlem apartment. A scratchy voice on the other end, speaking broken English with a thick Italian accent, said, "I am trying to reach the Buffalo Soldiers."

"They're not here," Herb said.

"I need to reach them."

"Which one do you want to reach? There were fifteen thousand of them."

"Any one."

"What do you need?"

"Nothing. I just want to talk to them. I want to thank them."

"For what?"

Herb heard what sounded like choking, or perhaps sobbing. "I was at Sommocolonia. I remember the tower."

"What tower?"

"The church tower. *Grazie. Mille grazie.*"

The man hung up.

Herb went to Sylvia's and cornered Maddy, the restaurant cook. "I've got to see the Judge," he said. "It's important. I know he's been avoiding me."

Maddy looked at Herb for a moment, saw the desperation in his face, and felt sorry for him.

"Go 'round on a Monday morning to Mr. Pitt's grocery store on 136th," Maddy said. "He plays the number over there on Mondays. Don't say I told you."

Herb did as Maddy directed, and was rewarded by the sight of the old Judge leaning on his walking stick, standing in line inside the grocery store, waiting to play his number. When the Judge saw Herb, his face darkened a moment, then relit, like a candle that's just found new air. He was all sunny optimism. "Ain't you outta school yet?" he said.

"I only have one more question."

"I already told you all I know."

"There was a town down in the Serchio Valley. A place called Sommocolonia. And there was a church tower. What happened there?"

The Judge blanched, looked at his feet, pawed the floor with his walking stick, then stepped forward as the line shuffled ahead. He looked straight ahead as he talked. "I haven't heard that town's name in thirty years. Where'd you hear it?"

"Army records. And a partisan. He called me and said he wanted to thank the Buffalo Soldiers."

"The Italians don't owe us nothing," the Judge said. "We owe them."

The line moved forward again. Herb felt the Judge pulling away from him. He could sense the old man closing down. He piped up: "The reports say three companies were destroyed in Sommocolonia. How'd that happen?"

"Oh, that was so long ago I can't recall," the Judge said evenly.

"You weren't there?"

"I was there, but I can't remember too much. Just a bunch of shooting. Running around, dodging. I don't recall it too good, actually."

"Neither does the Army apparently," Herb said. "They called it a skirmish."

Herb felt like he had punched the old man. The Judge, standing in line, swayed, pursed his lips, then looked down at his feet, then behind the counter, then out the window, averting Herb's gaze. His eyes seemed to shift focus, gazing at something far away, like a crystal ball in the ceiling. Suddenly his eyes teared up. He wiped them with his hand and coughed. After a moment, he said softly, "Of course they would."

"Would what?"

"Call it a skirmish. They hated us."

"Who hated you?"

The Judge was silent. The line moved forward. By now the Judge had reached the counter. Herb stood behind him as he played his number, then watched as the Judge, holding his cane, limped past him to the door and out into the Harlem sunshine and stopped, leaning on his cane, one hand resting gently on the storefront glass. Herb followed him.

From the sidewalk the Judge stared at the traffic on Lenox Avenue. Several passersby greeted him as he stood against the window. A couple of cars honked. The Harlem air seemed to revive him. He was home. In Harlem, everybody loved him. He took a deep breath, stood taller again, waved at a couple of friendly faces, then reached into his pocket, pulled out a pen, and wrote on the back of a piece of paper. He handed it to Herb. It was an address.

"Talk to Carlos," he said. "Ask him if he's gonna dance this Christmas Eve."

"What's that mean?"

"You wanna finish your little report or not? Ask him if he's gonna dance this Christmas Eve. Tell him I'm coming."

"Christmas is in eight months."

But the Judge was already gone, limping away, moving fast, down the crowded sidewalk, chin up, smiling in the radiant sunshine, greeting people, waving. A car honked at him, a woman stopped him, and leaning on his cane he shared a laugh with her, his hand on her shoulder. A passing motorist yelled out his car window on Lenox Avenue, "Hey, Judge!" and the Judge waved. A second pedestrian stopped, now a third, gathering around him. The Judge talked to them all, his arms open wide, cane in the air now, an old lion spreading his paws over his kingdom, laughing, the three gathered around him. Herb drifted closer to hear the conversation, which wafted into the crisp Harlem air.

"Judge! My boy is eight and wants to be a lawyer," one said.

"Judge! We missed you at church."

"Judge! Lemme ask you a question. If your ex-wife can't find your kid's birth certificate and you gotta pay child support, what's that called legally?"

"A loophole," the Judge said.

Laughs all around.

THE NEXT DAY Herb found himself standing before the door of a silent, battered brownstone on 147th Street, knocking with his heart in his mouth. Carlos answered.

"Mr. Ph.D.," he said. "I already gave at the office."

"The Judge said to talk to you. About dancing. On Christmas Eve."

Carlos's face darkened. "Judge talks too much," he said. But he turned and walked inside, leaving the door open. It was an invitation. Herb entered and followed him through to a door and down a set of dimly lit stairs.

Carlos sat in a darkened armchair in his basement parlor full of old leather furniture. A yellowed black and white photo of a pretty young Puerto Rican woman hung over a leather armchair that faced an old and dreary television set. The lamps, the furniture, the rug—everything was old. A Puerto Rican flag, mounted on the wall, crisscrossed an American flag that lay underneath it.

"Did Judge tell you anything else?" Carlos said.

"No. Just said you're a great dancer."

"He said that?"

"Twice."

For the first time, Carlos's dark face lightened and a grin cut the corner of his mouth. Herb was amazed at the transformation. Dazzling. Handsome. Then the smile disappeared. The light went off, and the grimace returned.

"He ain't too bad hisself," Carlos said.

"At dancing? He can dance with his cane?"

"Naw. He can't dance for shit. Never could. He talks good."

"What does that mean?"

"Just what I say. He's the talker. The narrator. He talks while I dance. The Judge can talk the horns off the devil's head."

Herb exhaled, puffing his cheeks. "Mr. Carlos: I got three weeks before I have to turn in my thesis. I spent all my tuition money. I got loans. Bills. No job. Everything depends on this thesis. If I don't hand it in, I'm cooked. And you're talking in circles. Jeez . . . Isn't there a straight story anywhere around here? Just tell me what I need to know. Were you there or not?"

"Where?"

"In Sommocolonia."

Carlos paused. A full minute passed before he spoke. "Just 'cause you can tie your sneakers and read a report someplace don't mean you know more than a turd, kid."

"What did I say to offend you?"

"You offended yourself! By reading the white man's books."

"I'm trying to find out what happened."

"You need a Ph.D. to know the white man writes history any way he wants?"

"I don't trust the books either."

"Find another book then. It's too late now anyway."

"For what?"

"Everybody who was there is dead. And everybody who wrote it up is white. White officers. What you expect?"

"What happened?"

"Ask the Judge! He likes to talk. That's all he does."

"He won't talk to me. He just laughs and makes jokes and said you'd explain it all. You guys are screwing with my head. I gotta finish school. I need a job *now*. That's why I got to finish this Ph.D. Without this oral history, I got no Ph.D., sir. None. And without this Ph.D., what do I got? Nothing. No job, no future. Just debt. Because I was depending on him—and you— to talk straight! How I'm gonna get a teaching job without a Ph.D.? You think they'd hire me to teach at any decent university without a Ph.D.? I'm gonna end up teaching kindergarten after eight years of graduate study—thanks to you guys. I gambled on you guys. I thought you'd want people to know your story. But it don't mean squat to you, does it? I should've found some white soldiers to write about!"

Herb grabbed his backpack, snatched his baseball cap off the couch, popped it on his head, and rose to leave.

"Wait a minute," Carlos said. He tried to stand and a terrible coughing spell stopped him. He hacked a few moments, then gathered himself. He blew his nose, then glanced at Herb with watery eyes. He cleared his throat and shifted in his leather chair, as he rubbed his nose and hissed through his teeth, his lips parted slightly. Herb noticed the gold tooth gleaming in the streak of sunlight cutting into the dark room.

"You drink brandy, son?" Carlos asked.

"No."

"Good. 'Cause I only got enough for one."

He poured himself a brandy from an old cabinet, then despite saying he had enough for only one, poured another for Herb. He raised his glass into the sliver of sunlight in the room and regarded it. Then he leaned forward and sipped deeply. The glint from the glaring sunlight struck Carlos in his hair, slick and smooth. Carlos's upturned face, silhouetted by the yellow window light, looked noble, almost statuesque, and Herb decided again that Carlos must have been quite the looker when he was young.

"I signed up for the Army with my cousin Joaquin," he said. "Joaquin was eighteen. Three years younger than me. When we reported they put us in a room. A captain came in and looked at Joaquin and pointed to a door that said 'White.' He pointed me to the other door marked 'Colored.' So Joaquin got sent to Belgium. He got his ticket punched there."

He eyes glazed.

"He was a great little carpenter."

"Did it bother you going with the black troops?" Herb asked.

"Shit no."

Carlos sipped the brandy and absently flicked a blind of the window.

"Old Judge was right about one thing, though. Me, I couldn't do nothing but dance. I used to imagine that I would one day really do something with my dancing. See, dance changes people. Dancing makes you free. It makes people happy. I used to practice all the time when I came to Harlem. I was seventeen. I never took dance lessons. I learned from the Cubans. Mario Bauzá. Machito. I learned in the clubs, dancing to their music. They liked me. I traveled with 'em as a dancer. That's how I met my wife, Angela. She used to say, 'Every girl I meet in Manhattan says they danced with you.' I'd say, 'That's because I danced with every girl in Manhattan—till I met you.' She loved to dance. We were a pretty good team."

"Then what happened?"

"Same thing that happened with Joaquin. You find yourself in a room with somebody you care about, except now it's not your cousin, but your wife. And this time it's not no Army room, but a hospital room. And the Big Man comes in Himself—and he says, 'You, Angela, go this way. And you, Carlos, go that way.'"

Carlos was silent for a moment.

"I got a son living in Florida," he said. "But he don't come home much. I don't see why he should either. I'm the last to leave the room, son. Me and the old Judge."

"Because his wife's dead too?"

"That's the least of it," Carlos said.

FOUR HOURS LATER, Herb walked into the blaring sunlight of 147th Street, the sun pressing his eyelids and his head, making them feel like a hundred hammers ringing around his ears. He staggered home to his apartment, set out his books and typewriter, and began to write. For the next four days he pushed deep into his thesis, writing into the night hours, and was nearly finished when he appeared at Sylvia's at the time he knew the Judge usually came to eat. Sure enough, the Judge walked in. When he saw Herb, he grabbed a tray and sat with him.

"I saw Carlos," Herb said. "I drank his brandy."

The Judge chuckled. "That means he likes you a little."

"I didn't know he was your commander."

"He was second lieutenant. I was just a grunt."

"What about your captain?"

The Judge smiled. "The captains were white. The good ones were killed early on. The rest of them didn't know shit. Most were rejects. Castoffs from other units. Southerners mostly. Couldn't find their ass with two hands. The first and second lieutenants ran everything. That was Carlos. Did he tell you about his buddy over there?"

"He didn't say he had any buddies. He had a cousin who fought with the white Army who died."

"Not him. Carlos had another buddy. A hell of a buddy."

"When he left, he said don't call him again. He's done. He ain't talking to me no more."

"I ain't either. I'm done with it."

"But he told me to tell you that he would dance this Christmas."

"Eve, son, Christmas Eve. He can dance like the dickens, Carlos can. You know, back before the war, he danced for Machito, he tell you that?"

"Yes."

"And Mario Bauzá. Lionel Hampton. They all wanted Carlos. He was something. He only dances once a year now. At Minton's. Every Christmas Eve. When Count Basie comes for the annual Christmas Eve ball there."

"With who? His wife is dead."

"We dance together."

Noting Herb's silence, the old Judge said, "What's wrong with us dancing together?"

"Y'all are . . ." Herb paused and wiggled his hand in a wavy motion to signify homosexual. "Special friends?"

The Judge laughed. "We're special, all right. He didn't tell you about the Christmas dance?"

"He didn't say that. He just said he was a star dancer. And that you can't dance. That you're the narrator."

The Judge laughed. "I ain't the narrator. I'm the producer. I'm like the guy in the sound booth who tells the musicians what to play."

"I don't understand."

"Didn't he tell you anything?"

"He told me everything."

"No, he didn't."

"What else is there to know?"

"Well, it don't matter. Ain't you got enough for your thesis now?"

"Yeah, I do. Except for this stupid dance business."

"Well, you ain't writing a thesis on dancing, son. Carlos gave you the info. So run along home now and don't stop for bread. Go finish your report."

"I'm about worn out with the games between you two," Herb said.

"You don't have to stick around us now, son," the Judge said, smiling. "I ain't seen Carlos in a month of Sundays. Not since we saw him in the restaurant together. We got no conspiracy against you. We helped you get the monkey off your back. You're finished now."

"But I just don't understand the dance, is all. I understand what happened over there. I'm not stuck on that. I wish y'all would come together and tell me what I don't know."

"Well, you got what you need. I gave you all I could. Carlos did the same. Now write your thesis and live happily ever after."

Herb sipped his iced tea angrily and set the glass down hard. "Jeez! No wonder black folks got nothing. No money. No houses. No history. Nothing. Without the right history, how are people gonna know what you did? They think all we did was float balloons in the war and serve as quartermasters! There were a million blacks who served in World War Two! Fifteen thousand in Italy alone. Most were casualties!"

"You don't have to tell me about casualties, son."

Herb was silent. The Judge's smile was gone.

The Judge peered out over the restaurant, then down at his tray.

"If I give you a chance to see Carlos dance—no promises— but if I give you the *chance* to see him go at it on the dance floor, would you promise to leave me alone?"

Herb felt hurt. He liked the Judge.

"I thought we were friends."

"We are, son, but you remind me of things I can't think about no more. I'm in the last October of life looking for a few more Aprils. I don't want to remember no more. I expect Carlos is the same. You promise or not?"

"All right."

The Judge scribbled yet another name and address on a piece of paper. He slid it over to Herb. "Lillian Johns," he said. "She lives in Brockton, Massachusetts. Here's her address. Go and see her. She knows everything."

"Was she there?"

"I already gave you everything you need," the Judge said. "I'm finished now. I ain't answering no more questions about the war. Got no more time to talk about the past. It's all done."

LILLIAN JOHNS was eighty-eight and lived in a neat house on a quiet street in Brockton. She was a slim, dark brown woman with dancing eyes and a wide smile. There was a deep beauty to Mrs. Johns that Herb, even as a young man, found attractive, and she was as warm and as kind as her smile suggested. She sat in her modest living room with pictures of grandchildren and silverware in a tall wood cabinet.

"I don't know why the old Judge sent you here," she said. "He knows more about what happened at Sommocolonia than I do. I wasn't there."

"I explained that," Herb said, "but he said you could explain it better."

She smiled sadly. "Is it about the dancing?" she asked.

"Yes, it is. They won't talk about it."

She smiled. Herb noticed a sadness behind the brown eyes. "I guess my generation is not that good at talking about old things. Can't blame us. I don't like old things myself. How do you know the Judge?"

"I met him through school. He introduced me to Carlos."

She chuckled. "You know those two only live five blocks from each other? I'm told they don't see each other that much. I told them they oughta talk to each other more. But men are so stupid. Still, I love them both."

"Were you married to one of them?"

"Heavens no," she laughed.

"Why do you care for them then?"

"Because . . . Have you ever been to New York Christmas Eve? At Minton's ballroom, where they have this big dance? With the Count Basie Band?"

"No. What's that got to do with the war?" Herb asked.

"It's got nothing to do with the war," she said. "It's got to do with a man."

.   .   .

THAT DECEMBER, six months later, Herb Melton—newly
christened as Herbert Melton, Ph.D. History, Columbia University, and enjoying winter break from his university teaching
job in Burlington, Vermont—got up at 5 a.m. and drove nine
hours through a heavy snowstorm to New York City. He mo-
tored to 118th Street in Harlem, filled up the gas tank, then
swung around the block for a good hour, patiently waiting for
a parking space to open up. When it did he squeezed his ancient Plymouth Duster with 134,000 miles on the odometer,
heat running full blast, into a space across the street from Minton's Playhouse. He was careful to note the "No Parking" signs.
He was an old hand. This parking space was good all day and
night.

He sat in his car all day, heat running, ducking in and out of
a nearby diner to get food, coffee, and use the bathroom, then
sitting in the car again, waiting until evening. The snow came
on and off all day, packing the sidewalks and streets. But at
night the people came, young and old, pouring out of cabs onto
the snow-packed sidewalk to hear the Count Basie Band per-
form their annual Christmas Eve set.

The Basie Band performance at Minton's was a throwback
to the old days, something everyone in Harlem loved, an annual Christmas Eve performance by a glorious swinging band
that demanded old-style glory, dancing and fun, which still
drew new fans.

Herb watched and waited, half expecting to be disappointed. Then, just before 8 p.m., to his relief, an old Lincoln Continental pulled up with "Judge" on its license plates. It unsteadily swerved into place and parked crookedly in front of a fire hydrant. Only the Judge had the nerve to park like that, in front of a hydrant—a judge in New York City could park anywhere. The driver's door opened and the old Judge, wearing a black tuxedo, held the door open with one hand and, using his stick with the other, pulled himself out to stand on the icy, snowy street. He surveyed the terrain, then slowly made his way over the slippery snow humps to the passenger side of the car. As he did, the front passenger door opened and Carlos, his back bent from years of carrying mail, his hair slicked neatly back, also dressed in a tux, emerged. Carlos turned to the back door of the sedan and opened it. Lillian Johns, clad in a fur coat, fur hat, and high heels, emerged. Carlos helped her out of the car and the Judge shut the door. The three converged for a moment, talking together, a tiny football huddle. Herb saw Lillian throw back her head and laugh, and the two men chuckled. Then she headed inside, followed by Carlos and the Judge.

Herb cut the engine of his Plymouth, straightened his tie, quickly bought a ticket, and scrambled inside.

When he entered, he saw that the foyer led straight into the ballroom, so he cut to the right and made for the stairs to the balcony, so as not to be seen. Upstairs seats lined the bannisters where tired dancers could come and rest their feet, order a drink, and watch the ballroom from above. Herb ordered a

Coke from a waitress, perched himself on a seat at the edge of the bannister, and leaned over.

The band was already in full stride, blasting the walls with hard swing. Herb watched the dancers spin in circles and waited to see if one of the three on the floor would jump to Basie's blasting, swinging, deep-grooving big band.

The three were seated at a table talking. It was there, as Herb waited, watching them, that he ran the story over in his head, the story that Carlos had revealed to him months before in his basement living room.

WE WERE AN *artillery company. Cannon company is what they call it. Me and the Judge. They called him Booker back then. Walter Booker. He was a funny, skinny motherfucker back then. Laughed all the time.*

We were forward observers. Our job was to go forward, scout enemy positions, then set up artillery. See, when a company attacks, before the combat troops charge, you drop artillery. You soften 'em up with artillery for the ground troops that follow. But oftentimes you can't know where to fire that artillery until forward observers go out and radio back to tell artillery where to fire. That's one of your jobs as forward observer.

There were four of us: me, my buddy Clifford Johns, who was first lieutenant, Booker—that's the Judge—and another man named Schaefer, a college man out of Oberlin, Ohio. We were the forward team. We'd get sent out on patrols. We'd go out ahead and scout the territory for the company and then come back and say if it was safe to set up. Nobody said nothing about firing. Just scouting is what we did mostly.

Well, they sent us out on a ridge called Lama di Sotto near a little town called Sommocolonia. Tiny little place. We went out there several times. We saw some movement. German troops. Guns being pulled around. It's not hard to see if the enemy's moving. Shit. An .88's a big gun. You need a mule to pull it up the mountains. In Italy, we all used mules with Italian mule skinners. The Germans and us. And I knew every Italian mule skinner in the Serchio Valley. I was one of the few Americans who spoke Italian, 'cause I lived in Harlem. There were plenty of Italians in Spanish Harlem back then. But the white American commanders didn't like the Italians, see. They treated the Italians like peasants. They told us: "Don't trust the Italians. They could be the enemy." Shit, if it wasn't for the Italian partisans up there, I'd be dead. They were some brave sons of bitches. Them's the ones who told us, when we were scouting, "There's a bunch of Germans up on that Lama di Sotto Ridge. And more coming."

I asked them, "How many?"

"Hundreds," they said. "Maybe thousands. They're building up for something big."

We passed it on to the captain. He didn't believe us. He was an idiot. He was out of engineering. He couldn't read a map. Neither could the guy before him. We changed captains in the Ninety-Second like most people eat lunch. Them white captains would rather eat an elephant's nuts than command a bunch of niggers.

They didn't like us. We didn't like them. They felt we were second-rate soldiers, and they were mostly rejects themselves. Most transferred out as soon as they could. Southerners, most of 'em.

Well, this guy didn't believe us, so we took it to S-2 Intelligence. Took it over the captain's head. S-2 didn't do nothing. They sent the shit right back to the stupid captain of our unit—with our name on it.

So Christmas Eve, about nine o'clock, the captain calls me and Johns in to see him. See, Company F, our company, was more forward in that valley than anyone else from the division. Right in front of us was a ridge going down, and on the other side of that valley, the Serchio Valley, was the town of Sommocolonia. And beyond it, going up, was the Lama di Sotto Ridge, going up higher over the town.

So the captain called me and Johns into his tent and said, "I got this report you sent to S-2 over my head. And since you know so much, I want you two to get a squad together and go down into that church in the valley down there and look out for the Germans."

They had a tall church tower down there in Sommocolonia. It was to the left of our position, but it was on a hill and from that tower you could see straight over the Lama di Sotto ridge, where we heard the Germans were.

Johns said, "When?"

"Tonight. At 0300 hours. Under cover of night."

Well, Johns didn't like it. He'd scouted that position enough to know the Germans had big numbers up on that ridge. Clifford

Johns was a smart man. Lt. Clifford Johns was his name. Out of Brockton, Massachusetts. A braver man I never met. He went to Wilberforce University.

He told the captain, "I don't need to see out over that ridge to tell you what's over there. It's Germans. A lot of 'em. They're moving artillery and men. The Italian partisans say the same thing."

The captain said, "I don't trust anybody who crushes grapes with their feet. I want y'all to climb to the top of that church tower and tell us what you see."

This idiot was from Florida. He was a replacement captain. Far as I know, this fella didn't even know how to fire a .124 millimeter. He didn't even graduate from college—and he was commanding a cannon company with guys like Clifford Johns, who had college degrees and had ten times more battle experience than him.

Johns said, "If I'm in the tower, how am I gonna get back if I'm rushed?"

The captain said, "We'll get you back."

Johns didn't say a word, but he didn't trust him. When he came back to the squad, he asked for volunteers. The only two who volunteered were me and Booker. I was Johns's second lieutenant. I had to volunteer. But Booker—the Judge—was a private. He was an enlisted man, a draftee. But he was a nervy fucker. He said, "I'll be safer with you than here." He was scared stiff. Everybody was. But he looked up to Cliff. We all did. We all knew the Germans were close, and Booker didn't trust that captain any more than I did.

But Johns said, "No. You and Carlos stay here." He didn't say why. But I knew why. Cliff was smart. He knew that if the Germans came down that ridge in big numbers, his only chance of getting out of that tower was heavy shelling from our side to delay them. He didn't want just any old fool firing that artillery to cover his ass. He wanted somebody he could depend on. Because if our line breaks or if they shell us too hard, the captain might quit the game and pull the company out, and then who's gonna send the artillery to help him out? He wanted us—me and Booker—firing them cannons.

So he picked seven men. I can name every one of 'em: Jefferson Jordan, Wade McCree, Sergeant Schaefer the music man from Oberlin, and four more. He told 'em, "Get ready," then took me and the Judge outside the tent and said, "When we get up there, watch out for us. If we have to get out quick, send the mail hard as you can."

"Send the mail" means to fire that artillery. See, when a forward observer goes out, he sights the enemy, he calls out the grid on a map where the enemy is, and you fire on that grid. He calls out the grid by radio. And you fire it at those coordinates. He wanted us to get him outta there if he was stuck. We knew he depended on us.

I said, "We will do that."

I can't say I was sad to be staying behind. I wasn't happy either. I was torn. Like most people, I wanted to live. But I told him, "We'll watch you. We got your back."

He picked up his squad and said, "Let's go." They cut out at

217

three a.m. in the snow. It was so dark you couldn't see your hand in front of your face. The rest of the division was mostly asleep in houses they'd taken over, about to have Christmas Day breakfast and all, because the white captains assumed the Germans wasn't gonna fight on Christmas Day. Who wants to fight on Christmas Day? The Germans have Christmas just like us. But I made my gunners and my radio man sleep in tents next to their guns. I was the only one who had his men sleeping outdoors that night. The captain came by and said, "Why you making these men sleep in the snow? Put a watch outside on the radio and send the rest inside." I said, "Okay, sir," and the minute he left I put them right back outside in tents. I didn't give a fuck. I had five .90 millimeter guns pointed at that valley when Cliff Johns and them went down there.

Well, I didn't hardly move from the radio. I had the radio man right next to me. Not an hour later, about five a.m., just before light, I heard the radio crackle with Johns's voice and a bunch of German .88s sailing over the valley towards us at the same time. I reached for the radio and by that time the Germans had knocked the entire division on its ass. It took about a half a second. The first volley blew my tent away and threw me about ten feet. It knocked out two of our five .90 millimeter artillery guns, disabled the third, killed three gunners plus the radio man, who was next to me. He was thrown with the radio several feet away clean to the edge of the ridge. We was down to two artillery guns before we even moved an inch. You gotta remember, Johns and his men were ahead of us by half a mile down in the valley. They were in the tower in front of us, positioned where they could see over the ridge on the other side. But it was full-on night when the Ger-mans fired, and their soldiers were coming down that ridge in white snow suits at night, so we couldn't see them—it wasn't dawn yet—and John couldn't have seen them, and he couldn't ever see where the artillery fire was coming from, I guess. It didn't matter. The Germans had noted our artillery, sighted us, fed that grid position to their gunners before daylight, and fired half blind, thinking it might be close. They scored big, 'cause they hit our artillery fire control center dead on.

I got hit so hard, it took me a minute to figure out where I was. When I sat up I was ten feet off the guns and a third of the cannon company was dead, and the first thing I saw was three guys crawl-ing out of a tent on fire. Booker's squad managed to get gun one pumping, and squad two got theirs going, and I looked around and managed to find the radio man, who'd been blown right near the side of the ridge. I ran to him and pulled the radio off him and glanced out on the valley before running back to the artillery guns where Booker and the other gun was. Then I looked over the ridge.

By God, there was so many Germans coming down the ridge and running up the other side towards us they looked like ants. I mean there was hundreds. They was already past that tower where John and his men were. That was at the crack of dawn. That's the first thing I saw Christmas morning, 1944. God knows I'll never forget it.

I had the radio to my ear by the time I got to Booker, who was firing, and the radio was still working so I yelled, "Cliff, get out."

He didn't. He said he was in the church tower and started calling artillery on the grid. There was nothing to do but follow his orders. I had four men left, two on each gun. Booker was sighting and firing the gun closest to me, and I called Johns's grid numbers to him, and Booker loaded and fired, sighting and firing. He was moving fast.

I kept saying, "Cliff, you got to come out." But he kept calling the grid. He'd call out 32/3. Then 34/3, then 35/3, like that. And I'd call that number to Booker and he was bringing it. I had both guns going. Then after a few minutes we got the third gun going again. But the Germans were dropping .88 rounds right on us, and worse, German soldiers started making their way up the ridge around to the side of our position. I heard gunfire ringing through the camp behind me. I looked over my shoulder and seen clerks and cooks dropping typewriters and pots and pans and grabbing rifles and shooting. They formed a line to our right and engaged the Germans who were working their way that way, just at the edge of the tree line to our right, about two hundred yards off. It was a fucking mess.

As for the captain, if I found that fucker today, I'd part his face with my knife. He was long gone. I ain't seen him from that day to this. I heard he went back to Pietrasanta after he ordered Cliff down into the valley. He was nowhere to be found.

Cliff kept calling the grid to me, and I kept feeding the grid to Booker. And then it got . . . chaotic.

Booker and his man was firing that .90 millimeter fast as they could load, and I was calling the grid, but Cliff kept changing the grid, and when I called out one of those grids Booker hollered, "It's getting awful close."

I didn't have time to ask what he meant, because I could hear hollering on Cliff's end now. Every time he pressed the call button on his radio I could hear yelling and rounds landing and small-arms fire, so I knew he was in trouble. So I said to Booker, "Shut up and fire!" which he did. Cliff called another grid number—34/7—he called—and I called it to Booker and he stopped. His man had loaded the shell and Booker had the firing pin in his hand—it was a ring you pull—and he just stopped cold, with the firing pin in his hand. He wouldn't pull it.

I thought he was crazy. I could hear Cliff yelling and the small-arms fire in the tower. I said, "Send the load!"

He said, "That's Johns's position."

I radioed back. I said, "Cliff, what's your grid position?"

Man, when Cliff Johns pressed the call button that last time, it sounded like hell on earth. Small-arms fire and screaming. But he was calm as a glass of water. And he said it clear. He said, "I know where I am. Send the mail, Carlos. Send it now. There's a lot more of them than us," and then I heard a burst of firing and yelling.

I yelled, "Book, fire it."

Book wouldn't move. He shook his head.

"Fire it, motherfucker!"

Book froze up. He had his hand on the firing pin and just stared over my head. Like he was hypnotized. He was shell-shocked, like a deer in the headlights. By now we was taking *heavy, straight rounds from the German .88s, one after the other. Dropping right on our position. Our three guns was back down to one, Booker's gun. Cannons two and three was out, and whoever had been firing 'em who wasn't hurt or dead had grabbed rifles and was firing out towards the right-side ridge where the Germans was coming.*

I was so fucking mad I drew my .45 sidearm. Booker was about four steps from me and I was on him. I said, "What the fuck is wrong with you?"

I remember standing over Booker with my pistol thinking I had to shoot him and suddenly it got so quiet, I said to myself, "Why is it so quiet?" I didn't realize till later that all those rounds hitting so close had knocked my hearing loose. There was a lot of smoke and I couldn't see much other than Booker crouched on his knees like a coward, staring over my head like he was looking for an angel to come from the sky and save him. I wanted to kill him.

I said, "Stupid mother—" and I had the pistol in one hand and reached over to pull the firing pin myself with my free hand. I had to reach over him to do it, and as I did, he snatched the .45 out my hand and pointed it at my head and dropped the hammer on it. That thing went off right at my ear. The noise almost busted my eardrum.

And a German soldier dropped dead right at my feet. He'd been running up behind me and Booker saw him coming and shot him as he came. That's what he was staring at out that way.

The guy fell right at my feet and then Booker cooked him again where he lay.

I turned around and it was just chaos. The Germans had bro-ken through the tree line on the right and was overrunning them cooks and clerks who'd set up that position down there. Men was fighting all around the camp, shooting at each other using jeeps and mules as cover, spinning the mule around, trying to shoot each other that way, fighting in the tents, hand to hand, some of 'em.

I reached over Booker and pulled the firing pin. Fired it myself. Sent that last shell right into the tower where Cliff was. And in the distance, I saw the top of the church tower pop. Booker had dialed it in perfect.

And then me and Booker got the hell outta there best we could.

HERB WATCHED from the edge of the balcony as the Basie Band played and the dancing night progressed. The Judge and Carlos still hadn't danced. They sat together, both talking to Lillian, all three laughing, drinking. They didn't seem to be in a hurry. They seemed to do nothing but talk. After a while, though, the band vocalist, a young man in a tux, came down to the floor from the bandstand and approached their table. The singer leaned over the Judge, who whispered something in his ear. The singer went up to the leader, the great Count Basie, and whispered in his ear. The Count nodded, leaned over to his great guitarist Freddie Green, who cued the band to a halt after the number was done.

Basie, who normally never strayed from his piano during concerts, rose and walked to center stage to speak in the microphone.

"And now, ladies and gentlemen, as we do every year, we dedicate this one to Mr. and Mrs. Clifford Johns."

Herb watched in wonder as the Judge, Carlos, and Lillian Johns got up and proceeded to the middle of the floor, surrounded by other dancers. The Basie singer strode to center stage and began to sing "Polka Dots and Moonbeams."

Herb watched, entranced, as the threesome danced. Carlos danced like a ballet dancer, graceful, holding lovely Lillian Johns like she was a gardenia, guiding her around tenderly and cautiously, spinning a web on the floor. They moved like angels, while the old Judge circled them like an attentive, clumsy, soused guardian, using his cane as a magic wand, a conductor's baton, waving it over the couple's heads, conducting a symphony only they could hear, smiling, laughing, joking, *narrating* as the couple whirled. With each twirl and glide, the Judge spun his cane about in the air, following along, half dancing, half limping, dancing with the cheer and lift of a thousand ballerinas. The macabre trio floated about the dance floor as couples smiled and noted them.

Because that was what Clifford Johns promised his wife. That's what Carlos told Herb before he sent him on his way. That after the smoke had cleared and the Americans had driven the Germans back, he and the Judge had walked down into Sommocolonia and found the body of Clifford Johns in the church tower, along with seven Americans and some forty-three dead German soldiers, and in Johns's pocket was a letter he was set to mail to his wife, Lillian, which said, "I may not be the greatest dancer in the world, but when I come home, I am going to take you Christmas dancing every single year. We will dance to Count Basie at Minton's on Christmas Eve while he plays 'Polka Dots and Moonbeams.' And at that moment I will be the best dancer in the world, because I am dancing with the best woman in the world. And we will do that every year until we die."

Herb watched them spin across the floor, an odd trio: Carlos leading the way, smooth and suave; Lillian following gracefully; and the old Judge floating alongside, waving his cane and dancing like an angel, clearing the way, narrating, dancing the promise a man made to his wife thirty years before. Dancing in a way that only an angel can make possible. Making good on a promise made so many years ago.

THE FISH MAN ANGEL

During the Civil War, it was not unusual for the great President Lincoln to take long, solitary walks to the War Department in the dead of night. The War Department was just a few blocks away from the White House, and Lincoln often went there alone, to review telegrams and the latest news from his generals on the front. He took this solitary walk much to the dismay of his secretary of war, Edwin Stanton, and his personal bodyguard, Alan Pinkerton, who deemed his midnight walks foolhardy. He had received numerous death threats, which he dismissed. His walks, the president insisted, were the only way for him to escape the daily madness of the White House, his quarreling Cabinet members, and a faltering Union Army led by a bumbling George McClellan, who called up reinforcements again and again, only to be whipped by the cunning of the great Confederate general Robert E. Lee and Lee's gloriously talented Southern counterparts.

So it was on this chilly March night when the tall and melancholy figure in a stovepipe hat emerged from the basement west side door of the White House and made his way toward the main gate that led to Pennsylvania Avenue and the War Department. The figure nodded at the sentry who was posted there, glanced over his shoulder, and then, instead of walking toward the War Department, turned away from the gate and doubled back along the side of the building to the rear of the White House. He nodded at a second, silent rear sentry who patrolled the south side of the White House, then stepped into the alcove of a rear doorway. He waited in the shadows until the sentry had turned away, then slipped into the nearby tree-lined grounds and strode with purpose across the weeds and thick bushes toward the horse stable.

At the stable, he checked over his shoulder again to make sure he was not being followed, then silently slid his giant frame inside, closing the door quietly behind him.

There, along a row of stalls, he found Tinker, the pony belonging to his son Willie.

The child had fallen sick with fever two months before. One day he was fine, the next he coughed and lay down, complaining of chills. His wife summoned the best doctors in the city—in the land. The best nurses. Long days passed, long nights, with the anxious president, his giant, six-foot, four-inch frame pacing up and down the dim corridors of the White House in dressing gown and flapping carpet slippers, anxiously consulting the doctors as his wife sat fretfully at her son's bedside. Everything possible had been attempted to save their son, but in the end, nothing could be done. Neither the greatest doctors in all America nor the will of its most powerful citizen could supersede God's will.

The boy's suffering had been long and painful, his breath coming in slower and slower gasps until he was gone. He succumbed to death at age eleven, when most boys are climbing trees and turning the corner toward young manhood.

The sight of the president wandering aimlessly down the halls of the White House sobbing, "He's gone," was a memory that most of the White House staff preferred never to recall.

The president entered the stall, withdrew from his pocket an apple, and offered it to the pony. "There now," he said brightly. "How's that for a treat?"

The pony, having eagerly climbed to his feet when the president entered, gave him a good sniff and gobbled up the apple. Even in the stable's darkness Lincoln could see Tinker's eyes shine with delight.

"Easy now," Lincoln said. "Don't want to eat my hand, do you? I'll need it to pick a few more in your favor—" and suddenly he burst into tears. He leaned his head upon the pony, his long fingers draped over the creature's back, his stovepipe hat falling to the floor as he sobbed.

He cried for several long minutes, his huge shoulders wracking with loud, debilitating sobs, his head bowed over the pony's back, his high-pitched voice echoing eerily through the empty stalls and passages like a knife clattering across a marble table.

Finally he came to himself. He wiped his face on his sleeve, patted the pony, and with a sigh reached his long arm over to the edge of the stall and grabbed a blanket. He wrapped it over the creature's back. Grabbing a pitchfork from the corner of the stall, the president of the most powerful army on American soil, whose single pen stroke across a piece of paper sent tens of thousands to their deaths, pitched the hay into a neat pile. He led the pony to the corner of the stall, coaxed the animal to the floor, then removed his tie, opened his waistcoat, unbuttoned his shirt, and lay down next to the pony, resting his head upon a bit of straw. Within seconds he fell asleep.

He was awakened several minutes later by the noise of footsteps. He lay without moving. His first thought was that he was dead. Many times Alan Pinkerton had warned him that assassins lingered about the White House, anxious to lure him out. He had ignored him and now was sorry for it, for there was only one doorway in and out of the stable, and judging by the number of steps he heard, the contingent that entered was more than one in number.

"Over here," he heard a voice say. It was that of a Negro.

The president lay immobile, listening intently. His eyes, now used to the dark, watched through the spaces between the slats of the stall as the aisle was illuminated by a gas lamp. The light shown on the face of a Negro he barely recognized, a stable hand whose name he could not remember. The man was followed by a Negro boy of about eleven, and then another lantern, and the president, with relief, recognized the familiar coat, shiny brass buttons, and tiny paunch of his regular coachman, Walter Brown, who led into the barn the team of horses that drove his presidential coach.

"Put 'em up, Simmie," Walter said. "President's gone to the War Department by foot again."

"Maybe we ought to keep 'em out a little longer," Simmie, the stable hand, said, "less'n the president might summon them for the ride back."

From his place, Lincoln watched as Walter's face, a glittering mass of white teeth and shining shimmy-sham that greeted him every morning with a joyful grin and a hearty huckabuck good morning, twisted into a grotesque mask of derision and rage.

"Who is you to sass me, Simmie? I am the president's coachman. I could have you throwed right back to South Carolina to the bondage of masters you runned off from. You and your boy here!"

"No disrespect intended," Simmie said. "Just thinking that the president might want his coach."

"Don't think beyond yourself, nigger! The president don't need you to think for him about his horses or his laundry or his cooking. If this country was left up to niggers like yourself, we'd all be slaves still. Keep your coat on, pus head! And learn to work slow. Don't be calling for more work. The man wanna walk, let him fool-walk! The runnings of *this* coach is for *me* to decide. Not you. Not him, even. He gived me this coach to run. So you coming at me to make me run it more makes me look bad to myself. You wanna make more work for me?"

"No. I was just thinking of the pres—"

"Shush now! Don't backtalk me. Being that I works for the president, I am practically a white man," Walter said. "And you is just a stable nigger. So as to teach an unstable stabler like yourself to be obedient and sanctified by the white man, you best get to practicing more. From here out, nigger, call me sir, since I am doing a white man's job. Besides, we in wartime now, you unstable stabler, and no-count niggers like yourself cleaning up all the time, picking up dust and trying to make me look bad in front of the white folks, is not good. This white man's army's fighting for freedom, nigger. *Your* freedom. Understand?"

"Walter, just 'cause you wasn't in bondage like I was—"

"What you call me?"

"Sir. Mr. Walter, sir. Just 'cause you wasn't in bond—"

"Shush your mouth and do as I say. You get your black ass 'round these horses and put 'em up, water 'em, and have 'em ready. You understand?"

"Yes."

"Yes what?"

Lincoln watched the stable hand's face. Simmie was a tall, regal man, dressed in tattered clothing with battered shoes. Simmie's face twisted in painful recognition as he separated the horses while his son stared. Simmie glanced at his boy and addressed the coachman.

"I reckon it ain't necessary, Walter," Simmie said softly, "to speak to me that way in front of my boy here."

Lincoln watched as Walter's face twisted into a deeper rage.

"Nigger, I will take this horsewhip and do you and your boy with it. Y'understand? I am tired. I want to sleep. I been setting up waiting for the president all night. And when he takes it to his mind to walk, I still got to sit there in the cold and rain. Now you, you broke-horse, low-country, wool-headed, yellow-bellied, dirt-faced nigger bastard. You *will* feed, water, and wash these horses. You *will* clean them down to the bottom of their hooves. And you *will* call me sir. And if you don't call me sir from here on out, I *will* see that you is sent out into the road. I can get any number of starving niggers wandering 'round these parts to take the warm food and shelter from out your mouth and your boy's mouth. You understand?"

"Yes."

"Yes what?"

"Yes, sir."

Walter turned on his heel, the bottom of his white horseman's tailcoat flickering in the lamplight as he stomped toward the barn door, where he stopped and, his back to Simmie, said: "I gots a hard job. I got to keep this yard tight, y'understand? I'm the president's man, y'see. Closest thing to a white man this yard has. Being 'round the biggest white man of all has gived me smarts, Simmie. You can learn from me. If I decides to, I might even learn you a thing or two."

"Yes . . . sir."

"Good night, nigger."

With that Walter departed, closing the door behind him.

Lincoln watched as Simmie silently led the team of horses to adjacent stalls across the aisle from him. He gently led them inside, then closed the gates. He stooped to grab a bucket as his son addressed him.

"Pa?"

"Yes, son."

"Why does he sass you so?"

"He don't mean nothing by it, son. Don't you worry 'bout it."

"But he ain't got to sass you so."

"His words don't hurt me. He's tired, is all. The Lord brings all evil to judgment. Let's get to these horses. And when we're done, we'll clean up Willie's pony and run him 'round soon as it's light. You feed him?"

Lincoln watched the boy's face droop. "I don't wanna feed him no more, Papa. He reminds me of Willie."

"That again," Simmie sighed. "Son, Willie's gone to glory. God knows it. He's resting in the arms of the Lord, bless his soul."

"I don't care. I don't wanna touch Tinker."

"But Willie was a good friend to you, weren't he?"

"As good a friend as any."

"You wouldn't want your friend displeased when he looks

down from Heaven and sees Tinker all muddied up and not being proper cared for, would you?"

"No, sir."

"G'wan then. Clean up his pony and water him good, and I'll tend to the coachman's horses."

Lincoln's heart froze as the boy turned and reluctantly shuffled his feet to the stall where he lay hidden. Then the boy stopped.

"Why do it please the Lord to take Willie, who was so good and kind, and when the coachman hollers like the devil . . ." And he burst into tears.

The president, blinking back his own tears, watched as the old stable hand set down his bucket and stepped over to his son.

"I ever told you the story about the Fish Man Angel your ma met?"

"'Bout a hundred times."

"Lemme tell it again," he said.

"What's the point?"

"'Cause the retelling of a thing makes it come more and more true," Simmie said. He was holding a pitchfork and set it down. "C'mere," he said.

The boy moved to him and Simmie gently placed an arm around him, then grabbed a nearby lantern and moved down near the gate of the stall, where he sat on the floor, the boy next to him.

"Your ma, 'fore she passed, couldn't have no children—"

"You told me this before."

"Well, set tight, Mr. I-Know-My-Letters, for I'mma tell it again."

The boy sighed and settled into his father's armpit as Simmie continued.

"Your ma, she was what you call a barren woman. Couldn't have nar child. When we married, we two was bondaged to a white man named Frank Dunbar. This was before the war. Well, Master Frank wasn't a good master. Weren't a bad master. Just a drylongso type boss. He was planning on going to the market and told your ma, 'I'm going to the market in the morning. Get the eggs and butter ready,' for he wanted to eat first. So she got up early to make his breakfast, but it was too early to go out to the barn and milk the cow and feed the chickens. And she looked—she thought it was gonna rain—and she went 'round to the side of the house to fetch water. And standing by the well, just near the woods, she saw this man, covered with fish scales, standing by the well. Looked like a fish, but he was a man—"

"Was she scared?"

"A little bit she was. But he spoke to her and said, 'Don't be afraid. There's something buried beneath the stones here.' There was flat stones around the well. He pointed to a flat stone and said, 'Take that stone and dig.'

"She dug down and lo and behold there was a chest there. And inside it was all the master's money. Every bit of it. Gold and jewel pieces. Enough to make a soul rich for the rest of his life. Master Frank had buried his money there so nobody could find it.

"The Fish Man said to her, 'Take that, it's yours.'

"She said, 'No, sir. I couldn't take that any more than I could snatch a crumb from a bird eating it off the ground.'

"He said, 'You can buy your freedom with it.'

"She said, 'But this is marse's. It ain't mine's.'

"He said, 'You worked for your master. You raised his corn. You pulled his cotton. You picked his tobacco. So it is by rights yours, too.'

"She said, 'If I take this I'll be a slave forever to the wrong I done. I serve a living God, and I want my freedom clear.'

"The Fish Man Angel said, 'Well, you are honest and true. So I'm gonna ask the Lord to bring you something special. I'm gonna ask Him to deliver to you a son, and I'mma ask him to give a promise to your boy that His Will and Deliverance will come to your boy's life. I'mma give you four magic words . . .'"

And here the old slave paused, and his eyes twinkled and sparkled as he turned to look at his son. "And the words was these: *here . . . thenceforward . . . forever-more . . . free.*"

Simmie waited for the response. The boy's face was blank.

"Them's the magic words, boy. There's four of 'em. Gived by the Fish Man Angel hisself. For your reckoning someday."

"I'm hungry," the boy said.

Simmie chuckled. "How can you fuss 'bout food when I'm giving you the word of the King of Kings? We got a place to live. And food to eat. And good friends. Like Master Willie and Father Abe and his wife, and all the people about us, even old coachman, with his crazy old self. See, God favors the righteous. He favors us with words! The Bible. Words, boy! Not a pistol or knife or cannon lingering in the whole bunch! Just words, passed from one ear to the next! Oh, yes, I wish I was lettered. Them four words just lingers in my mind. They floats about me from day to day. Just four words they is. But powerful enough. Righteous, I'd say. Them four words got bones in 'em! They say, 'Stop the train! We ain't going no further! It's over! Quit it! Har up that mule! Git off! Clip it! Ship out your troubles! Stop everything!'"

And here Simmie paused and dropped his voice to a near whisper: "*Here . . . thenceforward . . . forever-more . . . free.*"

He turned to the boy, who had placed his head on his father's chest now, eyes drooping. "What you think?"

"Mmm." The boy's eyes blinked slowly. Sleep was coming.

Simmie piped on. "Course, them thoughts is just my guesses. To be honest, I can't know exactly to the dot what them four words mean. But there's good to each and every one of 'em. I reckon if I had to boil it down, I'd say they mean hating on somebody takes too much work."

"Mmm," the boy mumbled drowsily.

Simmie cradled the boy's head in his chest and smiled at him, rubbing the boy's smooth, brown, downturned face. Simmie murmured aloud, almost to himself now.

"Your ma died in bondage, she did, but with a knowing in

her heart. That the Fish Man Angel's four magic words is gonna shine on you someday."

He sighed happily, then looked about, glancing at a tiny upper window of the barn where the first glimmers of dawn were appearing.

"There ain't but a few hours left till light," he said. "Father Abe do need these horses, and Angel Willie do need his pony cleaned up. Let's finish up. We'll do the horses first, then do Willie's pony last. First we'll fetch some fresh water."

He looked down, but the boy was fast asleep. He shook him. But the boy would not awaken. The old man gently slid away from the child and lay him curled in a ball, asleep, on the straw of the barn floor, then stood and leaned over the sleeping child, his hands clasped and eyes closed, praying: "Lord, listen in on the Fish Man Angel, God Almighty, listen in. Hear them words in the name of Sweet Jesus: *here . . . thenceforward . . . forever-more . . . free.* Amen." With that he unclasped his hands, stood erect, grabbed the bucket, and left the stable for the well, leaving the boy asleep on the floor.

Lincoln watched him leave, Simmie's words turning over in his mind, clawing at his chest, a reflection of his own aching heart, churning in his mind . . . *here . . . thenceforward . . . forever-more . . . free.*

He rose too, stepped over the snoring child, and crept to the door of the stable. He peeked out to see that the way was clear, quickly thrust his stovepipe hat upon his head, and headed back to the White House, a tall, stooped figure, hurrying across the yard in the night.

EIGHT MONTHS LATER, on a freezing New Year's morning in 1862, the president of the United States delivered, in twenty-two minutes from his Telegraph Office, the statement that changed the war and America for the rest of time.

There was no thunderous applause from the telegraph room when Lincoln was done. No standing ovation. No clapping on the back, no murmurs of approval; only a nodding of heads and a general flurry of excited activity in the office among the five telegraph operators who delivered the news to cities across America with somber and driven purpose.

Lincoln, in his usual fashion, had delivered a bomb that no one expected. He had changed the tenor of the war. The war between the states was done. It was now a war against slavery.

As was his habit, the president sat on a chair in the War Department while the operators worked to send his words across the wires, his boots resting on a desk. He waited, ruminating silently, to make sure the telegraphs had gone out to the most important cities in the largest states.

When he was certain they had gone, he rose and, accompanied by his staff and several generals, left for his carriage to head back to the White House. The telegraphers were sending them to smaller cities by the time he reached his coach. As he did, the president complained of thirst. An aide disappeared and returned with a glass. Sitting in the coach, Lincoln drank, then handed the glass to the man and thanked him. He opened his door to the crisp January air and spoke to the driver overhead.

"We got a long day, Simmie. Might as well get at it."

"Yes, Mr. President," Simmie, resplendent in coachman's outfit, top hat, and white gloves, said. He grabbed the traces to har up the horses.

"Wait," Lincoln said, glancing around. "Where's the boy?"

"He went to fetch you some water, sir."

The president seemed irritated. "But I have had it," he said.

"Yes, sir."

"Wait a moment, then," Lincoln said. He closed the door of the coach against the cold air and waited inside, his aides milling about outside the coach in the freezing weather until after a few long moments a black boy, Simmie's son, appeared from around the side of the building running at full sprint, holding a bucket and a ladle. He tapped at the door of the coach.

Lincoln opened the door. Standing outside the coach, the boy offered up the ladle. Lincoln motioned with his hand that he was not thirsty, and motioned for the boy to toss the water. As the boy turned to do so, even in the chill winter day, Lincoln noticed the sweat on the boy's head.

"Wait. You thirsty?" Lincoln asked.

"Yes, sir."

"Drink then. Hurry now."

The boy quickly slipped the ladle in the water and sipped.

Then, as an afterthought, Lincoln took the ladle and in plain sight of his generals, aides, and several pedestrians who stood on the wooden sidewalk, the president of the United States and commander in chief of the Union Army dipped the ladle in the bucket and brought it to his lips, where he drank deeply. He handed the ladle back to the boy, who dumped the water from the bucket and then hopped aboard the driver's seat next to his father.

The president stuck his head out the window.

"How about it, Simmie."

Simmie raised his reins. The carriage pulled away.

As the coach charged forward, the telegraph operators continued banging away, sending the words of the Emancipation Proclamation to cities all across the land, the words of the Fish Man Angel: ". . . *here, thenceforward, and forever-more . . . free.*"

MR. P & THE WIND

Chapter 1

The 24th Hour

I am a lion. I live in a zoo. But I was once a free lion, and never forgot it.

Many years ago, before I was captured and brung here, I knowed a lion who ate a Man. His name was Box. I don't know how Box come to that name, for lions got their own names for their own purpose, and that name was a puzzlement to me. Box is a Human name, you see, and it stands to reason maybe a Human gived him that name. However it happened, or whether Box got a reason for telling it or not telling it, it ain't my business to know, for most lions know that Man-things often ain't got no purpose, and no creature of the jungle is gonna sniff around something that ain't purposeful, especially something big as a name, for lions got their own names that's particular to 'em. Like Monkey Tricked Him, or His Wife Don't Visit, or Feet Smell Funny, or Don't Trust Her 'Cause She's a Son, or Orange Head, and all like that. For example, Humans call me Hal. But my real name is Get Along, Go Along. No Animal in his right head would dare call me Hal unless they want me lunching on their guts. But Box come to his name some kind of way. That was his first mistake, I think, to call himself by a Man-name when he had his own mother-called name.

I never knew Box's real name, by the way. Never stupid enough to ask neither, for Box was what you call a plain old drylongso lion. He was a hard lion, set in his ways. He didn't take no shit off nobody.

Now because Box was hard-set in his ways, he couldn't adjust to nothing. He didn't like fancy things. No springboks, rhinos, ostrich, monkey, and all that kind of shit for him. Just straight-out blood and guts. Zebra. Snake. Whatever he could get. He was what you call old country. He didn't slaughter a lot, but what he did slaughter he did eat. Most of what he ate was bigger creatures so the smaller, scarcer ones could grow big for better eating later. He didn't waste nothing, including time. So when he seen me walking 'round one day when I was but a little cub and said, "Set here a minute. I got to tell you something," I set down to listen. For Box wasn't nobody to ignore.

Now I heard many a story told to me when I was a cub running free back yonder in the plains of Africa, and a bunch of them stories was lies, for Animals ain't no different than Man that way. The story starts out one way and five days later it grows tree branches and leaves and before you know it, it's the size of a mountain with caves and rocks and you can't see the top or bottom of the thing while standing on it.

But Box told me this story hisself, and Box wasn't the type to lie.

This is what Box told me.

He was coming through the jungle one day and a hunter surprised him. Got the drop on him. Box walked right past him. Never smelled him or sensed him. Nothing. The man jumped out of a bush from behind Box holding a spear with dead lion scent all over it. He had Box dead to rights. He had old Box cold. Wasn't nothing Box could do.

Box knew his big head was gonna hang from the wall of the Man's lair for the rest of time while the Man apologized to Box and all his relatives for taking his life and so forth, for that's how the old-time hunters did it. They put you to the Big Sleep and thanked your relatives afterwards by praying and so forth so your souls can live together for the rest of time, while he uses your claws as plates for his smoking sticks and so forth.

There wasn't nothing Box could do, so he said to hisself, "It is a good day to die," and turned on the Man and waited to sleep.

But this Man knew too much. Instead of throwing his spear when Box turned on him, the Man spoke to Box in Thought Speak. Know what he said? He said this:

"I know it ain't your 24th hour."

Well, that threw old Box. I don't know what threw old Box more. Man talking in Thought Speak, which is how Animals speak, or Man speaking about the 24th hour. Both had never happened to Box before. But Man spouting off about the 24th hour put the thing in a different light.

See, a lion won't eat but one hour a day. The other 23 hours we mostly sleep or look for fun or pussy. That's our game. Lions is Higher Orders, which is what all Animals call ourself. It's mostly a pleasure trip being a Higher Order, except one or two rules you got to stick to. For this group of Higher Orders, lions that is, the 24th hour rule is our line in the sand. See, we're harmless 23 whole hours a day. You can do whatever you want 'round the King of the Jungle for them 23 hours: throw a dance, write your auntie letters, take your clothes off and dance naked, don't mean nothing to us. But that 24th hour, that lone hour we *is* eating, you don't want to be around us then. You might wanna go play cards or visit your aunt Thelma across the woods or do whatever it is smelly humans do during that time.

Box, old-fashioned soul that he was, was just floored by that whole business. He just plain didn't know what to do. First, hearing Man throw Thought Speak around like that. Then him going on about the 24th hour. Box got chicken-hearted. So he said, "Excuse me?"

"You heard me," the Man said in clear Thought Speak. "I know this ain't your 24th hour. You know how I know? I been tracking you, Box. You still in your 23 hours of wandering around, sleeping, looking for water, and fun, and pussy, all that. So I won't kill you, for I don't want your head now. I want your head in the 24th hour, when you are hunting, for I'm a great chief myself. And I'm looking for something mighty like me. So I'm going to let you live. I am even going to suggest a few things for you to do in your free 23 hours. For I have traveled many places and I knows many things. And I can help you." Then he patted Box on the shoulder and turned away.

That's when Box jumped him.

He knocked the Man down. Grabbed the Man's spear with his mouth and stuck the tooth end down into the earth so the stick stood up like a pole. Then he snatched him up in his mouth and whipped the Man across the stick, back and forth. Beating the Man with his own stick. Beating the stick with the Man. And when he was done, he threw him down and tore him up, ripped him up, ran a paw across the Man's face, and killed him dead. Then he ate him, or a good part of him, and slept a good two days without waking up.

Many a day I've thought about Box, while setting in this cage, pacing back and forth, night and day, year in and year out, thinking about it. That hunter did no harm to old Box. The Man had him cold and didn't kill him. He even offered to school Box on how to live good in his free time. Still, old Box killed him.

You know why?

He was insulted, see. If Man had walked off and said nothing, Box would've walked on into the jungle and gone about his business. But Man had to turn around and tell a Higher Order, a grown lion, what was in his head. Box didn't want that Man defining him and telling him who he was and what all his plans was and what Box was supposed to do with his free 23 hours and how Man knew everything Box was supposed to do in his 23 hours. That was Box's 23 hours to do with as he pleased. And just so long as Man wasn't fooling around in that magic 24th hour, that *one* hour where nothing in the world is safe from a lion who's got to eat, then he was all right. But he threw himself in Box's business them other 23 hours, telling Box what he could be doing with his time and how he was supposed to be sleeping and so forth. He was counting Box's 24th hour like it was his own. Well, Box didn't like that. He figured if the Man was so big in his britches to count up to his 24th hour, he might want to tell him how to count his free 23 hours, and tell him what to do in his 22nd hour, and the 21st, and so forth. So Box cleaned him up, beat him with his own stick, and sent him to the Big Nap, because he knew it wouldn't be long before that Man told him what to do with his one eating hour, and every other single hour.

I asked Box later, "What did Man sound like?" for I had never spoken to Man.

"You can't handle it," he said.

"What do he taste like?" I asked, for I had never tasted Man neither.

He said, "Tastes like chicken."

I REMEMBER HOW I got caught. I was crouched in high grass tracking a reebok that had wandered a bit off her pack. I was trying to figure another angle to take her before the wind threw my scent at her, because those creatures can smell a fart at three hundred yards and will run like the wind. I was crouched on all fours, ready to spring—then I heard a pop and I come here.

It wasn't bad getting caught, compared to how some around here got nabbed. My buddy She Scratch Backwards—the black jaguar who lives across the hall from me—she says they ran her down for four days in a rainstorm in Brazil before they got her. Shot her eight times in the ass, she claims. "I coulda got away but for that last one," she says. But you can't trust Scratch too much. She likes to preen and lie and carry on, licking and scratching herself all the time in wrong places while she's telling whoppers and so forth. They shot her four times, is what I say. I'm a lion. I know what the hell I'm talking about.

One of the problems of being here, besides the obvious one, is that the pecking order of nature's ways is all screwed up. You got pigeons here telling monkeys what to do. You got giraffes making deals with tigers. You got eels, fish, turkeys, ducks, all manner of Foreigners living one to the next, and each one willing to turn in their neighbor for a crumb of bread. Nobody got purpose here. Higher Orders without purpose are like Man: They get dangerous, often to themselves, which makes living here a task, for when you're taken out of your element, your mind slips. Sitting around bullshitting ain't no problem for Man, who can ignore his own heart and treat his own with all kinds of trickerations and cruelty to twist the truth so he can get what he wants, shutting off parts of his mind to let evil run things. But no Animal can do that, for Animals is Higher Orders, and we talk in Thought Speak, which don't allow but so much wiggle room when it come to truth and consequence.

And that's right, we do talk. Oh, I know you all got scientists and machines and people studying it and folks climbing into tanks with whales and sobbing tears on horses' necks and all, whispering and carrying on, fooling theyselves with bullshit about speaking to us. We don't pay that shit no mind. We talk through the mind.

When we're free, that is.

Caged up, though, that's a different wheel. Your mind ain't right. Hell, I had a Man who come into my cage for fifteen years to leave rotten meat and take my nature things away and I learned nothing from him. And he learned nothing from me. We gave each other nothing. The only thing he gave me was his fear. And I gave him my ambivalence. When he left this cage forever he cried, but I felt nothing. He used to waste hours trying to color my Thought Shapes with his own, but I didn't understand him, for he was without purpose, and no Animal can understand something that ain't purposeful. I confess my thoughts were polluted by his thoughts a little. I even walked like him a little, and sometimes I came to the door when he arrived, for I grew accustomed to him. But I always kept a small part of me for myself. Doing that kept me free inside, allowing me to remember things like Box, and what Box said about Man, and hearing what all the other Thought Shapes the Animals 'round here sometimes make about their keepers, for stilted as it was, we still talked. There's no such thing as silence in the zoo. That's the worst part of being here. It ain't the cage or the food. It's the noise. You got owls hollering about seeing their reflections in the looking glass. You got chimpanzees screaming 'bout rooms full of dead pelicans, and free rats screaming bloody murder and making threats because they're running free. You got mothers calling children's names that disappeared twenty moons ago. Everybody's looking for an angle and willing to kill their neighbor over a piece of old meat, trying to get out, to get in, to move on, to move over, their minds wound up tight, so the general Thought Speak is roaring loud and you can't read it clear like when you do in the wild. The upshot is your mind don't think right the moment you step into the zoo because the noise of sorrow is unbearable. So you just close it off. That's the way it was for me, and for every creature in here.

Till Mr. P arrived.

I don't know why he came here. I heard a rumor that he

worked at the circus before he come here to the zoo, but Rubs Her Head, an old girl gorilla, says she remembers Mr. P as a little boy coming to the zoo when she, Rubs, was just a tiny gorilla. That could be, for Rubs is the oldest Animal in the zoo and that she-thing got a lot of respect around this place and ain't prone to lie. She said Mr. P's real name was Peter and back then he was a pale little something, with hair that laid on his head like yellow grass, and even as a child he knew all the postures and gestures and facial expressions of Animals even before he knew what Animal he was aping. He howled like a banshee and "urred" like a baby leopard, all in Thought Speak. "He had the Gift of Tongue," Rubs said. Them two talk a lot. Rubs favors Smelly Ones.

Smelly Ones are Humans. I don't know why they're called Smelly Ones, by the way, nor do I know why we're Higher Orders. It's got something to do with how Animals use Thought Speak and Smelly Ones speak with their tongues going one way and their heart going another. Mr. P once ran this tale by me about a Smelly One named Adam and his wife and how they got an apple from a snake and ruined the world for Smelly Ones forever. But Irving, a boa constrictor who lives here at the zoo, he got real insulted by it.

Wherever he come from, he walked into a world of trouble when he first got here.

See, we'd been on a sort of general talk-silence that hatched out a dispute between a frog named Sniffs Meat and a girl whale that lives in over in Water World named Blows More Oil, who we calls Blows Oil for short.

I have known Blows Oil for quite a while, and Sniff too, though I got no real liking for frogs as a group. I ain't one of them frog-eating lions. Just never liked frogs and crocodiles and water creatures much when I was free. I only ate true, live frog once in my life, when I come upon one by accident at a pond called Meeting of the Waters. I wolfed him down quick before his wife seen it. Never had no frog before then. Didn't cotton to the taste neither. All bones, wrinkled up, no meat on him. I've tasted shirts that was better. But I done him a favor just the same, for he Jumped Souls, which all Animals do. When you get eaten and take the Big Nap, you come back as another Animal, usually up the food chain some. Happens to all Creatures. Well, wouldn't you know it, not long after I sent him down my throat, I was over at Meeting of the Waters and seen a frog colored different from him but bigger, staring at me from the water and sending me a Thought Shape that said, "You wolfed me down right near my wife over on that shore there last moon."

I said, "While I do believe I did that, I have no taste for you now."

He said, "Good, 'cause this time I got poison skin that'll give you a rash for eight days and nights, you fat butt-sucker." He was a nervy little critter, sitting in that pond outta reach. He turned and jumped into deep water and threw another Thought

Shape over his shoulder that said, "It worked out 'cause I got a better wife this time," and he grabbed my own Thought Shape that told him I didn't have no wife nor lioness the first.

So on that account, I ain't got no more kind feelings to frogs than a dog do to a cat. But Sniff was an amusement, for he was a joker, and he and Blows Oil had been going at it for quite a while. Like most things troublesome, their dispute come out of something heard from Man.

Sniff had got wind of a story about a Smelly One named Jonas who got swallowed by a whale and lived inside the whale, eating up all the whale's food till a gigantic Smelly One named God came down and got this Smelly Jonas out. Then the whale died.

Now I don't know about you, but that's the funniest thing I ever heard in my life.

Animals come and go all the time, but grub that's already in the stomach, that's serious. Nobody in the Higher Order, not even the tiniest fish, would ever let somebody down his gullet to snatch his grub. It don't make no sense.

Sniff got to teasing Blows Oil pretty hard about it, and he come up with a song he called "Smelly in the Belly." There ain't nothing like a song to get a Higher Order going, and he started crowing it one afternoon and we all took to it and sung along together, making quite a racket:

Smelly in the Belly,
Eat drink stinky

Smelly in the Belly
Put 'em in your gut,
Smelly in the Belly
Eating out your tummy,
It's not even funny
When your Smelly is all runny
And he can't find your butt.

Hell, I know it's silly, but this is a zoo. I was roaring it out myself, not thinking it was hurting nobody's feelings, when suddenly there come a loud boom that cut the song short and throwed me right to the floor of my cage. It felt like a big rock hit me upside the head. A sudden pain rang right through my body. I rolled on the floor of my cage, bellowing like a cub. I thought I was runned through by a spear, or worse, killed by one of Man's magic spears that go kaplooey but I didn't feel nothing enter nor see no blood. Whatever it was, it come from inside my head. It was a Thought Shape, but bigger. Stronger. Like a clap of thunder that kept rolling.

No sooner did it quit than a second Thought Roar hit me worse than the first, and I rolled on the floor some more. That noise cut through my head something terrible, pouring over me like boiling water. I wriggled around like a cub trying to get out from under it, rolling on my back, which ain't no small thing, for in the world of Lion where every twitch and itch says something, rolling on your back means you give up, you quit, you had enough, you's a goner. But it didn't stop. That

racket just beat on. Meanwhile the Smelly Ones outside my
cage looked on and laughed, thinking I was doing tricks to
please 'em.

After a few seconds, the sound quit.

I lay on my side, dizzy. Then I felt a torrent of regular
Thought Shapes come through as Animals all over the zoo
started hollering in panic at once. The Bird House was in an
uproar, with squawking and howling, and the free creatures,
Mice, Rats, Birds, Bugs, even a few Peacocks who roamed the
zoo grounds, hauled ass for the exits. Across the hall, my buddy
Scratch was flat on her back in the give-up pose too, her paws
in the air.

"What happened?" she said. She throwed a little Thought
Shape out there. She throwed it out small, for even that brag-
ging, dotty, bat-eating ding-dong was feeling chicken-hearted.

Then I heard Sniff the frog holler out in panic: "It's Blows
Oil! She's going crazy in the whale tank!"

And sure enough, the noise came again and it rung my head
so hard I singed my nose with my own claw and hit the deck
again. It was Oil, all right, but big, like I never heard her before. Whale Thought Shapes is powerful beyond ways you can
tell it. Whales is big creatures, they got a lot of room to be insulted.

I heard Rubs the gorilla cry out, "Sniff, what you done?"

Sniff tried to fix it, sending little froggy Thought Shapes
saying he was sorry. Oil responded by blasting out another
burst that made the first two seem like pigeon squat. I'm telling

you, it weren't no Thought Shape I ever knew of. These wasn't no mind pictures. You could feel them things deep inside you.

Sniff tried to apologize again, and Oil sent out another mind-stabber that sliced me so deep I almost emptied my nature onto the floor and lay on my side with my back curled and paws bent. When she finally whirred it down a little, the whole zoo got to raging and cussing at Sniff.

"Sniff, you stupid, sing-song, yellow-bellied tadpole . . ."

"Sniff! Feed yourself to Oil right now. Hurry along!"

"Sniff, you're my supper!" That was Can't Trot, an elephant. Trot don't even eat frogs.

The entire place was letting Sniff have it. Everyone was hollering and making a general fuss. When it died down a little, Scratch, who was across the hall lying on her back, looked at me and sent out a Thought Shape that said, "Well, Get Along, what you gonna do?"

Which figures. Only time I'm King of the Jungle around here is when there's problems.

Well, I couldn't just lie there. Everybody heard her ask it, and I could feel their minds pointing at me. So I got up, gathered myself, and let out the biggest Thought Shape roar I could muster. I even put a little zing on it by throwing the picture of a little half-eaten whale in it, which wasn't too good since I never seen or eaten whale to my recollection. Nor do I recall ever Jumping Souls to *being* whale, but I done my best. I reared back and threw it out there, then followed it up with a big, old-fashioned, open-mouthed roar, and let that whole business ring far and wide. I covered the whole zoo with them two roars, which every Animal in there knew I was entitled to do, given my position and responsibilities being that I'm King of the Jungle and so forth.

Well, no sooner had I closed my flytrap than Blows More Oil let go with a high-frequency mind-stabber that was worse than the first three all together and had every four-legged creature running around in circles eating their tails. I lay on the floor of my cage whimpering myself to a frenzy, and in fact did empty my nature to the floor that time with a pip or two. I couldn't help it, which it don't matter since I ain't got to bury my own pip here nohow, but the embarrassment of the thing wasn't too good, since I was the one that brung the added trouble.

I wasn't the only one who lost it, by the way, for there was howling everywhere on account of the pain. I remember thinking, "This is a good day to die," which is what every Higher Order says when troubles is coming at 'em in threes or they're about to go belly-up on account of doing something stupid or picking the wrong Animal to munch on, or fooling with Man, whose word ain't no good when he's holding his magic claw that goes ka-boom. It was bad, for Oil was calling in the dogs.

That blast lasted only a minute or two thankfully, but that was enough. After that I kept my mind shut. And everyone else kept their minds shut. And we all thought only deep thoughts, which is Thought Speak of your own that nobody else can't figure out.

And we were stuck that way for quite a while.

When we tried to talk amongst ourselves, she would blast us. When we tried to talk to her, she would blast us. I was trying to figure out a way to unsore Blows More Oil, like getting a big old grandfather Free Rat they call Born Fat, who owes me a few favors, to sneak into the frog house and give Sniff the old one-two and put him to Sleep. But the Free Creatures was long gone when Oil started up, and that included Born Fat and his whole rat family.

That's when Mr. P came around.

The first time I saw him was at night. He always did come at night. The only time I saw him during the day was at the end, when things got crazy. But generally, Mr. P was a nighttime Smelly, not like the rest.

He was standing outside Scratch's cage, wearing the green skins with flaps on it that Smelly Ones who work at the zoo wear all the time. He was a little Smelly and old by zookeeper standards, with an extra pair of glass over his eyes that the Smellies use to help them see. He sidled up to the railing outside Scratch's cage, climbed over the railing, stuck his face between the cage bars—which is a hell of a thing to do if that black panther's in a bad mood—and said, "Hello there."

Scratch looked back at him, then looked at me, then back at him.

"Hello there." Mr. P said it again. A Thought Shape. Clear as day. Didn't say a word of Human Speak. Just thoughts.

Scratch blinked a few times.

And then Mr. P says, "How are you today?"

I swear on my life this happened, and if I'm lying you can set my tail on fire and stretch it around my shoulders. It was the first time I'd ever heard a Smelly One Thought Speak. I couldn't believe it, so I stood on my hind legs and leaned on the cage bars to look. I wasn't even thinking how sore my legs was from being in that position.

He had a kind of Thought Shape voice I'd never heard before. Not like an Animal. It felt light and windy. The shapes he made was jumbly and coarse, like a little cub would make. He stood there with his head between the bars of Scratch's cage, smiling and showing his teeth and Animal Speaking. It was a hell of a thing to see for the first time, a Smelly One talking without moving his jaws, showing his teeth as he threw baby Thought Speak around, crude as it was.

Scratch stared at him frozen, just blinking.

I could feel everybody listening in real close.

"Don't be afraid," Mr. P says to Scratch. "Can you Thought Speak?"

Well, I could see Scratch was in a predicament right off. If she Thought Spoke, Blows More Oil might send out a charge that would knock out everybody's teeth. On the other hand, nobody had never spoken to a Smelly One before, and it was a hell of a thing.

So what Scratch did, she nodded.

Mr. P picked right up on it. He said, in a real kind way, "No need to be shy. I'm Mr. P. I just got here. What's your name?"

Scratch stared at him a minute, then wiped a paw across her face and looked away. That panther can be a cool son of a bitch when she wants to be.

Mr. P looked at her and sighed. "So terrible," he said. "I've heard of Higher Orders who have been in zoos so long they've forgotten Thought Speak. I didn't think they were real. But . . . it seems so quiet around here . . ." He looked at Scratch in a sad way and said, "It's a shame. And you're such a handsome, beautiful creature."

Scratch, that vain devil, she smiled.

Mr. P laughed. "C'mon now. What's your name?"

Later on, there was a few that criticized Scratch for what she did, because we is Animals, Higher Orders living under the Orders of Life, and we are bound to things and creatures of purpose, and nobody ever said anything about that including talking to Smelly Ones through the mind. It don't seem natural, and if it was, Smelly Ones would've been able to make Thought Shapes long ago. But I don't believe Scratch knew what she was on the edge of. Hell, none of us did, and I told her later I would have done the same thing.

What Scratch did next, she scrunched up her face, the hair on her back bristling, closed her eyes, and whispered her name. Real soft.

I braced myself.

Nothing happened.

Mr. P said, "What?"

Scratch opened her eyes. Seeing that she was all in one

piece, she opened her mind to send a second Thought Picture with her name in it. Before she finished Blows Oil came through with a mind-stabber that felt like a hundred spears sticking in my eyes and everything went black for a minute.

When I come to, I seen Mr. P lying on his back outside Scratch's cage holding his ears. He had got blowed off his feet and knocked clean over the railing. Howls were coming from all over the zoo, and through the pounding in my head and blurred vision I saw Scratch rolling around on the floor of her cage and I knew she was sorry then.

I tried sticking my head in the corner of my own cage for relief, my tail swinging high in the air, my rear end exposed, but it didn't do no good. Blows More Oil had let her rage out full blast, just a-roaring.

Finally she finished, and when she did, Mr. P, who was on his back, sat up. The extra glass he wore was blown clean off his face. The fur on top of his head stood on end. He raised himself up from the ground slow, crawling around on all fours just like an Animal till he found them windows for his eyes. He put them on, got back on his hind legs, and shook his head clear.

"Holy Jesus," he said. "Is that a whale?"

Scratch didn't say another blessed Thought Shape. She nodded.

Mr. P left.

I don't know what passed between Mr. P and Blows More Oil that night. Rubs the gorilla later said Mr. P put on some funny skins to cover his bare Smelly One body and went right in the whale tank with Oil for a heart-to-heart. Then he went to Sniff, who started it all, and talked to him private one-on-one, in a way I suppose that only Smellies can.

Whatever went on between 'em I never knew, for Smellies got ways of doing things that no Animal can quite understand. But the next day Mr. P came around and shouted to the entire zoo with big Thought Shapes that all of us could feel:

"From now on, no more Smelly in the Belly songs. So childish and cruel to treat one of your own that way. Have you got no pride? Are you Man? Or are you Higher Orders?"

Well, that sort of hit everyone where they lived, and we all agreed that we were Animals, Higher Orders all, descendants of the Highest Order of Things, and we apologized to Blows More Oil and she accepted it and we were all happy and excited, because we had ourselves the most interesting new friend we was to know for the rest of our days.

Chapter 2

Higher Orders

The nice thing about Mr. P wasn't so much that he was a Smelly One who could Thought Speak, but that he thunk Animal thoughts. For example, the first thing he said to me when he came around to visit me the next night was, "How big is it?" That's something no Smelly One would say right off. What he meant was how big my cage was.

"Twenty-one steps the long way, five the short," I replied.

"How many steps a day?" he asked.

"67,698 in the cold season, less when it's warm."

"Not bad," he said. "How's the vittles?"

"Real bad."

"Ever get anything from the outside?"

There wasn't no sense trying to fool him since Thought Speak don't allow no lies—well, it does, but everybody knows it's a lie when you tell it, and they more or less forgive it even though everybody knows you lied, but here it weren't no use trying to lie, for he'd likely be able to tell it anyhow, being that he seemed to know Higher Orders well enough. So I told him plain. "Two mouse I caught, and also a rat they call Born Fat, but I let him go 'cause he promised to catch me a dog. He got the dog into the zoo, but the beast wouldn't come inside my cage. That dog stood right where you are and laughed at me. I hurt my nose trying to get at that damned dog. Jumped into the bars. I was so hungry . . ." I stopped to scratch myself. "Rough life," I said, "when you scrounging 'round for a damn dog."

Mr. P laughed. "Serves you right, since you were out of Order."

"I'd like to see you live here, tight as they are with the food," I said. "I was hungry. Plus, that dumb dog might have enjoyed coming back as a lion."

Mr. P looked at me and smiled. "Maybe. But . . . the Order."

Sometimes this Order business works my nerves, though he was right. I couldn't eat that dog because it would've messed up the Order. You can't just go around eating any old thing like Smelly Ones who then eat their catch after burning it up over a fire and breathe smoking sticks that makes them dizzy and crazy. We ain't Humans here. Higher Orders got rules to follow.

The main one is that once you supper an Animal, that feller Jumps Souls and comes back as the next Higher up. He gets upgraded, see, on account of him getting torn up by your jaws. Therefore little fish who gets suppered come back as bigger fish, and bigger fish who get swallowed come back as sharks, who come back as whales, who come back as bird critters, then land critters like mouse, monkeys, gorillas, giraffes, elephants, and so forth until you reach lion. After you're on my level you're at the top of the heap and the next time you sink all the way back to the bottom and it's back to the water for you, buddy, and from there you work your way up to air creature and finally back to land creature again. Jumping Souls ain't simple and most don't like thinking on what they were before they Jumped Souls, for there ain't no purpose in it. Plus getting runned down till you is out of breath and then having your throat wrenched out and getting put to Big Sleep by your fellow Animal makes you chicken-hearted on the notion if you tarry on it too long, so it's best to forget it till it comes. My ridings from the high end to the low end happened three times to my recollection. I'm not favored of it, because being a small fish means from the moment you draw your first breath you're running full out. You got to move brother, swim Jim, scramble, git going, hit it, before somebody comes along, because to my recollection of Water World life, everything's eating everything down there. Most tiny fish the size of my eyeball get gobbled five minutes past breakfast before they even start running, which means you hit Big Sleep three or four times before you come back as anything substantial enough to prosper for a while. It's troublesome Jumping Souls. It hurts.

Of course, Higher Orders screw it up all the time, like a weasel killing a hound dog, or a herd of zebras kicking a wounded hyena to death and sneaking in a bite or two as they do it, or a hippo whipping an alligator. But working outside your business always causes trouble. I once wiped out a young elephant named Slurps Leaves during a rough dry season. Slurps was my friend, too, nearly my age. He even got me to try a couple of them big leaves he favored chewing, but it was a tough time and we were sitting there trading Thought Shapes and he'd wandered a bit away from his herd and nobody was around, and his coat was so shiny and oily-looking and he looked so good I couldn't resist. I said I was sorry before I wiped him out, but elephant ain't bad. A little salty, not sour.

Well, a few seasons later I was sitting around chewing the fat with a young lion named Don't Rest Mostly. It was afternoon, and we were setting at the bank of Meeting on the Waters trying to decide whether it was too hot to go hunting, or if we should stay by the water and hold out till maybe some female lioness would come along and do the work for us, when Don't Rest suddenly turns to me and says, "Get Along, I'm Slurps Leaves."

"Naw," I said. "That's impossible."

"I am," he said. "You wiped me out right by that banana tree over there," and he nodded at the exact spot where I rubbed him out back when he was a young elephant.

I sized him up good. He was a pretty big lion. Strong. And Young. Younger than me. With leg muscles like rocks. I couldn't take no parts of him. I was fat and pretty for him. I wouldn't have no chance against him.

I stepped back on my haunches, quivering in my hide. "I'm sorry about that, Don't Rest," I said. "It was a bad rainy season. But it's a good day to die."

"Oh, forget it, old fella," he says. "My dad was a hell-raiser and I needed an out."

So sometimes you can get away with dodging the Order of Things, though I never told Mr. P that, being that he was a Smelly One and wouldn't likely care nohow.

"I wouldn't have wanted to eat that dog," I told Mr. P pointedly, "if the Smelly Ones around here wasn't so tight with the sour meat."

"I'm not blaming you," Mr. P said. "I'm not God, y'know."

"I don't know who that Smelly One is," I said, "but please don't mention him to me no more. Blows More Oil don't like him."

"You got plans tonight?" he asks.

"Nah. I need sleep. I'm leaving in the morning. Gonna tour the jungle for two months and kill Animals. Like the Smellies do."

"That's too bad," he said. "We're all meeting at Rubs's cage tonight for a Fashion Me. Everyone's invited."

That nearly blowed me off my haunches, but since he was new, I sat silent tight for a minute and kept a straight face. I didn't get this old, even here in the zoo, being a fool. But he was pulling some high meat off the shelf, talking about a Fashion Me. That's a fashion show, see. No Animal can resist showing hisself to other Animals. But I kept my face straight and yellow as a daisy.

"Rubs's cage?" I asked.

"Yes. Everyone's invited. You. Scratch there. Everyone. At Rubs's Cage in the Monkey House."

"I know where Rubs lives."

"Well, you coming?"

"You say it's a Fashion Me. Right here? At the zoo?"

"Yes."

"You're kidding. How I'm getting out?"

"I got the keys," Mr. P said, and he pulled out a bunch of jangly keys the Smellies at the zoo carry around. "But no hunting," he snapped. "I mean it. And Thought Speak only. No roaring out loud."

"Hot damn!" I roared out loud.

"I just said no roaring out loud," Mr. P said. "You want to give it away?"

"Naw, naw. Can't give it away."

"Remember. No hunting." He stared at me real serious.

"Sure, sure, brother. I can't eat no Higher Orders here. I wouldn't have nobody to talk to."

He smiled and nodded.

"When can I go?"

"Now."

"Right now?"

"Yes. Right now."

"Well, what we waitin' for?" I bounded to the door of my cage. Then it hit me. I stopped in my tracks and sat on my haunches again.

"Hell, Mr. P. I been in this cage nine years. I need a minute to get myself together."

"Take your time," he said, "but I got other Animals to see. If you want out tonight, just call Looks Old. I gave him some keys." Looks's a monkey. Then he left.

I sat there a moment, then looked over at Scratch. I gathered up a Thought Shape and hollered it over to her. "Hey, Scratch. You hear that?"

"Yep." She scratched herself.

"I can get out, lady."

"Yep. Me, too."

We were quiet a minute.

"Hey," I said, feeling cheery, "we can take a walk around the zoo, you and me."

"Yep."

"Can walk outta these cages right now."

"Yep."

"Anytime we want. Just call Looks, he'll open up the doors, and we're out. Me and you. Walking around. Fully loaded. Still got all our teeth. Sniffing the grass, smelling around . . ."

"Yep."

"Watching the birds."

"Yep."

"Scout some hiding places, maybe."

"Yep."

"Hunt a little bit. Forget what Mr. P says. We'll hunt little stuff. A mouse or two . . ."

"Yep," she said.

My heart was thumping so hard I could feel it in my feet.

"So, panther, what you waiting for?"

"I'm waiting for you, lion."

"Hot damn! *Looks!*" I roared it at the top of my Thought Speak lungs.

"Yah, boss." His Thought Shape voice was faint in the distance.

"Swing by here and let me and Scratch out."

"I need five minutes, Get Along. I'm working on Rubs's lock."

"Make it three, son, or your black hide is mine. And the name's Get Along, Go Along. *Mr.* Go to you. Y'understand?"

"Yessir, Mr. Go. Be right there."

One of the nice things about knowing you're getting out is you can be King again. Creatures pay attention when they know you ain't behind bars.

ME AND SCRATCH didn't have no trouble knowing where to go, for Rubs has been sending Thought Pictures of the Monkey House around the zoo for the longest. But seeing a place from Thought Pictures and venturing to it in a zoo once you free and outta your cage is two different things. If you don't got no encouragement and a strong heart, you just can't make it. I never knew so much sadness till the moment I first peeked out the Lion House and seen that where I was living wasn't a zoo at all, but rather Man's prison for his own self.

The sight of the trees, the walkways, the sadness floating in the air all about the zoo stopped us in our tracks right at the door. We couldn't move, for the zoo is a downright ugly sight. The smell—the unnatural odor of the toilet of Animal creatures that had no place to go natural to join up with the air, sand, and soil from which everything come—was gone. Instead, Man's footprint was everywhere. The blend of hard things and lights, paths that lead to hard edges, everything ordered, numbered, and placed here and there in sequence and order. Cages. Boxes. Squares. Lines. Animals boxed here. Man boxed there. Nothing circular. Everything leading to something with points and edges and order. Man, I come to understand at that moment, was jailed as Animals was. He ain't free. That was the worst part of it, I reckon, standing there and feeling the downright sadness choking the place. I felt sorry for Man then, even as his unholy stinking scent was tearing at my nose. Everything before me was planned out. Clean. Go this way. Go that way. Take shelter here. There's light there. No bumps. No dirt. No rocks. No plains. No fun. Everything all smoothed over with the exception of a plant here or there. The life of the land beneath gone, drained forever. I never felt so much sadness in my life till that moment. It threw me and Scratch outta whack right off. We got so chicken-hearted we couldn't move. We lingered in the door of the Lion House afraid to leave.

Looks Old the monkey, he was setting on the top of the doorway over us as we tarried. "I know," he said. "It do take some getting used to."

"Does Man live like this all over the world?" I asked him.

"Dunno, Mr. Go," he said. "But I got others to let out," and he was gone.

Me and Scratch stayed in the doorway, staring, and finally that panther stuck her head out the door and put a paw to the outside and said, "It feels all right." I got ashamed and pushed past her and stepped outside into the air and she followed. We spent a few moments standing there, still rattled, for the sacredness of freedom is something you feel, not necessarily see, but it just plumb wasn't there. It made us scared to move at all, but finally I hopped up and hid behind a bush and she followed. We scrunched behind every bush and tree like cubs as we made our way to the Monkey House, for the stinking odor of Man got worse as we moved, and that too spelled danger.

It was worth it when we got to Rubs's, though, and I had to keep my face low, being a lion and all, for you don't want Higher Orders seeing the King weeping like Can't Trot the elephant and the rest of them sorry sensitive beasts like them hippopotamuses, who was choking like a bunch of cubs and smelling righteous since they was far from their watering hole. All the Creatures had waited on us knowing that a fashion show ain't no small turnips and the King of the Jungle do have to preside. Lions are the top of the heap when it comes to showing how much we can grunt, sniff, fart, and roar while showing how shiny our fur is but most others ain't far. Them Creatures standing around waiting for us was pumped up and ready to strut their stuff. It didn't matter that they was different breeds. Fashion Me's is for everybody. Of course, mostly the preening is confined to your breed, but we had some mixed-breed Fashion Me's back in the jungle too, mostly in emergencies, like when the Order was screwed up by some creature who'd gone too far left or right, like the time a baboon named Grunt started killing everything in sight 'cause a Smelly One shot him and didn't rub him out completely. A bunch of us tracked him and put him down. I remember we had just laid him down and was about to put him to Sleep when I felt sorry for him and said, "Nothing personal, Grunt." He looked up and said, real clear, "I understand, Get Along." Then he died and we ate his victuals.

Anyway, that place was loaded. There was flamingos and giraffes and peacocks and deer and wolves and the one female tiger named Pout Face from the Lion House and Urge Me, the one polar bear who came over and sweated it out. I seen more Higher Orders gathered in one place in that one time than I'd ever seen before. There was Animals whose Thought Speak I'd heard for years and never laid eyes on. And though I was hungry as all getup watching the zebras cavorting around, for I have a weakness for them sweet-tasting beasts, I kept my promise to Mr. P and didn't lift a paw.

He was standing over in a corner and didn't say nothing when the Higher Orders come into the Monkey House. Instead, he watched as Rubs welcomed everybody who came.

This was her house and she was host and let everybody know it, walking around like a den mother on two legs, greeting the different Higher Orders who come in by twos and threes. She come up to me and Scratch and said, "Welcome, brother and sister."

"I didn't know you was so old, Rubs," I said. She was the oldest gorilla I ever seen. Rubs is so old her hair was almost gone. She looked almost like a Smelly One.

"You ain't so young, Lion," she said.

"But I'm pretty, though."

"And I ain't pretty?" Rubs scratched herself. "I know I'm pretty, baby," and she sent out a little Thought Shape like gorillas know how to do, showing herself all done up eating a shoot covered with ants, with a shiny coat and looking young. Everybody laughed. She been drawing that Thought Shape of herself for years.

I didn't know if I liked them other Higher Orders laughing so free around me, being that I'm the King and all and mostly supposed to strike terror in 'em, but Rubs got everyone straight. She stood up on her hind legs tall like a Smelly One, spread her ape arms, and said, "C'mon here, y'all. Come look at Get Along, Go Along. See what the King of the Jungle look like up close. He been a good King. Never shouted at nobody or nothing." And the other Animals, they come up close, even the zebras, and they sniffed me a little and I sniffed them. It was strange, scenting them zebras, for my goodness, they smelled irresistible. There was a family of 'em. Don't Murder Me was the daddy and the whole family gathered 'round and got a good whiff of me and that was a test with delicious things like that so close, but it was kind of nice, too. It was like we was all brothers and sisters for that moment, and after I got used to 'em standing there for a minute or two, I felt like I could never eat a zebra again without feeling like I was eating part of myself.

I said to Don't Murder, "You and yours smell righteous."

"Who you telling?" one of the little ones said. That was Don't Murder's son. He was a cute little feller, and he went over and sniffed Scratch just as bold as he wanted to be. Scratch looked downright rained on. I could tell that old panther wasn't all the way pleased and was fighting the urge to plant her teeth in the little one's neck and stuff the leftovers in a tree someplace to throw down her gizzard later. But she knew where she was and lay low and kept her word about hunting. She sniffed him back and asked him his name. That little fella wasn't scared one bit.

"Mr. Nelson Whippie," said the little zebra proudly.

Scratch scowled. "Ain't Don't Murder your daddy?"

"He *is* my daddy, but my daddy named me after Mr. P now," the little critter said. "And he's *Mr.* Don't Murder Me now, like *Mr.* P, ya dig? Hey, can I stick my hoof in your mouth to see if you got any teeth?"

"If you do, I'll close my mouth to see if you got any hoofs."

"Cool it, Scratch," I said. She cooled a little and said she was sorry. But she couldn't hardly take it. She glanced at me. "Jeez. Ol' Mr. P's moving up," she said. "Next thing you know, all the Higher Orders is gonna be named Mr. P and walking on two legs. Does Man gotta take over everything?"

But Mr. P wasn't taking over nothing. He didn't hear her.

He was off by himself in the corner of the Monkey House, watching from atop a tree branch in one of the open cages, smiling his little Smelly One smile. I could see that he loved watching us, being with us, and he didn't need to say it. He was a Smelly One, for sure, because he stunk so bad you couldn't stay close to him for long. But deep in his heart he was an Animal, and that's a fact. I was never sorry about what I did to him later.

Chapter 3

The Wind

There was times in Mr. P's four years here at the zoo when Looks would swing by my cage with the keys to let me out and I would tell him I wasn't interested, but that didn't happen much. Most every night I spent at the Monkey House with everybody else, gathered around Rubs's cage scratching one another and listening to Mr. P tell stories.

He liked to sit on a little branch in a tree like a gorilla and flap his little paws in the air when he told his stories. They was fantastic yarns, too, but we almost didn't get to hear them, for after he told the first two or three he had to quit and go make peace down at Water World, for the Water Creatures down there had a revolt and threatened a big conglomeration when they couldn't hear every word he said. The only one who could hear was Blows More Oil—she had ears big enough to catch his Thought Speak—and she sent his yarns on to the rest of them fish who couldn't hear him. But she got tired of it quick and quit on account of not being able to enjoy them herself. It wasn't an easy job, for them stories was fantastical, but in the end them complainers down there threatened to turn loose one of their own, a feller in the shark tank named Jug who ain't right in the head. They threatened to sic Jug on every shark in the shark pen and gobble every one of 'em alive, for he was a thirsty, mean devil. A cantankeration like that would surely get Man suspicious.

So Mr. P went down there again and straightened out Blows some kind of way. She's a big old baby.

It was worth it, I do believe, for Mr. P enjoyed telling the stories as much as we loved hearing 'em. When he got his story going good, he'd flap his arms and legs together all at once, and his eyeballs would sparkle and the extra fur what he called clothes would stretch around him and almost swallow him up. He was a little Smelly, even by Smelly standards, but the stories he told was big. And most of 'em, of course, was about Man.

He told us, for example, that Smelly Ones marry two or three times in life, that they hate one another for not looking exactly the same, they all speak different tongues, and that the smoke-breathing-sticks they favor will eventually kill them. He said most of 'em who come to the zoo are scared of Higher Orders, even mice. We roared when we he heard that.

"Those Smellies are something," Scratch howled.

"Why would they be scared of something small as a mouse or frog like Meat Eat Sniffer?" Rubs asked.

"Germs," said Mr. P.

"Germs!" Rubs exclaimed. "They got more germs on their tongue than a dog do. That can't be true."

Sniffer, who was setting right there, piped in, "He ain't lying." He told a story about how he was once in a Smelly One's house and a Smelly saw him and ran away. Then the Smelly set a trap for him that had a little metal bar on it that was supposed to slam down on his nose, but Sniff didn't touch it because he doesn't like peanut butter. That made us laugh even more.

"Laugh if you want," Mr. P said, "but there are some other things you should know." He told us that some Smelly Ones kill Higher Orders and don't eat them. Instead they stuff the head with feathers and what all. "Then they hang it high in their house so the others can see it."

Everyone got quiet. "That's something I already know," I said.

"I'd rather a Smelly eat me and boil my bones," Rubs said, "than keep me around. Even if I already Jumped Souls."

"What do it matter?" Scratch growled.

"It matters a lot when you get older," Rubs said.

"It works out," Scratch said. "If I were to eat the Twisted-Mouth Smelly who comes to clean my cage every day, when they hang me, they're hanging him too, being that I have eaten him."

"Why would you eat a Smelly?" I asked.

"If they're gonna hang my head someplace, why not?" Scratch said.

"Keep your fur on," Mr. P said. "First of all, not all Smellies do that."

"Which ones do?" Scratch asked.

"Certain ones. Most of 'em wouldn't be here at the zoo."

"I'm glad," Scratch said. "It'd be bad to go to war with them anyway." And we all agreed on that. For by then Mr. P explained to us that only a fool would fight Man. Man, he said, remembers every wrong you done to him, whereas a Higher Order, well, if it don't involve food and you got to run around to revenge your neighbor for what they done to you in the past, why, we'd just as soon forget all about it and take a nap. Animals ain't never organized. Smelly Ones, Mr. P said, they write their little hates down on a piece of paper and pass the paper around. They leave them papers for their little ones and the little ones that follow their little ones, so they can all remember the hate from long ago.

It was a depressing thought, and we all got gloomy over it. So Mr. P told us some funny stories about how Smellies like to have fun. He said they like to throw a ball around and kick it, then throw each other to the ground to get the ball. Sometimes it's little white balls, sometimes it's big brown balls. Other times, two Smellies get in a little square and beat each other with fancy cow-skin paws just for fun. And sometimes to relax, they like to lie around in the sun to make their hairless hides look dark and pretty.

"Now hold on a minute," I said. "Only a fool or a cold snake would lay in the hot sun."

"I'm telling you it's true," Mr. P said. He drawed a little Thought Shape in his mind showing a female Smelly laying on a beach with the hot sun over her. "That's called a tan," he said.

"That's called a lie," I said. "You told us before that White Smelly Ones, which ain't white really, not like Urge Me the polar bear here"—that poor bugger was standing there sweating it out—he come every night—fascinated like the rest of us—"don't like the black Smelly Ones, which ain't black really, not like Scratch here. Now you're saying that the White-Pink Smelly Ones lie out in the hot sun to look like the Black-Brown Smelly Ones, which they don't like? Why would a body do that?"

"It's complicated," Mr. P said.

"They must not like each other much," I said.

"It's true," Rubs said. "Let me tell you what I seen before I come here."

Setting on a low branch of her tree, she told us a story about how she was a tiny gorilla captured in the jungle a long time ago. They brung her to the lair of a White-Pink Smelly. Inside the lair was a Black-Brown Smelly who worked at the lair, cleaning up and burning the food for the White-Pink Smelly. This Black-Brown Smelly raised Rubs and gave her a name and taught her everything. Then not too long after, they both died off and Rubs came to the zoo.

"But before she died, the Black-Brown Smelly hated the White-Pink Smelly something terrible," Rubs said. "Every time she walked out the room, she talked about her like she was a Human Being."

"That's not so bad," Mr. P said. He didn't know that's the worst thing you could say about an Animal.

"I'll tell you something else," Rubs continued. "That Black-

Brown Smelly One who raised me was real superstitious and had all sorts of bones and powders she carried in a sack around her neck. At night sometimes when I was setting alone in my cage looking, she'd kneel next to her bed, fold her hands together, and—" She stopped. She looked around the room pensively. "Forget I brung that up," she said suddenly. She sat on her haunches, a look of fear on her face. "Let's change the subject," she said.

But now everyone sitting in a semicircle around her was fascinated, and every Animal howled in protest.

"Finish the story, Rubs!"

"Don't stop now, Gorilla. Spill it!"

Rubs looked around the room, fearful.

"I can't!" she said.

Scratch was lying on a high branch above Rubs's head and swung down, hanging from her front paws. "Rubs. Remember that time you asked me to howl like a chimpanzee so that big Ape Mingo they brought in to mate up with you would loosen up and laugh? Didn't I do it?"

"His face was so ugly his looks could curdle a cow," Rubs said. "I'm glad I didn't mate him."

"That was 'cause of me, too," Scratch said.

"How's that?"

"I said I'd kill him. So the zoo got rid of him."

"Scratch, you lying like a dog," I griped. "You ain't never made a peep to any Smelly in the world till Mr. P come here."

That panther ignored me. She was slick as a piece of snot and don't mind lying her ass off to get her way. "Be a sport, Rubs," she said. "Finish the story. I love good endings."

"You ain't gonna like this one," Rubs said.

"Why?" Scratch asked.

"I can't tell why . . . I shouldn't've brung it up."

"I'll get you a box of bananas," Mr. P said, for he'd got on his hind legs about hearing the thing, too.

Rubs's furry face was creased with doubt. "I wouldn't tell it for a hundred bananas," she said. "I don't know what got into me for bringing it up."

"Can't be that bad," I said.

"It ain't bad or good. But there's some here who'll hate me for the telling of it."

"Hate?" Mr. P was lying on his side on the floor beneath Rubs's tree branch, and when he heard that he pulled himself over to her and gently stroked her on the head. He was crazy about old Rubs. And she was soft on him, too. "Man hates. Animals don't hate. You been in the zoo too long, Rubs. Who could hate old Rubs? Hate you because you're scared of something? We're all scared of something, Rubs. Just remember every fear that lives inside makes you smaller. But when you air your fears, they disappear."

"How's that?"

"They're out there to be seen, so you can address them. You can fight what's out in the open. That's why you put your fears to the air."

"That's just it. The air," she said. I got a bad feeling when she said that and started to open my trap on it, but quick as you can tell it, she took a deep breath and said, "Gather in close."

Everyone circled around and she whispered, "This Black-Brown Smelly every night, she'd kneel next to her bed, fold her hands, and speak to the Wind."

Well, that done it. A stunned silence followed. No Thought Speak. No grunting or growling. Nothing. But the wave of fear that swept through us was thick as forest fog. I felt the hair on my back rise.

"Now that's enough," I said. "I'm hearing all these stories and I've had enough. Rubs, you're old and your mind must be slipping, to talk about You Know Who."

"I'm telling you it's true," Rubs insisted. Even as she spoke, I felt a shaking of the ground and seen Urge Me the polar bear heading back to his tank. He'd had enough. Several Animals watched him go and looked soon to follow.

"Can't be," Scratch snapped. "And you know it's an insult to the Order to even speak of it."

"Damn right it is," I heard somebody say, and Step and Stop, a cheetah, sprang from the rear of the Animals gathered around and landed before Rubs. I knew Step since he first come to the zoo. It sure don't pay to fall in love with him. That scoundrel got a heart the size of a full-grown pea. He's a nasty little critter that'll eat his own.

He leaned in towards Rubs, gnashing his teeth, his tail curled and his eyes burning, the hair on the back of his neck high and stiff. "I oughta send your gorilla ass rambling to speak of You Know Who," he said.

"Hold up, son," I said. I rose up and stepped between him and the gorilla.

"Step aside, Get Along. You know she's wrong."

"In the jungle she is. Not here."

"Laws is laws, lion."

"I don't need no law to make you fresh meat."

"There's plenty here that agrees with me," Step said. "There's rules and there's blood." He turned to the creatures behind him. "Which one is this here lion for?" There must've been thirty or thirty-five standing there, staring at Rubs and me, and none of them looked pleased.

See, there ain't many laws to being a Higher Order, but of the few that's there, Rubs had broke the biggest one. Being of the Higher Order, you is allowed to communicate with just about anything that's living if you want, though some Animals do it better than others. Water is a difficult fellow to talk to, though fish do it pretty easy. Rain is hard to reach, though I know a snake who did it once. The Sun is next to impossible. Plants are easy if you's the plant-eating type and don't mind munching on your friends like us carnivores, and of course most Higher Orders can read Thought Speak from other Higher Orders. I would say the top of the list in terms of difficulty is Man, for Man's a lying idiot. And on top of that is the Wind.

It ain't possible to speak with the Wind. The Wind is different than any other thing on earth. A fella can get hurt trying to talk to the Wind. The Wind can hear everything you say, the tiniest strain of your heart, the smallest dot on your soul, ain't no secrets to him. Every creature on earth is taught from the time of birth to her Big Sleep that the Wind don't need you for hisself, for the Wind is sacred, the ultimate power. The Wind controls everything, the sun, the trees, the flowers, the water, life itself. The Wind brings all things. Good weather. Bad weather. Sun. Rain. You cannot live without water. You cannot live without food. But it ain't no crime to die from lack of those things, for life ain't never complete. You go to Sleep and come back again. But whether you're living or dying, sleeping or not, you live inside the Wind, which carries you in his pocket while you in your Big Sleep till he decides to drop you back as the Next Thing. You cannot be the Next Thing until the Wind decides it. When I was a cub the old lions used to say if you lead a good clean life, the Wind will lift you back to this life as any Animal you desire, even straight back to lion again without having to start at the Bottom. If you have any dream for tomorrow, give it to the Wind. If you have any dream from the past, give it to the Wind. But don't never *mention* the Wind, for nobody comes back from trying to fool with it. You're nothing if the Wind is mad at you. You are forever empty. Gone. Forgotten forever.

Rubs had crossed the line, and all the creatures there knew it. That's why they were standing there, surrounding me and Rubs, ready to kill. They would've done it, I think, had I not gived that nasty cheetah Step my words, see, that I wasn't going to take no backwater off him about Rubs. That gave 'em a little pause, for they had been in the zoo a long time and weren't particular to fighting and surviving in the middle of Man's land where none of 'em know one hiding or hunting place from the next, and I believe that's the only thing that kept 'em from leaping at my bones.

Step seen they wasn't jumping to his word, so he calmed down a little.

He said, "All right, lion. But just remember, you got a can tied to your tail, too. Rubs talking about the You Know Who put us all in hot water. I don't mind coming back as a fish or a mouse, but I don't wanna step out of the circle and be nothing forever."

"Maybe that won't be," I said. I turned to the others. "Rubs here," I said, "she's just telling what she saw and it ain't no insult to tell what a body *think* they seen. Of course she made a mistake, is all. Ain't that right, Rubs?"

"If I'm lying, I hope I come back as a small fish," Rubs said.

Well, that made it worse. A few Animals began to walk away. A few others growled. As the Animals peeled off and moped towards their cages, Rubs spoke to their backs. "Have I ever lied?" she said. "In all my years here?"

Nobody said nothing, but a few that was walking away slowed down, for Rubs is the oldest creature in the zoo. One of 'em stopped and said, "There's always a first time, Rubs."

That hit her where she lived. She slapped her forehead. "Carnivores! Put me down," she said. "Put me to Big Nap right now." She dropped down from her tree limb with a thud and lay flat on her back, her eyes closed. "C'mon back, everybody. Deaden me now. It's a good day to die. Eat my hams and all. Share me equally. And I hope I come back as a small fish."

The Animals who were walking away stopped. Several turned around.

Rubs kept talking, lying on her back. "Hurry up, y'all," she said, "I ain't got all day. I'm good eating."

Step the cheetah and a few other meat eaters including Scratch began to growl and edge up to Rubs.

"I don't understand," Mr. P said nervously. He watched, terrified, as they edged ever closer to Rubs.

I stepped between the meat eaters and Rubs and growled, "Y'all wait one minute."

"It's the law of the jungle," Scratch said, licking her chops as she eyed Rubs lying prone on the ground.

"This ain't the jungle, Scratch," I snarled. "The first one of y'all to touch Rubs goes home in threes."

"You ain't the law!" Step said.

"Be quiet and lemme think a minute or I'll bust you inside out," I said.

That threat didn't hold much, for there was several of 'em there, including two small tiger cubs plus their mamma, who was pretty big, Step himself, who's a cheetah, Scratch, who ain't no slouch when she's mad, and two or three elephants who was looking right upset. If they jumped all together, I wasn't no match for 'em. Even a lion got limits.

See, we was getting into a touchy area. Rubs thought nobody believed her and wanted us to wipe her out so she could take the Big Nap with honor, which is a natural thing for Higher Orders who are insulted or just want out some kind of way. If an Order asks to die, you obliged to give them their wish. But I wasn't ready to see Rubs off. Beside, this was new ground, being that we was discussing the Wind in the zoo rather than out running free. That, to me, made a big difference.

I took a deep breath and roared in Thought Speak loud as I could, "Hey, Blows More Oil!" I tried to sound as polite as I could shouting over to Water World.

"What!" Her Thought Shapes was tremendous and powerful.

"Listen, Oil, do me a favor. We're fixing to discuss the You Know Who. Would you mind . . . well, if you hear any crazy Thought Speak from outside somewhere, would you blast away? Sort of, er, explain things, run interference for us?"

"Okay," Oil boomed. She's a very reasonable whale when she ain't insulted.

I thought maybe Oil could tell the Wind we wasn't looking for no trouble. I turned to the others. "Don't nobody touch that ape. Rubs, get off the floor and tell us what you know. There must be more to what you is telling, or you wouldn't've started to tell it. I ain't gonna let nobody wipe you out on a humble."

Rubs sat up and seeing she wasn't torn to bits said: "What is there to tell? Like I said, this Black-Brown Smelly knelt by her bed every night, put her hands together, and spoke to that Smelly One they call God for a while. She'd go at him awhile and then start yammering away fast in Smelly Tongue, speaking all sorts of weird noises and such, and waving her hands. I couldn't make out what she was saying with her jaws, but in Thought Speak she was saying, 'Edward! Edward!'"

"Wow." There were gasps all around.

"And she would do that for quite a spell," Rubs said.

"Why?" Scratch asked.

"I don't know. But every night she did this, and one night the Wind did come right in the room and it spoke to her. He crashed the window open and hollered in Thought Speak in her ear, 'CUT OUT THAT CRAP!' He spoke so loud that it must've busted her brain open because she died right there, right on the bed with her hands folded.

"Then the Wind looked at me and said, 'Got any questions?'

"'No, sir,' I said. 'The name's Rubs here and I'm just visiting here against my will. As you can see, I'm in a little cage here. I don't have nothing to do with that and did not call you.'

"So he looked around the room a minute, and then he swept everything off the walls with a blink of his eye. Then he looked back at me and said, 'You been pure in heart?'

"'Yes, sir,' I said.

"'Shall I check?' he asked.

"I said, 'Check all you want.'

"'No need to,' he said. 'I already have. You want outta here? I'll blow the walls down and you can walk out.'

"I said, 'It's awful cold out there, Mr. Wind.'

"'I'll blow warm,' he said.

"'I'm a long way from home, sir.'

"'I'll blow you back. All the way to Africa.'

"I said, 'With all due respect, sir, I believe my family would not want me now that I've been contaminated by Smelly Ones. I would not want to spread my sickness around other Higher Orders. I think I better stay and wait till I Jump Souls.'

"'You're a good ape,' he said. 'You will lead a long, prosperous life and you will come back as a Higher Order on any level you want.'

"And then he swept out the window and was gone. They came and got that old Black-Brown Smelly One and brought me here. And that is the truth as I know it, and if it ain't I hope I come back as a small fish."

A long silence followed.

"Good God," Mr. P said.

"I wish you wouldn't mention him," I snapped. "Blows More Oil don't like him." But I too was knocked out.

We all sat there a minute. Finally Scratch spoke up. "Gosh, Rubs. I didn't know you had it in you. To speak to the Wind. Gosh." And we was all impressed.

A fresh breeze rattled the Monkey House and the leaves outside swished around. I shivered. The Wind was talking and we all got nervous thinking about it. It would be morning soon, and now maybe the Wind was mad, or maybe it wasn't, but either way, it was time to go. We split up, everyone heading back to their cages. I gave Looks a ride on my back to my cage so he could lock me in.

"I've had enough stories for a while," I said. "I got a headache."

"Me, too," Looks said. "Creepy. All this stuff about the Wind."

He sat outside my cage a minute, looking thoughtful. "Hey, Get Along?"

"Yeah."

"Can you tell Blows More Oil to stop now? I got a headache from all her Thought Speak."

I'd forgotten all about her. She was droning away. No wonder I couldn't think straight.

"Hey, Oil!" I hollered.

"Yes," she thundered.

"You can let up now. Thank you."

"You're welcome," she said. There was a whining noise as she brought her powerful Thought Speak voice home. I always liked that whale. She's a powerful nice creature. If I ever meet the Wind and get a chance to take my pick, I'm coming back as one of them.

Chapter 4

Rubs Gets Out

After that Mr. P never wanted to talk about Smellies no more. He wanted to talk to the Wind. Even after hearing Rubs's creepy story, he wanted to. He already knowed how to talk to Higher Orders. Now he wanted more. That's the problem with Smelly Ones. They got one thing Animals ain't got. They got ambition.

He was pretty obsessed with the idea and talked about it all the time. Of course we didn't want no parts of it. Not just because we was afraid, but Animals, you know, lose interest in anything real quick if it ain't got to do with throwing somebody or something down our little red lane. He wouldn't let it go.

We'd gather at Rubs's cage and sniff and tell jokes and no sooner did five minutes pass when Mr. P, setting atop a branch next to Rubs, would start up about the Wind again.

"Let us speak as one voice," he said. "We'll organize. We'll have study groups. And committees. We'll study ways to speak to the Wind."

"Nah, that's all right, Mr. P," we'd say.

"We can sing songs that will bring the Wind."

"Nah. No camels here, Mr. P. They're the best singers."

"What about we make up a message. Like a letter?"

"What's that?" somebody would say, and then they'd change the subject: "Hey! Y'all ever hear the joke about the mouse, the elephant, and the coconut?"

Of course that didn't stop Mr. P. He just went on and on about it. Finally we got so tired of hearing him moan about it, one night a bunch of us went to Rubs's and gave it a whack. Just to say hello to the Wind and make some friendly remarks. See, we liked Mr. P and tried to please him because he was a Smelly and therefore ignorant about certain things. We was hoping the Wind would take that into consideration.

It was a fool idea from the start, we knew, but we tried it anyway. Me, Scratch, Rubs, Urge Me the polar bear, Step the cheetah, and a few others. Even Blows More Oil pitched in to help. We tried for three whole hours, setting around Rubs's cage, but nothing happened except we all got a headache from Blows More Oil, whose howling sounded like fifteen elephants all hollering at once.

"This ain't no use," I said finally. "My head's gonna bust open. I got no business fooling with the Wind nohow. You got to have a solid clean record to talk with the Wind. It must've been that dog I tried to eat."

Mr. P sat on the floor, glum. "I don't see why he doesn't answer," he sighed.

"It ain't right," Scratch said, and she yawned and said she was going to sleep. The rest of us filed out of Rubs's cage to sleep it off. But Mr. P stayed up with Rubs. He tried to talk to the Wind all night long, and after a while he must've talked Rubs into helping him again because you could hear 'em both calling out to it. Rubs was calling the Wind "Sir" and Mr. P was calling the Wind "Wind," which just shows you the difference between Smellies and Animals. It's bad luck to call a person by their real name unless you're mad at them. For example, my real name, in Thought Speak, is Sir Harold Cornelius II of the Third Breed of Nimphius Lion of the Serengeti, but everybody calls me Get Along, Go Along, and Smellies call me Hal, short for Harold.

They kept at it for a while, till somebody told them to cut the noise 'cause they couldn't sleep.

The next day Looks swung by my cage and told me Rubs wasn't feeling well, so me and Scratch dropped by her box the first thing that night. Most everybody was gathered there when we arrived, and I didn't have to look at their faces but once to know something wasn't right.

Rubs was laid out on her back on the ground. Her eyes were bulging and yellow, and she looked like somebody had sucked all the air out of her. Mr. P was leaning over her stroking her face, and he didn't look too good neither. His Smelly face was long and drawn, almost pure white, his floppy zoo skin was practically falling off him, and he stunk like Smellies do when they ain't washed their hides.

Everyone stepped aside when they saw me coming.

"It's all my fault," Mr. P said.

"Rubs is ill," I said. "That ain't nothing new."

"Oh God, oh God," he said.

"Please don't mention him," I said. "Blows More Oil don't like him."

Mr. P ignored me. "Trying to speak to the Wind. Oh Christ . . . look at what I did to her," and he looked down at Rubs and sent out the strangest Thought Speak thing I ever heard. It wasn't no words, just a Thought Shape like the sharks know how to send out except it was softer. You couldn't hear it, but you could sort of feel it, like something inside his chest was melting and breaking up.

I went over to Rubs and sniffed her. "Well, you smell okay. You feel all right, old gorilla?"

"I feel old," Rubs said.

"You *are* old."

"How you know my age. You ain't supposed to ask a lady gorilla how old she is."

"I ain't never done it. But it'd be good to know now."

"Old enough to be tired, Get Along. Gosh, I feel sleepy. There's a noise in my ears. It's so loud. Can you hear it? It's going wooooshhhh!"

"I don't hear nothing."

"Put your head close to mine. Listen."

I brung my head close to her head and listened. "I don't hear nothing, Rubs."

"It's the Wind," she said.

"How come I can't hear it?"

297

She ignored me. "You think I'm on my way out?" she asked. She looked at me with her big ape eyes and blinked a few times.

"Hard to say," I said. "You're still coming in good over Thought Speak. You smell okay."

"Yeah, but . . . you think I'll come back in the Order I want to?"

"Long as you don't tell nobody what it was," I said. "I don't see why not. No reason for your friend not to keep his word." I didn't mention the Wind by name.

I sat on my haunches a moment and looked around, and of course they was all looking at me since I'm the King. Just about the whole zoo was there. Urge Me the polar bear, and Step the cheetah with his wicked self, Sniff the frog, and Scratch trying to look like she didn't give a damn. I could even feel Blows More Oil's whine, listening and sending all the news back to the fish—all of 'em listening in, waiting on me to speak. I can't stand it when everybody stares at me that way. It's the rudest thing a Higher Order can do, to stare, and I was about to roar them out of my head, when Mr. P did the oddest thing.

He started crying, out loud, in Man Speak.

Everybody gathered around him.

"C'mon, Mr. P," Sniff said. "It ain't nothing new. If Rubs goes to Big Sleep, she comes back."

"That's right," Urge Me piped in. "She's getting a new start. I wish I could get a new start, hot as I am around this damn place."

"Me, too," Scratch added. "I got all these holes in me where they shot me. I'm the holiest panther in the world. I'm aching for a new body." She scratched herself. "Rubs, you really think you're getting out?"

Rubs smiled at that. She seemed sleepy and droopy. "Yeah. I think I'm getting out," and she touched Mr. P's hand.

"Rubs," Mr. P said. He choked out her name in both tongues, Man Speak and Thought Speak. "What did I do wrong?"

"Oh, come now," Rubs said. "You ain't done nothing, Mr. P. But you ought to stick to Thought Speak. Because not everybody here understands Man Speak. A body just can't be in two worlds at once, y'know, love."

She was right about that. For right then she closed her eyes and her body stayed where it was. But the rest of Rubs got outta the zoo. All the way out. And her Thought Speak floated away, as it always does at them times, except for that last word she said, which hung in the air like a cloud for a long time, and then after a while it faded and disappeared.

Chapter 5

War

It takes a lot of energy to read a human mouth. Most Animals—Higher Orders, that is—can manage about a minute but it saps you right down, so I couldn't tune in too much when them Smellies was making a big deal over Rubs, though I heard enough to get the gist of it.

Boy, was they sad. All the Smellies that sweep the cages and harass us, the ones who came to the zoo with cameras and notebooks and all sorts of nonsense to write it down for other Smellies who can't Thought Speak, they was all bent up about it. I thought that odd, since Rubs was never too particular for Smelly Ones. Of course when they fed her ice cream and Smelly food she ate it 'cause she was an Animal and Higher Orders do like to eat, but she was never particular about Smellies for the small fact that she happened to be living in a zoo. Smelly Ones defy understanding. They lock you in a zoo all your life, feed you ice cream and Smelly food that taste terrible, spray you with water hoses, then cry when you get free. I don't think I'll ever understand them.

Which is why some of us had trouble figuring out Mr. P.

After the zoo people in the white suits came and took Rubs's body to the office building where they cut her up and put her head on the wall or stuffed her up or did whatever else with what was left, Mr. P didn't come around. We sent Born Fat the rat to follow him so he wouldn't do nothing crazy, but Fat said Mr. P only walked around outside the zoo for hours and hours and after a while Fat gave up because his feet were hurting and there were too many cats.

We didn't know what to do. Of course Looks still had the keys, so we got out any night we wanted. But we missed the old man and wanted him back. He was truly an interesting Smelly. As for Rubs, we didn't miss her at all and wasn't sad one bit, though it was fun talking to that ape 'cause she was a hoot and also wise. But that's the way it goes when you're a Higher Order. Rubs was pretty lucky. She had a choice of options, being that the Wind had cut her a nice break.

Finally, about a week after Rubs left, word came to the Lion House that Mr. P was back in the zoo. That was hot news, literally hot, being that he arrived during the afternoon, when we was all caged up tight and the Smellies were everywhere.

"That's good," Scratch said, getting up and yawning, showing her teeth to scare the Smellies standing outside her cage that were gaping at her. "I got a few questions about Smellies now that I know more about 'em. See them two there?" and she pointed with her mind to two male Smellies holding hands staring at her. She watched as they kissed. "Now them Smellies there, they're both male Smellies, holding paws and trading mouth spit. And the other Smellies standing around don't seem to like it. What you think, Get Along?"

"You ain't seen nothing till you seen two male giraffes necking in the forest, Scratch."

"Oh, I seen it," she said. "Chimps, too. So sweet. Makes me wanna mmmmm . . ." And here she closed her eyes and sighed.

"Wanna what?" I said.

"You know . . ."

"Don't you think it odd?" I said. "Two males going at it?"

"Not at all," she said, wistfully, opening her eyes. "Chimps, giraffes, Man. What difference does it make? It's love, lion. Real love. Not zoo love. Real love ain't got to do with species. Real love lives in a creature's heart. Look at ol' Rubs. Didn't she love?"

Well, it hit me right where I lived, her talking that way, and in that moment I seen that panther in a whole different light. Scratch wasn't the easiest leopard type in the world to know with her lying self, and with her being a panther and me being a lion, well, I just never seen her as anything but a pain and a friend. But we'd been staring at each other across that aisle and telling jokes and lies for years, and the combination of seeing them two male Smellies nuzzling and the excitement behind Mr. P suddenly being back in the zoo, and the last word that Rubs left in the air before she died, it all gave me a revelation. I seen Scratch looking at me, and said, "Gee, Scratch."

She said, "Gee what?"

I didn't know quite what to say then, for my nature ways had left me the moment I come to that zoo years ago, and now they was rising inside me fast. So I said, "Sit yourself down a minute while I roar in Man Speak and make them two Smellies turn around so I can study 'em, for they are giving me ideas."

"'Bout what?"

"You know what kind, missy. Sit down for a minute while I teach 'em a thing or two about being a lion. There's still a thing or two a lion can teach Man about us Higher Orders. They ain't the only ones in this world that can say two things at once, y'know. There's lots I can show 'em about what us lions can do."

"Like what?"

"Like how you roar in the air to announce that you're about, and how that same roar might be telling another creature in a roundabout, lion kind of way that you might—just might, even if you is a lion and all—got some special feelings about that creature, even if that creature ain't no lion."

Scratch sat down looking pleased, I opened my mouth to pull a big roar from the back of my throat, and just before I blew air into it, one of the two male Smellies turned around and looked at me and screamed, pointing. The other Smellies around him began screaming too. Then the pungent odor of a Smelly hit me from behind and I spun around. Standing there, near the back door of my cage, was Mr. P, and he didn't look none too friendly. His hand didn't look none too friendly neither, since he was holding one of them magic killing spears in it that goes kaplooey.

"You oughta knock before you come in here," I said in Thought Speak. "Where you been? We been worried about you. What's the magic spear for?"

"It's a gun," he said. His Thought Speak was thin and shrill. "Man uses it to kill."

"Myself, I use my teeth," I said. "You need me to kill somebody for you?"

"I want to come back as a lion," he said.

"I can't help you there."

"Kill me, Get Along."

"What?"

"What I did to Rubs, I can't bear it. Kill me. Please . . ."

Quick as flash lightning, the Thought Speak wires was hopping from one end of the zoo to the other. I could hear everybody shouting at once, not to mention the Smelly Ones who was screaming outside.

I sat down real slow. "I'm sorry, Mr. P," I said, "but I don't eat Smelly Ones."

"Then I'll kill you first."

"Please do. I need an out. Wreck my head afterwards please, so nobody can stuff it and hang it on their wall."

"I knew you wouldn't help. For God's sake. You don't understand. None of you. Rubs's gone. The guilt . . . I can't bear it . . . Kill me. Please . . ."

"Mr. P, let's talk—"

"No!" And he suddenly aimed the gun over my head, pointed it straight at Scratch, who was staring from her cage across the hall, and fired. She was struck right between the eyes, and bless me, she was dead before she hit the ground.

Now I will tell you how the zoo will change a Higher Order. If this was the old days and me and Scratch was in the jungle and she got it between the eyes, even in my newfound feelings for her, I would say, "It's a good day to die," and go on about my business, hoping she'd come back higher up in the Order if she lived a clean life. But I spent many moons looking across the aisle at that panther, and while I always didn't agree with her lying ways and never did look at her eight holes where she claimed they shot her eight times, she was a friend and had just become a special friend. And it ain't fun to watch a friend leave, even if you know she's free. I got a little bit of Smelly One disease inside me, I think, for I got truly mad.

I turned to Mr. P again. "You just put the ninth hole in Scratch," I said, and before I knew it I'd leaped on him and put him out. Tore out his throat, ripped off his arm, then tossed his head around the cage.

It happened so fast you couldn't really tell it all. The Smellies was screaming outside my cage and the Animals was howling in Thought Speak. I heard Step the cheetah hollering a warning that a bunch of Smellies was heading my way with more kaplooey spears and that it was war now and let's fight, and somebody else hollered that Trot and the rest of the elephants and Urge Me the polar bear had broke out of their cages and was coming my way, and Blows More Oil was screaming in the whale tank trying to bust out the side and the war was on.

I didn't have two seconds to think before a couple of Smellies stood in front of my cage with big, long kaplooey spears. I roared a warning at 'em once, and then I seen the spears blinking fire at me and heard them go kaplooey. Then I fell into the Big Sleep.

When I woke up, I could feel air blowing through my body, but I couldn't see.

"Darn," I said. "Just my luck. I came back as a small fish." Even though I knew I was just born and my eyes wasn't open yet, I started trying to kick my little fins, automatically dodging and scrambling to keep from being swallowed up right away by some big fish. Hard as I kicked, though, I wasn't going nowhere, and I couldn't see, so I said, "This is worse. I can't see. I'm a bat."

Then I heard a voice say, "Just poke your head up as high as you can, and breathe as hard as you can, and you'll see everything."

"Holy smoke. Is that you, Scratch?"

"Yep."

"Well, that's some affair! How I know you not lying? Where you at?"

"Do as I tell you for a change," she said. So I poked my head up as high as I could and breathed as hard as I could, and my eyes opened and I looked down on home. Real home. Africa. The place Where the Waters Meet, the lair where I'd slept and made my first catch. The big tree where my mother taught me to hunt, the mountain ranges and plains I used to run. All there. All unchanged.

"Why, I'm a bird," I said. "A bird in Africa. That ain't so bad."

"You ain't no bird."

"Is that you, Rubs?"

"It ain't no bumblebee, honey, that's for sure."

"I'll be damned. Where you at? Where's Scratch?"

"Over here."

And I seen Scratch's Thought Shape and Rubs's Thought Shape and said, "Jeez, your Thought Speak's awful strange."

"No stranger than yours," Scratch said.

"Stop back-talking. You know who you talking to, panther?"

"Be quiet. You ain't King of the Jungle no more," she said.

"Listen to you," I snorted. "Don't you know I put Mr. P to Sleep for you? And he was a fine Smelly. He should've been an Animal."

"Why, thank you," said another voice behind me. I turned around to see Mr. P, grinning to beat the band. I was glad to see him.

"I thought you wanted to be a lion," I said.

"I'll take this," he replied.

Then I remembered something. Something real important.

"I got it now!" I said. "Let's go back to the zoo and see if we can't raise some hell. Let's make us a hurricane and get the rest of the gang up here." And I breathed real deep and we was off.

It's nice being the Wind. You can do anything you damn well please.

AUTHOR'S NOTE

In 1986 I took my two nephews, Dennis and Nash McBride, who were little boys back then, to visit a major zoo in one of America's big cities. They were so horrified by what they saw, I wrote *Mr. P and the Wind* for them. The rest of the stories came as they came, over the years, as I traveled over hill and dale and dusty trail, moving through life. As for the particular ache or longing that brought them on . . . well, if I shared every Twitter feed and eye blink and snort and nose pick with every Tom, Dick, and Mary in the world every five seconds, I wouldn't have a thing left for me.

James McBride
Brooklyn, NY